Berkley Prime Crime titles by Hannah Reed

DRESSED TO KILT

HANNAH REED

BERKLEY PRIME CRIME, NEW YORK

BERKLEY PRIME CRIME

An imprint of Penguin Random House LLC
375 Hudson Street, New York, New York 10014

DRESSED TO KILT

A Berkley Prime Crime Book / published by arrangement with the author

BERKLEY® PRIME CRIME and the PRIME CRIME design are trademarks
of Penguin Random House LLC.
For more information, visit penguin.com.

ISBN: 9780425265840

PUBLISHING HISTORY
Berkley Prime Crime mass-market paperback edition / July 2016

PRINTED IN THE UNITED STATES OF AMERICA

10 9 8 7 6 5 4 3 2 1

Cover illustration by Jeff Fitz-Maurice.
Cover design by Sarah Oberrender.
Interior text design by Laura K. Corless.

Penguin
Random
House

CHAPTER 1

"It's like living inside a snow globe," I said to Vicki MacBride over afternoon tea at the kitchen table in my toasty warm cottage. We watched snow fall through the white-framed windowpanes, coming down fast and furious, whirling and swirling before softly landing and then drifting high against the stonework with every gust of wind.

Vicki's signature perfume with fragrances of rose and jasmine had accompanied her on the short walk from the main house to the cottage. So had her two white West Highland terriers, Pepper and Coco. The Westies were identical except for a small black mark on Pepper's smooth little belly. At the moment the two were snuggled together in front of the wood-burning stove, the only source of heat in the cottage, but it had served me well so far, since the cottage was small and cozy, having been built to retain heat in the cold winter months.

"The snowiest beginning to the winter season in decades," Vicki agreed, going on to explain. "We're only a week into December, and already we have our first official weather bomb. The weather alert has been upgraded from yellow to amber until sometime later this evening. Thirty centimeters yesterday, another twenty today."

That entire statement is Scottish Highlands speak, which I'm finally learning to translate after five-plus months in Glenkillen and some real concerted effort. Yellow means be aware. Amber, be prepared. And red, which we haven't encountered yet and I hope we don't, means better take action to protect yourself.

"Twelve inches of new snow already," I said, after struggling to convert the weather report from centimeters into inches. I doubted I'd ever become proficient with the metric system. "That on top of another eight inches from the last 'weather bomb.'"

At least we hadn't experienced any blackouts. In case that happened, Vicki assured me that we were well prepared for a power outage. My cottage and the main house where she lives have trustworthy wood-burning stoves, and we'd stacked plenty of wood inside after the yellow alert had been issued. Vicki had also made sure we had a supply of lanterns and enough fuel to keep them burning if necessary.

I've come to learn that the Scots are a well-prepared and rugged bunch. They don't let a few feet of snow concern them. My admiration for them and for their way of life has been growing daily.

The MacBride farm, where I've been residing since my arrival in Scotland, is on the outskirts of Glenkillen, an easy drive back and forth on a good day, which of course this wasn't. Eventually, after many harrowing experiences, I'd grown accustomed to driving on the left. After doing so almost every single day, traveling to the local pub to work on a romance series I'm under contract to write, I found my confidence level was running pretty high. Or it had been, before all this snow began falling and making the only narrow, winding road that connects the farm to the village slippery and treacherous. I expected to have to negotiate under these conditions sometime in the near future, because, as I understood from Vicki, this weather was going to stick around for the long haul. The "long haul" for me being December twenty-second, when I was scheduled to depart.

Vicki dipped the last of a chocolate shortbread biscuit into her tea for the precise amount of time, an act I consider a fine art, which is totally lost on me. "Not so long that it falls into the cup," she's explained often. "Not so short that the flavor of the tea isn't fused with the buttery treat."

Vicki popped the perfectly dunked morsel into her mouth.

"I don't want to go," I said, using a spoon to fish for the piece of shortbread I'd dipped too long, my mood turning as downcast as my gaze.

"What? You're joking, right? Most of the community would kill for an invitation to a private winter whisky tasting at Glenkillen Distillery!"

Vicki had misunderstood me.

Regarding the whisky tasting: I was really looking forward to tomorrow evening's event. Especially since the invitation had been extended by Leith Cameron, local barley supplier to said distillery, professional fishing guide, and the man who comes to mind every time I need to write a scene involving a hot, sexy male protagonist. He also is

3

a single dad, father to six-year-old daughter Fia, and on top of all that he also enjoys chumming around with his border collie buddy, Kelly. And sometimes me. He's easygoing and self-confident with beautiful Scottish blue eyes and ginger highlights in his hair and a short beard he's recently taken to wearing as the days become colder.

And that man can really wear a kilt!

White tie, the invitation had specified. The delivery had been formal, arriving in the mail earlier in the week with the inscription: *Leith Cameron requests the pleasure of your company at a special winter whisky tasting on Saturday evening, December 8 at 7:00 p.m.*

Of course, I'd responded as formally, on the advice of my current teatime partner, sending off a posted note with my acceptance. In Chicago, where I was born and raised, I would have picked up the phone. Or he would have. This was all so foreign to me. But who am I to criticize Scottish tradition?

I paused, a fresh shortbread hovering over my tea, to consider Leith's attire for tomorrow's event. A kilt, for certain, Vicki had informed me. But what should I wear? I hadn't brought much with me, but I *did* have a simple black dress and a few pieces of jewelry that Vicki had thought would be perfect for the occasion. Simple, elegant, classic.

I couldn't wait!

Which brought me back to Vicki's misinterpretation of my remark about not wanting to go.

It had nothing to do with the whisky tasting. Far from it.

No, my comment had to do with the quickly approaching expiration of my tourist visa, the standard maximum of six months. Soon I'd be on the flight from Scotland back to

Chicago. Ami Pederson, my best friend there, practically had to force me onto the plane for the flight over here, insisting that an extended visit to the Highlands would jump-start my imagination. And since the first book in the Scottish Highlands Desire Series needed to have an authentic setting, and since I'd never been to the Highlands . . .

"It's only reasonable to actually go there for research," she'd said, insisting that the village of Glenkillen was the perfect place to find inspiration. She'd done her own research to determine this. "It's right on the North Sea. Perfect. And reasonable to spend time there," she'd repeated.

Only I hadn't been reasonable.

I'd resisted from the moment she'd suggested it, digging my heels in right up to the last hours before I was set to depart. I'd complained and explained and made excuses—too busy, too tired, too, too . . . everything. I'd continued with attempts to worm out of it while packing, continued to explain ad nauseam why I shouldn't go, even as I checked in at the airport, whining, sniffling . . . but Ami had been more tenacious, refusing to capitulate. She'd driven me to the airport and followed me as far in as she could before security turned her back, waiting there until she was sure I had boarded.

Then I'd arrived—overwhelmed, jet-lagged, and culture shocked, especially by the Scots' so-called English language.

And, in spite of myself, I had instantly fallen in love.

I adored every aspect of the Highlands. The glens, munros, and lochs. The lush vegetation. The hillsides covered with heather and flocks of grazing sheep. The picturesque harbor village of Glenkillen. And especially the Scots. They are witty, fun loving, fiercely independent, fiery, and bold. My kind of people, I had discovered to my astonishment.

With the Scottish surname of Elliott (originally spelled Eliott and perhaps any number of other ways), I was doomed from the start. "It's in your blood," Vicki had said, "whether you want it or not."

She was referring to my Highland ancestry. The Elliott clan has a crest of its own—a hand couped at the wrist holding a cutlass. And a motto: *Fortiter et Recte*, which means "Boldly and Rightly." The rich history on my paternal side might have intrigued me even more, if not for the fact that I'd disowned my father and anything having to do with him. The man disappeared when I was six years old, right after my mother had been diagnosed with multiple sclerosis. Shortly after, he'd flown to Scotland for his father's funeral, and that was the last we ever saw of him.

What kind of person does a thing like that? No one I want to know, that's for sure. He'd vanished without a trace, and to say I was remotely interested in that branch of the family tree would be an overstatement.

Or so I told myself.

But the fact that I knew the crest and motto spoke volumes. To be honest, an occasional flicker of curiosity *does* pop into my head, but I'm not about to act on it, now or ever. As they say, you can drag a horse to water, but you can't make her drink.

Sometimes I think Ami did this on purpose—suggested the setting to get me involved with distant relatives.

But I've had over thirty years to build up walls of resentment and anger, and I'm not caving to mere curiosity. I owe my loyalty to the woman who birthed me, who lost her battle for life earlier this year.

Anyway, my time in Scotland has flown. I haven't had a free moment to do any family research, even if I wanted to, what with writing *Falling for You*, book one in the Scottish Highlands Desire series; turning it in; and working on finishing the first draft of *Hooked on You*, book two.

Then there was the unexpected volunteer work.

This unusual opportunity had arisen out of the blue. Detective Inspector Kevin Jamieson had approached me with an offer to replace his special constable, Sean Stevens, who had been accepted into the Scottish Police College in Fife and had taken off for training in September, leaving Jamieson forced to find another.

"It would appear," the inspector had said, "that I'm required tae have a volunteer special constable at all times, whether it agrees with me or not."

"But I'm leaving in December," I'd pointed out.

"Aye, we can cross that bridge when it's upon us. Fer now, ye're the likeliest tae get along with. At least in my mind."

I'd agreed. The inspector and I were very much alike. Both of us are introverts. Neither of us is shy, but we need more personal space than some people do. He and I tend to work best alone and are more comfortable touching base occasionally rather than investigating while joined at the hip. Most importantly, we respect each other. I consider him shrewd, intelligent, tough, but sensitive when he needs to be. We are even both left-handed, if that means anything significant, which I suppose it doesn't.

I'd accepted his offer without much thought as to the ramifications of the position as special constable. It was hard for me to believe that a country (or rather the entire United Kingdom) would allow untrained volunteers to run riot on the streets—wearing police uniforms (I'd been given a waiver on that requirement) and wielding all the power of real cops. I even carry pepper spray, which is considered illegal contraband, its possession a serious offense.

Unless one has a police warrant card.

Which I have.

I keep it close at all times.

It's been interesting, mixing fictional romance stories with real-life crime drama.

Not that there's been any police-type work in the village since the snow began to fly. Not even so much as a missing pet or a wayward teenager to track down and drag home. With the blanket of snow had come a perceptible quiet. It was a fine time to bake a batch of cookies, read a good book, or, in my case, write one.

I've enjoyed myself thoroughly, whether hiding away in one of the warrens at the Kilt & Thistle Pub in the center of the village. Or raising a dram or two there with Leith. Or stocking up on shortbreads from A Taste of Scotland. Or discussing a case with Inspector Jamieson. Or just walking the cobblestone streets of Glenkillen. I've savored every moment.

But in exactly two weeks, right before Christmas, the most magical time of the year to spend with friends and family, this will all come to an end. Vicki will drive me to Inverness. From there I'll take a short flight to London and make a connection at Heathrow, leaving behind this amazing world I've discovered, to return to the drabness and loneliness of my old life.

At thirty-eight years old, I find myself virtually family-less with the loss of my mother. And as to friends? Well, other than Ami Pederson in Chicago, my friends are here in Scotland. A controlling husband, now thankfully an ex-husband, tends to put quite a damper on establishing and maintaining friendships. And after I'd extricated myself from that toxic relationship, I'd focused on caring for my mother up until her death, at which time I gave up the apartment I'd shared with her in those final days.

Vicki had suggested a simple solution. Why not fly back to the States every six months, then turn around and come back? Simple, maybe, but with the exorbitant cost of airline tickets, that idea wasn't feasible. Ami had subsidized this trip and I really needed to pay her back with future royalties. Besides, the nomadic life isn't for me. I need someplace to call home, even if it means establishing new roots in Chicago. Which, unfortunately, it does.

Vicki and I sat next to each other on a connecting flight out of London into Scotland when I first arrived and became fast friends when she offered me the use of the cottage on her property. We've already had a cry or two over what would soon be our mutual loss. But tears weren't going to alter reality. Laws and regulations are too powerful to challenge. Time is against me. I have to go.

"How is Kirstine feeling?" I asked, putting my own problems aside, sure that I'd revisit them soon enough. "Is she any better?"

"Still in bed with a nasty cold," Vicki said.

Vicki's half sister manages the farm's woolen shop, and Vicki teaches knitting classes as well as running a skein-of-the-month club. The shop is called Sheepish Expressions and is a favorite with tourists as well as locals, specializing in rainbow-colored skeins of yarn and exclusive Highland wools. Now, with Kirstine out of commission, my friend has taken over all aspects of the business.

If not for the snowstorm raging and the deserted main road, Vicki would be at the shop instead of sharing tea with me. I've seen little of her the past several days unless I stop in at Sheepish Expressions.

"Gritters will be out before too long," Vicki said. At my blank expression, she added, "Salt trucks. You know, those big vehicles that spit salt out of the back ends."

Oh.

My friend giggled, grinning from ear to ear. She loves to see me perplexed by the little idiosyncrasies and foreign terminology I encounter. Vicki has an advantage over me. She lived in California most of her life, but she's Scot born and spent summers in the Highlands before deciding to move back here permanently in her forties. So she's been a great interpreter.

But I suspect most of her current delight, what is really causing her lightheartedness, has to do with Sean Stevens, the special constable I replaced and my friend's significant other.

He was scheduled to return later tonight from police college, his initial classroom coursework completed. Monday he would begin the next part of his training—following in the footsteps of a certain unwilling but resigned inspector.

"Well, I best get back to the shop," Vicki said, rising and going about the task of wrapping up—boots, wool coat, scarf, mittens, and beanie hat, which she tied under her chin. "It's unlikely that anyone will brave this weather. No one can possibly expect the shop to be open, but there's plenty of other work to be done."

I watched her pushing her way through the newly fallen wet snow with a Westie under each arm, since their short legs never would have made it through without her assistance.

My phone rang, turning my attention away from the winter wonderland outside my window.

"How ye be managin' out there?" came the inspector's voice. "Are ye good and buried?"

"Yes, but perfectly fine with that, thanks to a bin full of firewood and a shopping trip for supplies earlier. Vicki knows how to prepare."

"She's one o' us, and we know how tae manage in adversity," he said with a chuckle. "There haven't been any major tailbacks, thanks tae the gritters that have been treating the roads. And don't ye worry, it'll be over in plenty o' time fer yer big event tomorrow evening."

"So the gossipmongers are hard at work." Keeping anything quiet in Glenkillen was impossible. News spread almost before it happened.

"It's out and aboot that ye were invited."

"I *have* been wondering if it will have to be canceled."

"Fer a few snowflakes? Hardly. What are ye intending tae wear?"

That was an odd question, especially coming from this particular man. Since when does he care about my attire? Since when did he even notice? Oh, wait, he was up to something, judging by the teasing tone. "Don't even think it," I shot back. "I'm *not* wearing a police uniform."

That was worth another chuckle. "Ye're on tae me as usual."

"You're an easy read," I quipped, although that was far from the truth. Most of the time, he was completely unreadable. I suspected that the term "close to the chest" was coined after him.

"No drink drivin'," he went on. "And no stirrin' up trouble. Ye have an image tae uphold, Constable Elliott."

"I promise to be on my best behavior," I said, disconnecting soon after.

Inspector Jamieson's personal life was an enigma to me. In some ways, I understood him. In others, he eluded me. In spite of time spent together sampling local fare and talking shop, I never felt that I had him completely pegged. Perhaps that was because of his skill in circumventing any mention of his life outside work.

All I knew for certain was that he was in his fifties, that his wife had died of cancer some years ago, that he'd never remarried nor did he have any interest in the advances of the local women, and that he lived at some remote hunting lodge away from the village.

I added a few more logs to the stove, after feeling a bit of a chill in the air, and used the fire iron to arrange the wood for best results. Then I sat down and picked up my knitting.

I'd only recently learned to knit and had insisted (against Vicki's better advice to start with a simple scarf) on beginning this new adventure with December's skein-of-the-month club kit, which consisted of the appropriate yarn and a pattern that Vicki had named Merry Mittens. Some of the members had already whipped out their mittens and were wearing them, while I'd barely begun the first mitten, thanks to the confusing abbreviations associated with the pattern as well as my fumbling fingers. But I loved the color combination—apple green, lime, and sunshine yellow.

At this rate, though, I'd finish by next December, but I was determined. I also lived in terror of dropping my first stitch. Because once that happened, the mittens were sure to be doomed.

Soon after, my phone rang again. This time it was Leith Cameron. After several comments back and forth about the storm and a few minutes spent on arrangements to pick me up tomorrow night, he said, "I'm looking forward tae the event."

"So am I."

"This special tasting is as exclusive as the Glenkillen Distillery's fine whiskies. Bridie Dougal doesn't invite just anybody tae her private gatherings, ye know?"

"I'm appropriately honored."

From what I'd heard through the pub's active rumor mill via Vicki, Bridie Dougal was a crusty old woman who'd run the family distillery with a firm hand after the death of her husband, finally turning it over to her son in the last year when her advanced age began to slow her down. These days, she was rarely seen in public but still had managed to arrange this special night of tasting, thanks to her personal companion, Henrietta McCloud.

When the invitation had arrived, I wasn't at all surprised to discover that Leith's name had been included on the exclusive guest list. The barley he grows on his farm next to the MacBrides' is used for the production of the popular Scotch whisky produced at this particular local distillery.

Not only that, his family had been key suppliers for generations.

So I was taken aback when he went on to say, "I'm still wondering how ye managed tae get invited. How do ye know Bridie Dougal?"

"I don't understand," I said, after a moment's pause. "I don't know her at all. *You* invited *me*."

"I would have fer certain, if I'd been the one doin' the inviting."

We ended up comparing them. I read mine: *"Leith Cameron requests the pleasure of your company at a special winter whisky tasting . . ."*

"Ye're not foolin' with a poor Scot, are ye?" he teased.

"No. What does yours say?"

"Eden Elliott requests the pleasure of your company at a special winter whisky tasting on Saturday evening, December 8, at 7:00 pm . . ."

"But I sent a note to you accepting," I sputtered, while my mind raced to figure out how this happened. "Didn't you get it?"

"Sure, I did. I thought it was a wee bit strange, but ye're from the States and they're an odd lot." Now I heard the amusement. He went on. "Henrietta musta been confused when she wrote them out. She's come on pension age, not as young as she once was. Although anybody coulda made a mistake like this."

A reasonable conclusion.

"If it was a mistake . . ." I began, feeling disappointment at the thought of missing out.

"Only a slight one," he reassured me. "Henrietta hasn't gone dotty. We both are invited, I'm sure o' it."

"We're still on then?" I asked, hopeful.

"If ye're game, so am I."

"Great. I'm looking forward to my first whisky tasting."

Besides, I wasn't about to turn down an opportunity to get an eyeful of Leith Cameron in a kilt!

Chapter 2

That night dreams interfered with my sleep. When I awoke, they had disappeared into the recesses of my memory. The details might have faded away, but I was left with a sense of impending doom that was hard to shake off.

The day before, I'd been preoccupied with preparing for the whisky tasting and fearful of the unknown I'd encounter when I left the Highlands. Something there must have triggered the disturbances I'd encountered during the night.

It was still dark outside, making whatever visions I'd awoken from seem even more sinister. Checking the time, I realized I'd begun sleeping longer and later than I had during the summer months. Days were short and nights were long now as the shortest day of the year approached. Fourteen hours of sunlight were distant memories as we suffered through a mere seven hours at best.

Today's sun wouldn't rise until approximately eight thirty, and it would disappear completely by four, already beginning to fade from sight as early as three. That is, if we even saw the sun. Mostly we were grateful for the light it emitted through the cloud cover.

I wasn't about to dredge up the specifics of what I was sure had been a terrible dream. Let sleeping dogs lie, as the saying goes.

Speaking of dogs. John Derry, Vicki's brother-in-law and Kirstine's husband, had already shoveled a path from the main house to my cottage. He wasn't in sight now, but there was no doubt that he had done the hard labor. He always did.

Cup of coffee in hand, I assessed the white world outside my window.

Coco and Pepper ran along the path and began yipping at my door. They must have been snow pile diving, because they were coated in the white, fluffy stuff. Or rather, they had been, before they shook it all over my floor and pajama pant legs.

"I don't know why I let you in here," I scolded them lightly. The truth was I loved the little Westies like my own. I couldn't think of a better way to brighten up the day than with a visit from them. They were the perfect antidote to this morning's gloomy beginning, which had been inspired by elusive imagery produced by my renegade mind.

The two lounged by the fire while I showered in the hottest water my body could tolerate. Then I dressed in warm trousers with leggings underneath and a cotton sweater. The snow had stopped falling sometime during the night, but the weather report had forecast wind and a lingering chill.

I poured another cup of instant coffee, something I'd gotten used to over time and now found pretty good. Sitting at the table, I nibbled on one of the cheese scones I'd purchased from A Taste of Scotland, my favorite bakery. The Scots pronounce the name of this delicacy much differently than we do in the States. Here it phonetically sounds like "skon," rhyming with "gone." This one was baked with Scottish cheddar cheese from the Isle of Mull. It was delicious.

Vicki had finally installed Internet access at the farm, so I started up my laptop. I still did all my writing at the pub, finding it more conducive to the creative process. At home, I was easily distracted by pretty much everything and everyone, especially by my friend and her canines. But really anything could interrupt my thought process. A quick glance out the window now with a view of the hillside was enough to stop my brain from functioning as it should.

Because across the lane, framed by the hills, I spotted an enormous red deer stag, with a thick winter coat and a huge rack of antlers. He must have sensed my interest, because he swung his head in my direction, then turned slowly and sprang across the base of the hill, disappearing from sight.

Glancing down at my laptop, I found a short e-mail message waiting in my inbox. It had been posted several hours before and it was from Ami Pederson.

"I'm excited about tonight's whisky tasting," she wrote, as though she were the one going. "What do you think Leith will wear under his kilt?"

That again? You'd think she'd have some interest in what *I* was wearing. I suspected that Ami was living vicariously through more than her own fictitious tales.

Ami is a bestselling historical romance author. By bestselling, I mean mega-famous. And she's a push-and-shove kind of woman who always gets her way in the end.

"Shoes and socks," I wrote back, grinning as I hit the send button.

I owe so much to Ami in spite of her annoying persistence regarding my future and even though she has a one-track mind when it comes to my personal life—she's obsessed with getting me "hooked up." She feels it's her personal obligation to do so.

Immediately after my shoes and socks reply, an e-mail from her came bouncing through cyberspace. What was the woman doing awake? It was the middle of the night in Chicago.

This time, after one "LOL" and several "snort, snorts," she switched subjects. "Are you letting your characters get naked?"

"Of course," I responded, with more of a quip than I was feeling.

Sex scenes are extremely difficult for me to write. They definitely don't flow naturally, and I made the mistake of sharing this with Ami, who has always had a pat answer. "That's because you need more hands-on research. You can't write what you don't know."

In spite of her implication regarding my virginal sex status, she knows I've been married. As hard as I try, though, I don't remember any passion in our relationship.

Instinctively I must have taken her references to my lack of experience as a challenge, because I proved her wrong when I finished *Falling for You*, sex scenes and all. Once Ami read it, she'd changed her tune. Although she managed to stick with the same theme but with a new twist.

"All that fragile desire and suppressed longing bottled up inside you translated into some beautiful sexual encounters," she'd raved. "Keep doing what you're doing."

Which wasn't much in the way of romance, or even much

platonic male companionship. I'd had several outings with Leith, and the inspector has shown me a few sights, but that has been pretty much it. That night's whisky tasting was going to be the closest I'd come to an actual nighttime date. And as it turned out, it hadn't been initiated by Leith at all. He'd thought I'd been the one doing the inviting.

The more I considered the mix-up, the weirder it seemed. I picked up the invitation I'd received in the mail and reread it. So odd. But I told myself that I'd never met Henrietta McCloud. Maybe she was a flake.

Pulling on a quilted wool coat and knee-high boots, I made my way along the shoveled path, with Coco and Pepper racing ahead of me. Vicki wasn't at the main house. I left the dogs inside, walked down the lane, which had also been plowed, and found the open sign illuminated and her inside Sheepish Expressions.

"You don't have to open this morning," I suggested. "No one is going to be out unless they have to be."

"I need to take care of a few things anyway," Vicki said, seeming a bit subdued. "So I might as well. It's a good time to get caught up on inventory."

I did a little theorizing. Sean Stevens should have been back from Fife last night, but I hadn't seen his car outside the main house as one would expect if he'd arrived as scheduled. Either he was still away, or the snow had stopped him.

"How did you sleep?" I asked subtly.

"All right," she said with a shrug, removing a pair of reading glasses from the end of her nose. "Though I was expecting to get not a wink. But Sean couldn't get through. I knew in my heart he wouldn't make it, but I so wanted him to. The roads were closed. But, of course, they've reopened now." She sighed in exasperation. "All those weeks away from each other, and it doesn't seem right that we have to wait even longer. Why couldn't the snow cooperate?"

"There's always today," I said.

Vicki smiled and gestured toward the open sign. "Yes, and I'll pull that plug the minute he shows up. Are you ready for your big night?"

I told her about the invitation snafu. When I finished, she said, "Henrietta McCloud is usually more organized than that. But I hear that her health isn't good at the moment, so she could have slipped up. It doesn't matter, does it?"

"I'd like to look into it."

"Why on earth would you bother? Go to the tasting and enjoy yourself."

I shook my head, remembering the feeling of distress I'd experienced on awakening. "Something about it doesn't feel right."

"That police business you're involved in has you imagining dark secrets in every corner."

There might be some truth to that. Still . . . "I think I should call and speak with Henrietta McCloud. If there's a chance the invitation was extended in error, Leith and I shouldn't show up at all. I have absolutely no connection with the distillery or the family who owns it, so why on earth would I receive an invitation?"

"But you do have a connection," Vicki said. "Leith."

"Do you have a private phone number for Henrietta McCloud?" I insisted. "Or one for Bridie Dougal?"

Vicki didn't press it further, knowing by now that when I set my mind to something, I follow through. She replaced the reading glasses and shuffled through a phone directory she'd pulled from a drawer. "Henrietta McCloud is a member of my skein-of-the-month club, so I should have her contact information someplace. Yes, here it is." Then she couldn't resist and added, "But I still don't see why you're making such a big deal of a little misunderstanding."

Actually, at this point, I wasn't sure myself.

But true to form, I made the call.

A woman answered. I asked to speak with Henrietta McCloud and was put on hold. After a rather lengthy wait, the same woman's voice came on and said, "This be Henrietta. But herself wishes to speak with ye instead."

Herself? I attempted to explain myself. "I'm afraid there's been a mistake, which I hope to rectify. I was calling to speak with you about tonight's whisky tasting and the invitation I received. It seems that . . ."

She cut me off. "I'm aware o' the reason fer yer call, and as I stated, Bridie wishes tae speak with ye."

"That's fine. I'll need her telephone number unless you can connect me."

"In person, herself says."

"The roads will be slippery. Does she have a driver?"

There was a pause, then Henrietta said, "There's no fireplace like herself's fireplace."

Huh? Oh. I was being summoned. "An hour, then."

"Ye know the way tae the distillery, ye do?"

"Yes."

"Drive around the eastern end, and ye'll see the house. She'll be expecting ye."

I hung up. Things were getting stranger and stranger.

"I've been asked to meet with Bridie Dougal," I told Vicki, who had been immersed in sorting through a new shipment of woolen wear. At my announcement, she glanced up sharply and said, "Now what could you have done to catch the attention of the chieftain of the entire Dougal clan for a private audience?"

"Chieftain? A *woman* is head of a clan?"

"And why is that such a big surprise?"

I stammered around a bit, at a loss for words, embarrassed by the realization that I might actually have prejudices I didn't know about and they were raising their ugly little heads.

Why not? Why couldn't a woman be a chieftain? The idea appealed to my senses. This day was getting more interesting by the minute.

Vicki went on, "Not that the Scots care much about clans and lineage in this day and age. It's a much bigger deal in the States. But Bridie will enjoy being treated like royalty, if you decide to bow to her." Vicki giggled.

"Should I really bow?" I didn't know the proper protocol, having never met the head of a clan before. I imagined a Highlander wielding a broadsword, adorned in tartan, kilt, and sporran, living among misty Scottish hills. A reclusive woman residing in a distillery just didn't do justice to that romantic image.

Vicki was laughing now. "I should encourage you to bow for the fun of it. But really, in this more modern world, chiefs can be gardeners or hill farmers or pub owners. Clans were needed long ago—for basic protection and sustenance. Solidarity was necessary to defend territories. As to proper etiquette in this century, treat her with the same politeness and respect as you would any other elderly woman with massive wealth, privilege, and title."

"Oh, great, thanks. I feel so much more confident now."

Vicki was having great fun. "Call her Bridie. Everybody does. And she isn't the chief of the clan. She's a chieftain, which means she's the head of one branch of the Dougal clan."

I hadn't realized there was a distinction between chief and chieftain. Okay, that didn't seem quite so formidable. Which was what I told myself as I trudged to the barn where we kept our cars during the winter months. Predictably and thankfully, John had cleared away the snow that had drifted against the barn doors. Vicki's brother-in-law might be a burly Welshman of few words, but he knew how to keep the farm running on schedule.

Jasper, our resident barn cat, had developed his winter coat and appeared to be twice as large as he really was. When the days and nights grew colder, I'd made a fuss about leaving him outside in the elements and even tried to bring him into the cottage. But he wanted nothing to do with what he apparently considered nothing short of incarceration and was very vocal with his opinion on the matter. He also expressed himself physically by shredding my kitchen curtains in protest. After that, I was forced to accept his decision, but I still didn't agree with it.

I spent a few minutes cuddling with him now that we were on speaking terms again, enjoying his purring machine. Then I eased the old Peugeot out through the large barn door. I was an old hand at working the clutch and maneuvering through the gears that were housed on the left side of the driver's seat instead of the right. When I drove again in the States, I'd have to relearn what had come naturally to me in the past.

I focused on sustaining my continuing good health after

sliding out onto the main road from the lane, quickly realizing that the roads might be clear, but the surface was still snow covered and treacherous.

After white-knuckling the steering wheel for what seemed like forever, I turned off the main road onto the one leading to the distillery, which was located just above Glenkillen, directly before the descent to the harbor and the village. The distillery appeared and I followed Henrietta McCloud's directions, heading for the east end of the distillery, driving along the expanse of its nondescript brown stonework. A few moments later, what I first thought must be a royal castle appeared before me.

The stonework structure didn't have a moat, drawbridge, or battlements. And I would bet there wasn't a dungeon below a circular staircase. But the granite building was stately with Gothic gables and soaring turrets. Altogether fitting for what I imagined was the residence of the chieftain of Clan Dougal.

I drove the car into a circular driveway, got out, gazed around me at the carpet of snow, and then rang the bell, hearing it resounding within.

And resisted the urge to hum "Hail to the Chief."

CHAPTER 3

The estate had presence, but the individual who opened the door had character.

I expected a servant (manservant, wearing white gloves, carriage erect, formal air about him). Instead, the head of the household greeted me through the partially opened door. Or so I assumed. I'd been told that Bridie Dougal had turned ninety recently, and I didn't need to be a detective to know this woman was advanced in years.

"You must be Eden. I'm Bridie," she said with a strong and commanding voice that belied her size and age. She was small and delicate with a lived-in face, and she had trouble fully opening the massive door until I stepped up and gently assisted her.

Bridie Dougal wore a furry Cossack-style hat, better suited for outdoor activity, and a plum-colored dressing gown. She leaned heavily on a walking cane. Once she recovered from the ordeal of managing the door, she took a step back at the same time that I took one forward. As I entered the hallway, I saw an expression of wonder cross her face. She raised a liver-spotted, blue-veined hand and placed it over her heart.

"I would have recognized you anywhere!" she exclaimed.

Behind her, I heard thick-heeled footsteps approaching from down a long hallway.

"Ye're impossible," the arriving woman said. I guessed her to be around the same age as my mother would have been if she were still alive, midsixties. She was tall but very thin, with a raspy voice and coarse complexion. She wore a black housedress with a large white collar and a dour expression. I assumed she must be Henrietta McCloud, although she didn't introduce herself. Ignoring me, she closed the door and took Bridie's free arm without giving me so much as a sideways glance. "I coulda seen her in," she said to her charge.

"I couldn't wait," Bridie replied. "But now that you have taken charge, Henrietta, perhaps you can assist us to the sitting room. This old coffin dodger could use a helping hand." We walked slowly through the great hall with its elaborate stone fireplace, and past a well-stocked library into a brightly lit sitting room where tea service had already been prepared at a table set near a roaring fire. "I must say that it was great fun luring you away from your writing obligations and all the going-ons at the MacBride farm," Bridie said to me. "I'll sit nearest to the fire, Henrietta, if you don't mind. I'm a bit chilled."

"And right ye should be, opening the door, hardly dressed at all." Henrietta scowled, then was seized with a cough attack. Once she recovered, she settled her ward into an upholstered chair and went about serving tea after I chose an embroidered chair directly across from my hostess.

My attention was drawn to the chair next to Bridie where a most unusual cat slept on its back. White, long hair, a round face, and ears creased and lying flat to its head, it looked like an owl.

"That's Henrietta's feline companion," Bridie said, noticing my fascination. "Snookie is a Scottish Fold. Folds originally came from Perthshire and are quite affectionate creatures."

"She's beautiful," I exclaimed.

Henrietta watched carefully as I complimented her cat. I had caught her studying me several times when she thought I wasn't looking. She was especially intrigued after the cat roused, stretched, and sauntered over to my chair. Snookie leapt up onto my lap, arranged herself in a comfortable position, and began to clean herself.

"Well, I'll be," Henrietta said. "Snookie doesn't take tae just anybody."

I never considered myself a cat person, having been raised with the occasional rescued dog here and there. But I liked Jasper, enjoyed going out to the barn to spend time with him, even though I'd had to woo him shamelessly to gain his friendship. This one was warm and friendly.

When Henrietta finished pouring each of us a cup, Bridie said, "You may go now, Henrietta. We won't need anything more at the moment."

"I'd prefer to stay in case ye—"

"That will do fer now. Thank you." Bridie's voice had

taken on a commanding tone. Then more softly she said, "Go on. Put yer feet up, take a rest."

Henrietta shot a glance my way from the corner of her eye, picked up Snookie from my lap, and reluctantly left the room. I watched her go before turning my attention back to Bridie, who was now staring openly at me. I thought I detected something akin to awe in her gaze. But that was impossible.

If my name were Ami Pederson, I would be able to understand her fascination. Ami's full-color photograph adorns the back cover of every one of her bestselling novels, and fans are always recognizing her and asking for autographs. But my first book hadn't been published yet. And chances were that my picture would be in black and white and located on one of the back pages. If it was even there at all. So she couldn't possibly be a fan of my work.

So why did she say she would recognize me anywhere? And why was she staring at me?

A random and uncomfortable thought crossed my mind, one I hoped wasn't anything more than a figment of my imagination. I set my cup down. Bridie confirmed my growing suspicion by saying, "You're the spitting image. Ye have his eyes."

"What is this all about?" I demanded when I found my voice, already feeling my temper rising.

"Simple, ye see. I wanted tae meet ye," Bridie said, leaning forward. "So I had Henrietta arrange for ye tae come tae the tasting. This private tête-à-tête is an unexpected gift ye dropped intae my lap without realizin' it. When ye phoned, I chose tae seize the opportunity. Don't look so perplexed, my dear. Like I chust said, it's simple. I had tae meet Eden Elliott, Dennis Elliott's visitin' daughter, while I had the chance."

It was a good thing I wasn't holding my teacup, or I might have dropped it. "I wouldn't have come," I said, manners forgotten, "if I'd known that."

"Then it's a good thing I didn't tell ye." Bridie carefully lifted her teacup to her lips, managing to look innocent.

"You concocted this charade?"

Bridie slowly returned her cup to the table. "I see this foolish old woman has shocked ye," she said. "That wasn't my intention. Rumors have been circulating since yer arrival in Glenkillen. They say Dennis abandoned yer mum and yerself when ye were just a bairn. I couldn't believe that possible. Is it true? I can see from yer expression that it is."

Speechless, I listened as she continued.

"I wasn't sure if ye'd accept my invitation or turn it down, but I didn't want tae take the chance. I knew ye'd come if Leith Cameron invited ye. And the only way I'd get that rascal interested in a little hobnobbing is with an invitation from yerself. It almost worked, didn't it? Until the two o' ye compared notes. Am I right? Ye caught on tae my scheme?"

She didn't wait for a response. I caught the twinkle in her eye. Merriment at my expense? A little fun in an isolated life that must be dreadfully routine? I could just imagine her plotting. All good fun.

Except I wasn't having a good time. I felt manipulated and decided to extricate myself from this awkward encounter as quickly as possible.

"Thank goodness fer all the typical village gossip," she went on. "Or I wouldn't have known about yer friendship with Leith. Or is it more? Ah, humor an old woman. Do ye fancy the lad?"

"I'm not interested in discussing my personal life with you," I blurted, "or hearing about my father. Or learning of your connection with him."

"Why, dear girl, I don't know where he is or what he's been up tae since his father died all those years ago. Shamed by his actions, I suspect. It's yer grandfather who I cared very deeply about, taken too soon from this life. He would have been immensely disappointed in his only child." She shook her head in wonder. "Ye resemble him so much. Roderick Elliott, or Roddy as I called him. We were lifelong friends, and seeing ye sitting here in front of me is like having a few more precious moments with him."

Tears welled in her eyes. Great. She was going to cry. *Please don't cry!* It was going to be difficult to remain angry and indignant if this little old lady started to sob.

I sprang to my feet.

"Please," she sniffed. "Don't go! I'm sorry if I offended ye. But I have a much more pressing reason fer wanting ye tae attend the tasting tonight. Ye see, I've been following news of ye ever since I discovered yer connection to Roddy. I'm fully aware of yer value tae Inspector Jamieson as his assistant. That ye've solved several crimes since yer arrival in Glenkillen . . ."

"I haven't been responsible for closing those cases," I insisted, shaken that this woman knew so much about me. "I only assisted in small ways."

Bridie smiled. "Ye also have yer grandfather's humility and grace."

I started for the door. I'd heard enough about the wonders

of my grandfather. He was buried and gone. And in my opinion, so was his son. My so-called father might really be dead. If not, he was dead figuratively, at least to me. I was bitter and planned on staying that way. And some conniving dinosaur of a family acquaintance wasn't going to change that.

"Please. Ye can't walk out on me," she pleaded, and I heard desperation in her voice.

Just watch me, I thought.

She raised her voice. "I asked ye here because of a serious threat tae my person."

I could tell she was good at getting her way. Very good. Well, at ninety years old she'd had a lot of practice.

I paused and considered. It was one thing for me to take offense over a personal matter that wasn't any of her business. It was quite another to ignore a plea for police protection, having taken a pledge to uphold the peace. Although I was pretty sure she wasn't above conveniently embellishing her situation, judging by her recent deception.

But when I turned around, she was holding out a piece of paper; her hand that had been so steady only a few moments ago was shaking. I took it from her and read the crudely fashioned block letters. *You are skating on thin ice. Cancel plan for Saturday night. You only get one warning.*

"I never ice-skated a day in my life," she said, as I sat back down. "But o' course that isn't what the person who wrote this meant. Henrietta found it several days ago, mixed in with the regular mail. So ye see, Constable Elliott, someone really is threatening my life."

CHAPTER 4

Inspector Jamieson sat across the table from me inside the Kilt & Thistle Pub. We'd greeted the pub owners, Dale Barrett and his wife, Marg, and put in our order. From my position, I could see the local drunk, Bill Morris, slouched at a table close enough to the bar to eavesdrop, yet tucked in a corner far enough away to remain out of sight. I always wondered how much information managed to seep into his sodden brain.

"Blutered again," the inspector observed when he followed my gaze over to Bill.

The Scots have a bottomless pit of synonyms for drunkenness. I've heard "hammered" here, which is used stateside, and "guttered." I'd also heard it referred to as "legless," and now "blutered."

"Bridie wants to keep the investigation unofficial, at least for the moment," I told him while we lunched on brown bread and cock-a-leekie soup, a combination of chicken, leeks, carrots, and rice that warmed up my insides on this nippy winter day. "In fact, Bridie was adamant. She doesn't want you involved, didn't want you to know. She tried to swear me to secrecy."

The inspector humphed as I continued, "I refused. If anything were to actually happen to her, and I'd kept information from you . . . well, you see that I couldn't in good conscience. I told her in no uncertain terms that the only way I'd agree to attend is with your full approval. She argued, but finally acquiesced when she realized I wasn't going to change my mind."

"Ye did the proper thing," he assured me, finishing his soup and leaning back to study me with sharp eyes, a habit of his that still makes me uncomfortable. "Does she have any idea who might be behind this threatening message?"

"After the stunt she pulled to get me to come to her event, she could be making the entire thing up, might have created the note herself. The woman seems to be trying to get close to me."

"And that would be a horrible thing because . . . ?"

I busied myself with buttering a thick slice of brown bread since I didn't have an easy answer to his question. It had to do with my privacy, with this person knowing more about me than she should. And with my resolve to ignore the Elliott side of the family. It would feel like a betrayal after all the grief my mother went through because of my father. I'd intentionally left Bridie's connection with one of my relatives out of the conversation we were having at the moment.

The inspector went on. "Bridie's reason fer the game she played with ye was most likely just as she admitted. Tae have ye nearby in case o' trouble. She's a tough old girl, loyal tae her friends and always one tae stay two steps ahead o' everybody else. I can't imagine why she didn't come directly tae me, though, if she was in real danger. What else did ye chat aboot?"

I went on to relate the story. "According to Bridie, she's been dropping hints to her son, Archie, about selling the distillery. Bridie says she's tried to groom her son to take over, but he doesn't seem to have the ambition or the passion, and she's worried that he'll run it into the ground once she's gone. She told him she'd rather sell to an outsider now than have it lying in ruins later . . ."

". . . without a pound tae show fer years o' hard work," the inspector finished for me. "Archie's in his fifties. You'd think he'd have his nose tae the grindstone tae put aside a tidy nest egg. It's a shame in family businesses when the children don't care aboot what their parents have built."

"Well, Bridie made up the entire thing as a ruse to spark a flame under him," I said. "She reasoned that if he thought he could lose the family business, he might shape up and take his position as head of the distillery more seriously. She believes that the warning was in regard to an announcement she said she was going to make in private with the family after the tasting."

"So she thinks this warning was penned by her own son?"

"She refuses to accept that, saying there are others who are more likely suspects. Although she wouldn't mention names, only insisting that I shouldn't be prejudiced before forming my own opinion."

"Has she been bandying her thoughts tae sell all aboot the place?"

"Only to her son and his wife, Florence. But she believes

they could have been overheard, or passed on to the wrong individual. I'm thinking any of the distillery workers could be worried about a potential sale and their own futures. Anyway, after the note appeared, she didn't know what to do, if anything. For a day or two, she ignored it. Then she thought of me."

"Rather than coming tae me?"

I shrugged. "Unofficial, she said. And a perfect excuse to drag me into her net."

"She's quite the plotter. Are ye sure the two o' ye aren't related?"

I smiled. "Positive," I said.

"Ye could collaborate together," the inspector suggested. "Co-author a novel."

"You aren't taking her seriously, are you?"

"Bridie Dougal always enjoyed a wee bit o' drama in her life. She has some jinxter in her, and it must be gettin' dreary up there, since the snow started flying aboot. What's this big announcement o' hers fer tonight?"

"Actually, she claims her ploy worked. Archie has been much more focused on the business. She plans to announce that the distillery will remain in family hands. But of course, the implication was that she'd announce a sale."

"So why doesn't she make the announcement right now and save herself all this grief?"

"I asked her that. She refuses to change her plan because of a threat."

"More like she's enjoying the excitement. Archie and Florence have a son studying business and marketing. I expect he'll take over at some point in the future."

"That's Bridie's most fervent wish."

"Well, we can't be discounting the possibility that someone actually did threaten her."

"So you think I should go?"

"It wouldn't hurt tae have ye there. Ye've a fine eye fer seeing things in a different light than others do. Go and decide fer yerself if there's truth tae her tale. But she wants unofficial and that's what she'll get. Fit in, as I'm sure ye will, have a fine time, and don't think ye have tae play the part o' her security team."

"I shouldn't drink tonight."

"Wha'? And how are ye tae pull that off at a whisky tasting without making yerself the center o' attention?"

"Good point."

"Go and have a swell time. I could make ye redundant fer a day or two if that's what ye need tae feel better aboot sampling the whisky."

"You'd fire me!"

The inspector chuckled.

My thoughts flashed to the dress I had chosen for tonight. And to Leith Cameron and the kilt he most certainly would wear. If nothing else, it would be a new experience for me, hobnobbing with a clan chieftain while sipping fine aged Scottish whisky.

I came back from my daydream, to the table and the inspector sitting across from me, watchful as ever but with an amused expression on his face when he said, "Fer all I know, ye concocted the whole thing yerself tae get out o' wearing yer uniform."

"Don't worry," I said with a grin. "I'll be prepared for anything. I'll have my trusty pepper spray along in case anyone acts up."

"Heaven help the lot o' us," was his parting shot.

After that, I dug my laptop out of my tote with the intention of writing for part of the afternoon before I went off to get ready for the tasting. *Hooked on You* was coming along well ever since the weather had turned cold, and I was certain to have the first draft finished by the end of the year, as I'd promised my publishing house editor. Hunkering down inside the pub, feeling the warmth of the fireplace, hearing the murmur of voices in the background, a cup of hot tea beside me—all these things are usually conducive to my creativity.

The setting for my Scottish Highlands Desire series is a small village called Rosehearty, a harbor town much like Glenkillen. Where the hero (Daniel Ross) is rugged, gorgeous, and sexy. And the heroine (Jessica Bailey) is beautiful and strong-willed and doesn't need a man complicating her life.

I really intended to write for at least a short while.

But how does that saying go?

The road to hell is paved with good intentions.

Because instead of creating a whole lot of conflict, setting those two characters at cross-purposes, and watching the sparks fly, I couldn't help it—my mind wandered here, there, and everywhere.

And as much as I tried to rein it in, it refused to cooperate.

Instead of taking an imaginary trip to Rosehearty where I could control every character's destiny, I found myself firmly entrenched in Glenkillen, where I was powerless to change the future.

Instead of writing about sweet promises, I sat at the pub table worrying about my own future, about my remaining days here, and how I should be making the most of the time I had left.

Another saying came to mind, one that the inspector had used a few months back when reassuring an anxious woman whose baby was threatening to enter the world in the back of his police car.

It had applied then and it arrived now just in time to save me from a funk hovering over my head. A Scottish saying this time, one having nothing to do with pavement and hell.

Whit's fur ye'll no go past ye.

Later, Inspector Jamieson had translated it for me in two other languages.

In French: *Que sera sera.*

And in English: *Whatever will be, will be.*

CHAPTER 5

"What *is* this haggis I keep hearing reference to?" Janet Dougal said to anyone who was willing to respond. "Is it some sort of Highland animal like the Loch Ness Monster?"

Leith, slightly behind me, gave a snort of derision that only I was close enough to catch. I felt exactly the same way.

Bridie had given me a little background on her other guests in advance, laying the groundwork. "Seven o' us in total," she'd said, surprising me by the intimacy of the tasting. For some reason, I'd automatically assumed twice that many, or more. Seven expected guests turned into eight with the appearance of Janet Dougal.

She introduced herself as a widowed American who'd recently arrived from the States and checked into the Whistling Inn in the center of the village. Although she had taken Bridie's last name, she was not a close relative (as distant as they come, according to a whispered explanation by Bridie), and every time she opened her mouth, she proved exactly how far removed she was from this Scottish clan. Or any

Scottish ties whatsoever. Somehow, though, she'd wormed her way in at the last minute.

Heavily made up and with a pointed chin, she had managed to insult most of the guests in some way or another in the short time we'd been gathered in the tasting room. This I ascertained by the tight smiles whenever she opened her mouth. For starters, she'd referred to the men's kilts as skirts and to the men in the room as Englishmen. The current question drew several smirks along with Leith's muffled snort.

"Haggis is a national culinary dish," I told her. "You should try it while you're here."

I would have enjoyed mentioning that one traditional ingredient that went into the dish was sheep's organs, but I turned away from Janet to take in the visual delights of the room—rich wood, a solid oak bar, granite walls, low lighting that brought out the deep grains of wood.

Tonight's whisky was being served with a variety of breads, antipastos, dips, smoked meat, smoked vegetables, feta, sundried tomatoes, and one thing that I'd been eyeing up—caramelized chocolate brownies with sticky sauce.

I adjusted my black dress, pleased that I'd chosen appropriately. At the last minute, Vicki had produced a sash of gold and blue. "It's called Monarch of the Glen. It's a universal sash. Anyone can wear it," she'd told me as she fashioned part of it into a rosette and pinned it to my shoulder, allowing the long ends to fall down my back.

Most of the other woman also wore cocktail dresses, except for Bridie, who, as fit her station as head of a clan branch, had chosen a full-length soft olive-colored tartan skirt and silk blouse with a matching tartan sash over one shoulder and an elegant walking stick that matched her skirt. Bridie had also had her hair done. It was swept up in a formal do. She'd exchanged the Cossack hat she'd worn earlier in the day for a bow that matched her sash. The men all wore kilts.

My eyes traveled to my escort. Leith wore a red and gray kilt, red tie, white oxford shirt, and a gray kilt jacket left open. He was a man comfortable in his own skin, exuding warmth and self-confidence.

He caught me sneaking a peek and winked.

I smiled before looking off toward Patricia Martin. We'd been formally introduced, but I'd already known of her from Bridie's description. Patricia had to be at least six feet tall, carried herself like a queen, and was Henrietta McCloud's older sister by five years. Unlike Henrietta, who lived modestly as a personal assistant, Patricia had married into the political life. Connor Martin was well known as a member of the Scottish Parliament in Edinburgh, the main reason he couldn't leave the city to attend the tasting.

I'd expected Henrietta to make an appearance after all the work she'd put into arranging the tasting, but so far she hadn't shown up.

"Cup yer hands around the glass." Archie Dougal, Bridie's son, demonstrated while servers presented each of us with our first taste. His wife, Florence, stood beside him. She was short and chunky, with furrowed lines in her face. "Holding the glass in that manner will warm the whisky and change the nose slightly," Archie explained, looking distinguished with a touch of gray at the temples. "As ye will discover, some whiskies will be smoky, some spicy, some fruity. It all depends on the cask, the amount of smoke used in malting, the shape of the still, and"—here he raised his glass to Leith—"to the most favorably grown barley."

"And don't forget the water source," Bridie added. "Our River Spey flows fast and true when not frozen over, and is as important an ingredient as anything else."

Archie smiled at his mother. "Yes, we can't forget tae mention that." Then to us, he said, "Go ahead and try it. This one is an everyday dram."

I eagerly raised my glass and took a sip, tasting vanilla and a light hint of oak.

Moments later, when we'd hardly begun exploring the world of whiskies, Bridie said, "If ye will excuse me. I find I tire more easily the older I get." Then to her son, with an implication that only the family and I were aware of, she said, "If ye'll fetch me, Archie, shortly after the tasting." And to me, "Would ye be so kind as tae see me tae the outer door, Eden."

"Do ye need a ride round back tae yer home?" Leith asked.

"Thank ye, lad, but my trusted driver has the automobile toasty warm." She chuckled as the two of us walked out of the tasting room. "In my younger days, I would have gone after that handsome man myself. He'll be a fine catch for some smart young woman."

"He's a winner," I agreed before saying, "It feels strange letting you go off alone."

"Nothing's goin' tae happen tae me, at least tonight. If the warning was fer real, it would be a fool that would try anything tonight with me fair warned. Henrietta will see me in, and we have solid locks and a security system ready fer action. Ye keep yer eyes and ears open, and we'll speak tomorrow."

As I helped her slip into her coat that had been hanging on a rack with the rest of ours, she said, "Henrietta would like tae have a private word with ye after the tasting."

"I thought she might have attended after all the work she put into it and with her sister visiting."

"Henrietta was not feeling quite up tae snuff and decided tae stay in her room. She isn't much fer socializing. Even so, after ye left earlier today, she asked me tae relay her wish of a wee chat with ye."

"Did she say why?"

"No, she was mysterious, I have tae say. Will ye come round tae the house directly after?"

"I'll do that," I said, a bit flummoxed as I watched Bridie exit the distillery and watched her driver help her inside. What could the housekeeper want with me?

When I returned, Leith handed me another whisky sample.

"This one is a cracker," Henrietta's nephew and Patricia's son, Gordon Martin, announced. Gordon, fortyish, had wide-placed eyes, a broad forehead, and a strong nose. What "cracker" meant was beyond me, but taken in context, I assumed Gordon was pleased with the results.

Bridie had told me that Gordon, along with her son, Archie, oversaw operation of the distillery. "Distillation in its simplest form," she'd told me after I'd expressed interest, "involves heating the liquid until it boils, capturing and cooling the vapors, and then collecting the resulting condensed alcohol."

We continued to sample single-grain whiskies with each one more aged than the last as Bridie's son described the complex flavors. Archie Dougal sure knew how to wax poetic when it came to romanticizing whisky. "Lovely fresh banana flavors," "a smokey nose that doesn't mask the citrusy notes but rather complements them," "creamy and sweet with hints of coastal salt," "heathery," "chestnutty," and my favorite of all his descriptions, "creamy body like sweet caramel pudding on a cold winter's day."

As to my own personal imbibing: I tried to take it easy, sipping each sample and then depositing the glass on a server's tray. But somehow I must have lost track, because the world was beginning to tilt a bit. To counter the effect of the alcohol, I wandered over and helped myself to a piece of the caramelized chocolate brownie with sticky sauce. It was as wonderful as I'd imagined it would be. And if it soaked up some of the alcohol, that would be an added bonus.

"Did you make these?" I asked the young woman standing nearby. She'd been in the background since the beginning, dressed more for catering than partaking. She was slight, had medium-length dark brown hair with bangs, and couldn't have been more than twenty-five years old.

"Aye," she said, beaming.

"What's your name?"

"Katie Taylor."

I remembered reading somewhere that many of the oldest surnames in Scotland came from the trades or occupations. Katie's ancestors most likely had been tailors. The same was true of other surnames affiliated with family occupation. Mason and Shepherd were two examples I'd encountered.

"And what's that ye're eating?" Leith asked, stopping beside me, with a slightly crooked grin.

"Something wonderful," I said.

Katie offered him one and he accepted with enthusiasm.

"Where did you learn to bake like this?" he asked her after sampling the brownie, appropriately impressed as I'd been.

"From me mum and hers before her."

While we chatted about baking and family recipes, I remembered to keep an eye on the others in the tasting room. Nothing seemed out of place. Archie was playing the perfect host. His wife, Florence, and Janet seemed to be getting on well, in spite of the visitor's brashness and my aversion to her, which really surprised me. Gordon and his mother, Patricia, were engaged in light conversation. Nothing amiss that I could discern.

A few minutes later, Patricia Martin made her way toward us while Leith worked on getting the basic ingredients for the brownies from Katie.

"Are you enjoying yourself?" Patricia asked me, and like her son, Gordon, her features were strong. In fact, so were Henrietta's. It was easy to see the resemblance between the three of them. Patricia's accent, though, wasn't as thick as her sister's or son's.

"Immensely," I replied. "The food is delicious, the whisky is the best I've ever had the pleasure to drink, and everybody has been warm and delightful."

"I agree with you. A perfect evening."

"It's too bad your sister couldn't be here to see the results of her efforts."

Patricia knitted her brows in concern. "Henrietta has been quite ill," she said.

"I'm sorry to hear that. She seemed well enough earlier today, although she did have a serious cough."

"She puts on a good face, she does. But the truth is that she's far from healthy. I wish Bridie would quit making so many demands on her. Henrietta has done enough for the Dougal family. It should be her turn for a bit of pampering and care."

A moment passed when I thought Patricia might elaborate on her sister's health, but the topic seemed to be closed, so I asked, "Where were the two of you from originally? Glenkillen or elsewhere?"

"A small village on the northern side of Loch Ness called Tainwick. Have you heard of it?"

Had I? It sounded familiar, but I wasn't sure. "No," I decided. "I don't think so."

"Henrietta left Tainwick and came here to the distillery when she was quite young. I was twenty-four, so she would have been nineteen."

Her recollection amazed me. I could barely remember the most significant of dates, or ages when events occurred, so I was always fascinated by those who could dredge up less memorable happenings. Although some were wedged in my head for eternity—my mother's date of death, for example.

"And you stayed on in Tainwick?" I asked.

"No, I'd gone to Edinburgh to university, and shortly after finishing I met Connor." Her gaze shifted to the few morsels still on the dessert plate in my hand. "What's that you're eating?"

"You have to try one of Katie's brownies," I took her then to Katie, who stood alone once more, Leith having moved off to circulate. "If you don't do this for a living, you should."

"It's more o' a hobby than anything," she said. "My real interest is in Highlands history and local families. I'm hopin' tae write a book one day on mysterious happenings in the area."

That was impressive. If she lived in the village, I would enjoy talking with her about her aspirations. "I'd like to continue this conversation later," I told her.

"You won't find much mysterious in these parts," Patricia said. "You need a larger population base for that—Edinburgh or Glasgow."

Gordon joined us as I relinquished my plate to a tray, and he handed me another small glass of whisky that I vowed not to touch to my lips. I said to him, "I'd like to see the distillery. Can that be arranged?"

"This tasting room is attached tae the warehouse where we store the oak casks until they're ready to be bottled. Right through those doors." Gordon gestured to a heavy set of doors to the right of the bar. "The still house where fermentation takes place is much more complex and worth a more lengthy private tour at another time, but I'd be happy to show ye the warehouse."

"Now?"

"Right now, if that suits ye."

"Leith," I said, catching my escort's attention. "Would you like to see the warehouse?"

"I've been inside it many times. You go along. I'll be right here."

"Patricia?" I asked.

"I think I'll stay here and chat up Leith."

So it was decided. Untouched glass in hand, I followed Gordon into the vast stone-walled building attached to the tasting room. An aroma of earthy oak wafted through the air. Casks were mounted on shelving, rows and rows against every available wall. Only the closest bank of overhead lights was lit; the rest of the room was in deep shadow.

Next to me, Gordon reached for a panel of light switches on the wall. "There we go. That'll make yer viewing a wee bit easier." And the room came alive with light. My eyes swept along the shelves as I savored the combined aromas of the aging whisky and oak barrels hanging thickly in the air.

"That door over there," Gordon said, gesturing, "leads tae the rest o' the distillery."

We walked farther inside. In the farthest corner of the warehouse, I noticed several large wooden vessels of some sort, definitely not casks, because they had a different shape, more like open tubs than closed barrels.

"What are those back there in the far corner?" I asked. One of those tubs had been moved directly below the very last cask on that wall.

"Discarded washbacks. Washbacks are where the fermentation process begins," he explained after a brief glance in that direction. "With fine barley, pure river water, and yeast. We've gone to using stainless steel since. But let me tell ye a little about the casks themselves."

Something propelled me away from my tour guide.

"We get the casks from the States," Gordon was saying behind me. "Properly seasoned. 'Tis a great secret to fine whisky making and the exact sources are not shared amongst the distilleries here."

An object seemed to be protruding from the top of the washback, but I couldn't be sure. Warily, I walked toward it, no longer listening to Gordon.

Was that an arm hanging over the top rim?

I sped up, my heels clicking loudly, the warning Bridie had received burning sharply in my mind. *You only get one warning.* And Bridie's parting words to her son, spoken aloud so anyone could have overheard. *Fetch me*, she'd told Archie, after the tasting. Implying that she might be following through on her own threat to sell out. If only she'd told them the truth beforehand. What had I been thinking to leave her alone?

I reached the end of the row, heart hammering in my chest. The whisky glass slipped between my fingers and I heard it shatter on the stone floor.

My eyes took in the cask, stored above the washback. It had been opened, tapped to allow its contents to stream into the tub below it. I remembered later the intense fragrance of it, how I'd always enjoyed that malty, smoky effervescence. But at that moment, it was overpowering.

Without hesitating, I grabbed the arm and tried to haul the rest of the body out. But the weight was too much for me. Strong hands joined mine, voices surrounded me, other guests, whisky sloshing everywhere, and before long we had pulled out the drenched form of a woman.

Leith and several of the other men tried to revive her, taking turns administering CPR while others hurried off to call the police. Finally they realized their efforts were hopeless and gave up.

Gordon, sitting on the floor of the warehouse, let out a cry of anguish, tears flowing freely down his face.

Because his aunt and Bridie's longtime companion, Henrietta McCloud, was lying dead in his arms.

CHAPTER 6

"But why Henrietta?" Bridie asked with a tremor in her voice. It was the question we all wanted answered. "She never caused a moment's trouble as long as she lived here, not tae me nor tae any others. If anything she was a wee bit reclusive, never complaining about anything or anybody."

It took only a moment or two more for her to remember the threatening note.

"I thought fer certain that the warning was fer me!" Bridie exclaimed, sitting in a chair in the same room where she and I had had tea this morning when her companion had served us. Now Henrietta McCloud was dead. Drowned in a vat of whisky. At the inspector's request Bridie turned the note over to him. The distraught woman was barely in control of her emotions as he studied it.

I felt more miserable witnessing Bridie's anguish than I'd been since finding the dead woman. Bridie and Henrietta had been close for years and years. Telling Bridie that her longtime companion was dead had even been difficult for the inspector. I'd stood beside him, my knees threatening to collapse beneath me, and now, if she broke down, I might, too.

Bridie went on, "And all along someone was after Henrietta. When she brought that awful note tae me, we both assumed it was fer me. Poor Gordon and Patricia. I need tae go tae them."

"That isn't possible at the moment," Inspector Jamieson told her. "They've gone with the body. And the warning and its intended recipient are still tae be determined."

Several hours had gone by since the shocking disclosure and the subsequent follow-up—guests interviewed in the tasting room, the body and crime scene examined, results logged, items bagged for further study. Finally, Henrietta's body had been removed, after which the warehouse had been cordoned off.

Sean Stevens had been dispatched to the distillery to perform for the first time in his new capacity as constable-in-training. Because I was a special constable, only a volunteer after all, my role at the scene normally would have involved less-critical tasks than those performed by the inspector. I'd have comforted the victim's family, kept witnesses gathered together, and remained alert for abnormal behavior. Although we all were acting abnormal considering the circumstances.

However, as the unfortunate person who discovered the body, I was front and center instead of backstage, forced to relate my story multiple times, what there was to tell. Way too little, much too late.

I'd been so sure when I'd reached into the vat and begun pulling the body out that once the dead woman's face was revealed, it was going to belong to Bridie Dougal. So when Henrietta's openmouthed face had surfaced from the depths of the whisky vat, followed by the rest of her body still clothed in her black housedress now water soaked, its pressed white collar limp, it had taken me a few minutes to process that fact.

When I did, I'd been shocked for a second time. The first time being when I realized it was an actual body inside the tub. Then it was so unexpected that the drowning victim was Henrietta when I fully expected to pull out Bridie.

"Who would do this?" Bridie, very much alive, repeated. "And why? Do you think it was a case of mistaken identity? That Henrietta was thought tae be myself? It can be dark in there without the lights on, ye know."

I bit my lip, because I wanted to answer, to say that it couldn't have been a case of mistaken identity. Bridie was diminutive; Henrietta, though frail, was tall. They were as different physically as the lanky Inspector Jamieson and the much shorter Sean Stevens. But it was Jamieson's place as head of the investigation to answer, not mine.

It certainly wasn't a case of mistaken identity, but there still was some concern (remote, though) expressed privately with the inspector that Henrietta's death could have been the elimination of a barrier of safety. She'd acted much as a bodyguard, and anybody getting to Bridie had to get through Henrietta first. Unlikely, we agreed, but still a concern.

I'm not sure how the inspector would have addressed Bridie over mistaken identity, because Sean chose that moment to speak up.

"Haud the bus," Sean said, spreading his arms wide as

though actually attempting to stop the wheels of a bus. "Ye might be ontae something there, Bridie Dougal. But let's take it a step further down the path. Some bloke mighta mixed up the sisters. That other one is a politician's wife, eh, and that might have something tae do with it. *She* mighta been the recipient o' the note and shoulda been on the receiving end. Instead her sister got it."

Leave it to Sean to come up with a theory none of us had considered, although usually we hadn't for good reason. I expected an unlikely scenario from someone like Bridie, who'd never dealt with a situation like this, but Sean had jumped right onto the same bandwagon. He has a heart of gold, but he isn't the sharpest when it comes to detecting and the tedious process of rational elimination.

Sean tends to affect a stiff and proper pose whenever he wears the official uniform, which he does proudly on every occasion he can, and this was one of those occasions. The inspector, on the other hand, is rarely decked out, preferring a less obvious show of authority. Tonight he had on beige trousers and a white oxford button-down rolled at the sleeves.

A look of pained annoyance crossed the inspector's face, an expression not uncommon when he was dealing with Sean. "Please give us a moment. I need tae have a private word with Sean and Eden," he said to Bridie, leading the way to the hall, where he turned to Sean.

"So," he said to his constable recruit in a controlled, low tone, "ye think somebody sent a warning that was found by the deceased, as would be expected, since she always brought in the mail, according tae Bridie here. And somehow the warning was intended fer Patricia Martin? And, tae top it off, the killer followed her all the way from Edinburgh tae murder her in the distillery and then managed tae botch the job by doin' in the wrong sister?"

I added another point. "And what plans would Patricia have that she needed to stop? And why threaten her through Henrietta? And without addressing Patricia specifically in the note, how could anyone have guessed the warning was for her?"

"Eden's right," the inspector said, scowling at Sean. "That won't do."

"It could be her politician husband who thought he was doin' away with the wife," Sean insisted.

"We'll leave the speculation fer now," the inspector said, glaring at Sean. "And if ye have any more bright ideas, ye need tae express them tae me in private, not go blathering tae others."

From past experience with him, I was well aware that he didn't approve of voicing theories in public, where the rumor mill would grind and churn out something altogether unsavory and most likely untrue.

He went on addressing Sean. "Why don't ye tell the lot in the tasting room that they can go fer the time being. But not tae leave the village. I've already made that clear, but another reminder won't hurt."

"I'll put it tae them firmly that no one is tae go against yer orders," Sean said, hustling off on his new mission to warn the group against travel.

Staying in Glenkillen wasn't going to be an issue for those who worked daily at the distillery. Most of tonight's invitees were local and affiliated with the distillery in some capacity. I'd learned that Archie and Florence owned a home in Glenkillen and that they were renting out one of their bedrooms to Gordon until his financial situation improved to the point that he could purchase his own home.

Nor was it a problem for Janet Dougal, the tactless American, who had checked into the Whistling Inn upon her arrival in Glenkillen. Her departure date was a week out. Hopefully the case would be solved before then and she could be on her way.

The victim's sister, Patricia Martin, also had booked into the inn, and her original idea had been to depart by train after spending a few days with her sister. Little had she known that those days would be spent planning her sister's funeral.

Katie Taylor would have had an hour's drive home after the event, and based on the weather conditions, she had made arrangements in advance to stay with a friend for the night. She'd be imposing on that friend for a little while longer.

We rejoined Bridie and the inspector said to her, "Ye shouldn't be alone tonight. Where is Archie?"

"He's seeing to his wife," I answered for her. Florence had come completely undone at the sight of the dead woman and was demanding her husband's constant attention.

Bridie glanced at me. "I agree with ye, Inspector," she said. "I shouldn't be alone until ye track down the person who did this tae Henrietta. I could be in danger. The guest room adjacent to my bedroom is made up, and I would rest easier. Eden?"

Thankfully, Jamieson caught on instantly, the same moment I realized she wanted me to stay with her. "I hardly think ye're in mortal danger," he said, "but we've all had a terrible shock, especially yerself losing yer friend and companion in such a violent manner. I'll have Constable Stevens stay until yer son is available. Perhaps Archie can drive his wife home and return fer the night."

Bridie sniffed. "That's not aboot tae happen when his wife wants him home."

"Then I'll speak tae my constable about staying the night as ye said a bedroom is made up and ready fer a guest."

I shot the inspector a look of gratitude as we left the house to return to the distillery, a short enough walk under different circumstances, but this night we would drive in the inspector's police car. Before we got inside it, he turned sharp, intuitive eyes on me. "It's not yer fault this happened, ye know," he said softly while our breaths fogged in the cold night air.

How could he know that I was racked with guilt, plagued by my inability to prevent what had happened? Well, why not. Nothing much got past him. "This is my fault," I said with a catch in my throat, tears threatening. "I had advance warning. I was right there all night. And Henrietta was killed right under my nose!"

"We both took Bridie's claim more lightly than we should have," he assured me, assuming his own share of blame for the oversight. "If I'd had a crystal ball we woulda been on high alert. In law enforcement we do what we can."

"Maybe if I hadn't been drinking."

"Don't haver on with that nonsense. The note was vague, not even specific tae a certain person. And what was supposed tae happen if the warning wasn't taken seriously? Fer example, the sender didn't threaten tae throw anybody under a gritter, now did he? And Bridie didn't ask ye tae be her bodyguard, only tae make some observations. And I was clear as well from our little chat that ye weren't tae act officially."

That was probably the longest speech the inspector had made since we'd met. By now, we'd driven around to the front of the distillery and parked near the entrance to the tasting room. The inspector didn't turn off the engine. Instead he let it idle while we talked.

"Henrietta had asked to speak with me after the tasting," I told him, although that had been one of the first things I'd explained during our initial conversation right after the death.

"Aye."

"What do you think that was about?"

"Could be important or it might not be relevant. The reason will come tae light."

"You should fire me, you know?" I said. "Or I should offer my resignation."

"Tell me, if ye hadn't let Bridie out o' yer sight the entire time, would it have stopped the murder? Would Henrietta McCloud be alive now if ye'd done that?"

"No, but . . ."

"No, but nothin' at all. As it turns out Henrietta is dead instead, and we have a murder tae solve. And I'll be wanting the help o' a certain constable, and I need her tae be at her best. Not snifflin' around with a bad case o' self-pity. Are ye up tae continuing?"

Was I? I'd really botched this one, hadn't been able to save a life. Yet part of me was growing increasingly more angry by the minute. At myself, certainly, but much more so at the person who'd killed Henrietta.

"All right, yes. Bridie shouldn't be in that big house alone," I said, thinking of Sean's overnight protection. "And I don't mean just for tonight."

The inspector looked pleased that his pep talk had done me some good. "Aye, in case that warning was fer more than one o' them. I didn't want herself tae worry none, but I'd like tae make sure she's safe without creating too much fuss in front o' her."

So this would be my lot—to end up on security detail, protecting Bridie for the remainder of the investigation, until the case was solved. I'd be having tea and fending off questions about my past from a wily old lady while the inspector and Sean carried out the real work. But didn't I deserve it?

The inspector watched me, as though he could tell what was going through my mind. Then he said. "And I know just the person fer the job o' protecting her."

"Me, of course. I'm the obvious choice. After the mess I made."

The inspector shook his head. "No, not yerself. It's our Sean I'm thinking o'. He'll make a bonnie companion. And tae fire him up tae the task, I'll alert him tae the old girl as one o' our suspects. Ye never know. She might turn out tae be our killer."

The darkness hid my relief. Actually I was pleased with the arrangement. It would satisfy all three of us. I could continue to work on apprehending the killer. The inspector would be free of Sean and had a valid reason to postpone the routine training he dreaded. And Sean would consider his role of the utmost importance.

"You don't really believe Bridie could have murdered Henrietta!" I said, as we got out of the car and walked toward the tasting room to finish up for the night.

"Not fer a single second. Bridie can barely lift her walking stick. How would she manage tae hold down a woman such as her companion fer even a moment let alone long enough fer her tae drown?"

"My analysis exactly."

"Let's finish and get some shut-eye. Tomorrow we have our work cut out fer us. And look who is still here, waiting tae take ye home."

Leith was heading our way, his usually light manner gone, a solemn set to his jaw and concern in his eyes.

We didn't say much on the ride back to the farm. It was late; midnight had come and gone several hours past. Both of us were exhausted and lost in our own thoughts. But I did remember to ask Leith if he'd overheard or seen anything that might have to do with Henrietta's death.

"Not a thing," he replied. "Everybody seemed tae be enjoying the evening. I know I was. But if I think o' anything, you'll be the first tae know."

Using a flashlight to guide us, he walked me to the cottage and followed me inside, where he wrapped his arms around me. I buried my face in his winter coat, finding it comforting. Being so close to him on such a harsh and brutal winter night was comforting.

We stood that way for a long time.

CHAPTER 7

After I'd moved into the cottage, I'd rearranged things a little differently to make better use of the space and had even found two matching kitchen chairs in the barn to add to the original two. Which was a good thing, since they were needed this Sunday morning.

Vicki was at the counter, dishing up one of her baked wonders onto small plates. Charlotte Penn and I were prepared to sample whatever she was about to put before us. If the aroma wafting from the baking dish she'd arrived with was any indication, we were in for a treat.

Until recently, Charlotte was the MacBride farm's sheep shearer as well as the shearer for most of the surrounding area while she worked her way through college and vet school. Now that she's completed her coursework, she still tends to the MacBride sheep although she's had to delegate out most of the shearing, because she's a full-fledged veterinarian. Earlier this morning, Charlotte had paid a visit to the farm to attend to a new litter of border collies. She'd appeared at my door after she'd examined the pups and declared them fit and sound.

The vet is in her midtwenties, wears her hair in a thick braid down her back, and usually smells faintly of hay. Today was no exception. I decided I liked her "perfume." It mixed nicely with Vicki's roses and jasmine, and I wondered if we could create a new scent, perhaps call it L'Hay Les Roses.

"You two need to get out from underfoot," Vicki said to Pepper and Coco, who liked nothing better than to keep the kitchen floor clean.

"What is it called?" I asked as she placed the delicacy before me.

"Clootie dumplings," she said. "It's a pudding. With dried fruit, ginger, and cinnamon, among other things. Clootie is the fabric the dessert is cooked in."

"Dessert?" I said. "For breakfast?

"And why can't we eat it for breakfast?" Charlotte said. "It's usually served for Christmas, but Vicki wanted you to taste it before . . ."

She broke off, not wanting to spoil the morning by bringing up my departure.

"What's that you're pouring on it?" I asked Charlotte, happy to avoid that subject.

"Clotted cream." She poured some on mine.

"Go ahead," Vicki said, taking a seat. "What do you think?"

"Delicious," Charlotte and I exclaimed simultaneously after our first bites.

"In the evening, I serve it with a dram of whisky," Vicki added, which brought the subject around to the poor woman who'd drowned in a vat of the Scottish alcoholic beverage.

"Henrietta McCloud was one o' those unlucky individuals who always suffered one setback after another," Charlotte said. "Ye know the sort that seems tae attract bad luck, havin' one tragic turn after another."

"Unlucky how?" I asked, anxious to hear what Charlotte had to say. The vet practiced up and down the hills of Glenkillen, so she had to have a wealth of information on the locals.

"I'll only consider telling ye because o' yer position, Eden," Charlotte said, "and Vicki, I can trust ye tae keep this tae yerself?" Charlotte obviously was having doubts about whether she should continue. She disliked gossip and as I've discovered since my appointment as special constable, there is a fine line that has to be walked. As a doctor of veterinary medicine, my friend also has to maintain a certain professional standard.

"I appreciate anything you can share about Henrietta," I assured her. "We will have to look into her current situation as well as her past. Anything that you offer will be a great help."

"And you know you can trust me to keep quiet," Vicki added, which was true. She loved to discuss the locals with me, but I couldn't recall a single instance when she'd spread anything that she shouldn't have. Vicki was trustworthy.

"The first thing was that Henrietta was unlucky in love," Charlotte told us, having decided to continue. "There was a bloke in her hometown who jilted her when she was nineteen and thinking they'd be wed. She carried that pain fer life. She never did marry, resignin' herself tae bein' a servant fer the rest o' her days."

"Sounds like plain old life's knocks to me," I said, thinking the dead woman wasn't the only one who was unlucky in love. "We've all suffered disappointments." That certainly was true in my case. But that didn't mean I planned to sequester myself away for life, bitter and lonely. Most of us get back up eventually, dust ourselves off, and continue the journey.

"But Bridie treated her well," Vicki said.

"Aye, like family, but it isn't the same as havin' yer own husband and children."

"But she had a sister," I pointed out. "I wonder why she didn't move to Edinburgh to be closer to Patricia."

"I never could figure that out." Charlotte took another bite of the clootie dumpling and hummed. I did the same while I thought about luck. Personally, I think we have quite a bit of control over the quality of our lives. Henrietta had choices after that man ended their relationship. She could have moved on with her life, let go of her pain, and found love again. Instead she isolated herself within a self-imposed prison of her own making. She'd held on to a bitter past for a lot of years. If Henrietta had been nineteen at the time and was in her midsixties when she was killed, that added up to forty-some years of service to Bridie, instead of making a family of her own. Hardly my idea of random bad luck.

I really do believe we make our own luck.

"The second stroke o' bad luck," Charlotte said. "The poor thing developed a disease that woulda killed her soon enough anyhoo. The third, as ye know, was that somebody murdered her. A black cat or two musta crossed Henrietta McCloud's path, that's fer sure."

"What disease?" Vicki asked, on high alert now that she was about to learn something about the dead woman that she hadn't known.

"Yes, what disease?" I seconded, just as interested. Purely from the viewpoint of law enforcement, I told myself. But the truth is, at times, despite my best efforts to resist that particular temptation, I enjoy gossip just as much as the next person.

"Lung cancer," Charlotte announced. "But it was hush-hush. Not public knowledge. She wanted to keep it private among those closest tae her. Henrietta was havin' a hard time accepting her lot. It was as though she thought if she refused to acknowledge her illness it would go away."

The news of her cancer didn't surprise me as much as I thought it would. It explained Henrietta's cough, the hoarseness of her voice, and her extreme thinness. And it also explained Patricia's statement regarding her sister's poor health and her opinion that Bridie wasn't sensitive to Henrietta's needs. But from my observation, Bridie was kind and considerate. Perhaps Henrietta was the one who wouldn't slow down and face her prognosis.

"Her medical condition most likely will come out," I said, carefully. "And I don't mean from Vicki or me. Things like this have a way of getting out during an investigation as serious as this."

"I understand," Charlotte said. "She was a tickin' time bomb, she was. Musta felt awful fer a long time before the diagnosis, which came about due tae a respiratory infection that forced her tae see the doc. She always was a stubborn woman, not one tae run fer medical care unless she had tae, and so it was in the advanced stage by the time it was discovered. In her bones already, and the doc said it would get tae her brain next and that'd be the end of her. She refused tae go through any procedures, which is just like her, but it was probably too late by then regardless o' any efforts."

"When was Henrietta diagnosed?" I asked.

"About two months ago. The doc gave her six months tae live. At the most."

I studied Charlotte for a moment before asking, "How do you know so much about Henrietta McCloud? From what I'm learning, she was almost reclusive. Surely she didn't share all this with you."

"I was out at Bridie's house a few weeks ago fer a routine exam o' Henrietta's cat, Snookie, when Henrietta had a moment o' weakness. I had tae help her tae her room. That's when Bridie confided in me. She said Henrietta was trying tae carry on as always. She insisted and Bridie couldn't stop her. After a while Bridie resigned herself tae the fact that her companion was going tae take care o' her tae the bitter end. But she was trying tae make it easier on her whenever she could."

On that sad note, a moment of silence ensured. Then Charlotte stood up and said, "Well, I best be on my way. Vicki, that was the best clootie dumpling I've ever had the good fortune tae devour."

After she left, Vicki and I gathered our dishes and silverware and placed them in the sink.

"How's Kirstine doing?" I asked Vicki. "Is she back to the shop?"

"She's got some bug that's going around. The doc says

she should rest another few days before coming back to Sheepish Expressions. Which is fine with me. She doesn't need to spread around her germs."

"Do you need help?" I asked, wondering how I'd manage if she did.

Lucky for me, Vicki shook her head, looking a bit down. "I'm doing just fine."

"Let me know if you change your mind. Is something bothering you?"

"No, it's just that I have plenty of time on my hands, since the inspector needs Sean round the clock on this case. I still haven't seen him!"

I felt a pang of guilt over the joy I'd felt when Jamieson had assigned Sean to watch over Bridie. I'd thought that it benefited all of us, but I'd forgotten about Vicki and the hole it would leave in her personal life. *It's only temporary*, I reminded myself. And Vicki's happiness was another reason to solve this quickly.

Vicki bundled up and left with the dogs racing ahead of her. I cleaned up the kitchen, reflecting on the murdered woman's life. I didn't know much about her. Most of what I'd discovered had been this morning at my kitchen table. Henrietta had made a decision long ago to remain alone for life. Her choice. She'd ignored her health, resulting in a fatal diagnosis. But she hadn't deserved what happened to her in the end.

Lost love, terminal illness, and murder.

Had her killer known about her death sentence?

If so, why go to such extreme measures to shorten it? Six months to live. That had been determined two months previous. She'd be gone in a few months, so why take the risk? Unless there was some immediate threat, one that I couldn't imagine at the moment.

Either that or the killer wasn't aware that Henrietta was dying, which was a more realistic analysis based on the victim's private nature. What, then, had driven someone to drown her in a vat of whisky?

She had wanted to speak with me after the tasting. Bridie claimed she didn't know why. If that was so, and I had no reason to doubt her, the only way I might eventually learn the answer to that question was if it pertained to her murder and became obvious at some point. What would she have said to me?

While I gazed out the window, deep in thought, a familiar red Renault pulled up near the main house. I watched Sean get out and saw Vicki come running from inside her home. They met midway and embraced, then walked together out of view. The inspector's police vehicle arrived directly after that, and I couldn't help chuckling. Usually it was the other way around, with the inspector racing away to outrun Sean.

Jamieson walked along the path leading to my door, unaware that I was observing him. As usual, he was solemn and carried himself with an air of sadness. Inspector Jamieson never spoke of the loss of his wife several years ago, but I was certain he hadn't recovered from her passing. Instead, he threw himself into his work.

"Yer phone line appears tae be out o' order," he said with a bit of snarl when I invited him in. From personal experience, I've learned that he isn't an early-morning person, and I try to avoid contact with him until later. "So I had tae drive all the way over here tae speak with ye."

"Vicki knows about the outage," I responded. "She says it's not that unusual to lose phone service during a snowstorm."

"But ye could have had yer mobile phone handy."

"Duly noted," I answered, a little terse myself. I didn't mention that my cell phone had drained and I'd forgotten to charge it.

The inspector grunted. "Are ye ready tae do a bit o' police work?"

"Yes. I see Sean is taking a break."

"Chasing after Vicki MacBride like a schoolboy."

I smiled. "He wouldn't be here if you hadn't approved it."

I didn't get a return smile. "When Bridie isn't with her son, which she is this morning, he's tae stay out there, keeping her company and nosin' around. But that isn't yer concern."

"Oh, and what is my concern?" I asked, feeling even more bristly. The inspector sensed it, too, and wisely backed off.

"If I seem out o' sorts," he said, more gently, "it's because I've had a long night without results. News o' the murder is all over the village, and I'm under pressure tae solve the case quickly."

"Why don't you tell me what you need me to do," I suggested. "That's what I'm here for, to make your life easier. Then go home and get a few hours of sleep. You'll be more effective if you do."

"Are ye sayin' I'm not effective right noo?"

"You're on to me as usual," I replied, forcing a light tone, using the same line he used on me when I caught on to his subtle meanings. He ignored my effort to make peace.

"I say nay tae yer suggestion."

"Would you like coffee or tea? And Vicki made clootie dumpling. There's a little left."

"Not noo. There's no time fer socializing. The sooner I'm on my way, the faster a villain will pay the mail."

Pay the mail? I gave him that furrowed-brow look that means he's lost me, but this time he didn't notice my confusion. Nor did he enlighten me, but taken into context "pay the mail" must mean pay the penalty or piper or something on that order.

"So there's been no significant progress yet?" I asked.

"None tae speak o'. I intend tae have more words with Bridie, hopin' she'll think o' something relevant, although we've been over most o' the areas o' concern and she hasn't been able tae contribute anything significant. Same can be said o' the guests who were at the tasting, but I'm not close tae done with them. Have ye put questions tae Leith? If not, perhaps yerself would like tae do that?"

"As you know, we went to the whisky tasting together and left together. He wasn't in the warehouse when I discovered the body, and from our brief conversation on the way home, he didn't notice anything unusual or anyone acting strangely. Nor did I. But Charlotte Penn shared something this morning. Did you know that Henrietta had been diagnosed with lung cancer and was given six months to live?"

"Aye, Bridie told me. But I don't see a connection as o' yet. Do you?"

I shook my head. "No, but it's still bothering me that Henrietta had wanted to see me after the tasting. Did you question Bridie further on whether she knew why?"

"She claims tae be as much in the dark as we are, and I believe her."

That was disappointing, but expected. "I hoped Bridie might have some idea."

"Henrietta refused tae say other than she needed tae have a chat with ye. She was a stubborn woman when she set her mind tae something. Anything she gave away during yer earlier visit that might have bearing on her reason?"

"None. But what if she had a particular concern over the note? Since she assumed it was intended for Bridie, she might have had suspicions to share with me. Maybe she thought she knew who sent it. Although wouldn't she have said that earlier?"

The inspector sighed. "We may never know what she had on her mind. Fer now, I'd appreciate it if you'd go intae toon and have a go at Patricia Martin. Sean took her statement and I had words with her, but she was in no shape tae answer questions o' a more personal nature last night. Hopefully, she's managed tae pull herself together. And if she hasn't, we need answers anyhoo. We can't wait any longer. The sister could have an idea or two as tae the reason fer the drowning."

"I'll see what I can do."

"And while ye're at it, ye better speak tae that space cadet from yer part o' the world. I can't imagine that she'll be useful, but ye never know."

"Are you really referring to my countrywoman in that derogatory manner?"

"Aye, Janet Dougal. From our exchange last night, I'm guessin' she's too high up on her throne tae have noticed anything at all. And I wouldn't go acknowledgin' that ye share a country with the likes o' her if I were you."

And so, after he'd gone on his way, I bundled up against the cold and popped into Vicki's house before heading to town, noting that Sean's Renault was gone already. Neither Vicki nor I are in the habit of knocking, although we don't exactly barge right in. So I opened the door, poked my head in, and announced my presence.

Vicki was hunkered over her laptop and looked startled at first. Then she reddened and slammed the computer closed as though I'd caught her surfing inappropriate sites.

"You scared me," she said, stumbling over her words, making me wonder what she'd been up to.

"What's up?" I asked.

"Nothing. Nothing at all. Just looking up a recipe or two."

"Really?" I said, thinking that another treat like the recent one was on the horizon. "What are you going to make?"

"You're certainly nosy this morning," she said, with a weak smile. "Save that for your suspects." If not for that smile, however small, that accompanied her words, I would have felt hurt. Still, her reaction when I'd arrived was out of character for Vicki.

What was going on?

Not feeling particularly welcome, I went back outside. The world was a white blanket as far as I could see, my breath rode on the air, and I pulled up the collar of my coat.

A few minutes later, I warmed up the Peugeot and headed for Glenkillen.

CHAPTER 8

The Whistling Inn, the village's only lodging, is next to the Kilt & Thistle Pub, and I'd stayed here myself on my arrival in the Highlands. At this time of year, after high season, it has more vacancies than paying guests. Even Christmas sees few visitors, as sightseeing takes a back seat to family gatherings. Another three weeks, though, and it will be brimming with visitors celebrating Hogmanay, which is the Scottish version of New Year's Eve. Even a small village like Glenkillen will indulge in all-night partying—singing, dancing, eating, and drinking.

Or so I've been told. I won't be around to join in the revelry. It's back to Chicago for me.

After parking, I entered the inn.

A Scots pine, or Scotch pine as we call them in the States, stood in one corner of the reception area. The smell of fresh, woodsy evergreen assaulted my senses. The dark-green foliage was decorated with white lights and tartan ribbons fashioned into bows. On the banister leading to the guest rooms above, garlands of holly and berries wound up the stairs, and more garland graced the mantelpiece over a fireplace with a roaring log fire. The inn was warm, inviting, and cozy.

I greeted Jeannie Morris, the reluctant proprietor. She has her own cross to bear in the form of an alcoholic father, who isn't in any condition to help the young woman manage the inn. The inspector had referred to her father earlier when we'd had lunch together at the Kilt & Thistle. Bill spends his days and evenings inside the pub with one pint after another in front of him.

My heart went out to Jeannie now that I knew the woman better. She acted out in her own way, with shocking red hair and the defiance of a nose ring. Recently she's added a tattoo to the back of her neck—XX, which she claims is a Viking symbol meaning, "Where there's a will, there's a way." In spite of her appearance, the inn is immaculate and well run, and it appears that she has reconciled herself to her circumstances. At least for the time being.

When I gave Jeannie the names of the guests I wished to speak with, she rolled her eyeballs and said, "Janet Dougal is in the breakfast room. I haffn't seen hide nor hair o' Patricia Martin. She's in her room, grievin' I imagine. Ye'd think she'd need tae eat at some point. I can't believe Henrietta McCloud is dead. And murdered at that. What a shock! But ye'll sort it all out, won't ye?"

"Of course," I said, taking on the same positive attitude as the inspector. "I'll be in the breakfast room with Janet. If Henrietta's sister comes down, let her know that I need to speak with her."

"Haff fun with that one," Jeannie said, which explained

the reason for the eye roll. It seemed that my fellow American had a knack for creating that effect on people.

Janet Dougal had shoveled on her makeup with a trowel again, rouged cheekbones and aqua eye shadow along with ruby-red lips. In the light of day, it gave her a harsh appearance. Last night, she'd worn it just as heavy, but I'd assumed that was her nighttime look. Apparently it was her daywear as well.

"I've finished eating," she told me when I asked to join her. "So if it suits you, go ahead and sit down. I was just lingering over another cup of coffee. These Scotch know how to make a hearty breakfast. I can give them that much credit at least."

Jeannie appeared with a coffeepot, refilled Janet's cup, and poured a fresh cup for me. She caught my eye and did another eye roll before moving off, having arrived at the table in time to hear the reference to "Scotch."

"They're called Scots," I corrected her, taking a seat. "Not Scotch. I believe they find that term offensive. I'm going to hazard a guess. You're not Scottish, are you?"

I smiled to myself. That was hardly an educated guess. The inspector would have been amused if he were here.

"My husband certainly was," she said. "Otherwise he wouldn't be of Clan Dougal. I have never been active with our clan, although I'd hate to admit it to this bunch of relatives. My late husband dabbled in genealogy and was proud of his heritage. He liked to hang around with the clansmen. He and I planned this trip a year ago, prior to his death. I decided to continue on without him after realizing that he hadn't taken a travel insurance policy and the expense of the trip would be a total loss if I canceled."

"He was closely related to Bridie?"

"Not the way we think of connections at home, of course. By name, though, and I have to be accepted based on marriage to a Scotch."

So much for my effort a moment ago to socialize Janet. Let her find her own way.

She took a slow sip of coffee before adding, "That was terrible what happened to the housemaid. Have they caught whoever did it?"

"Henrietta was Bridie's longtime companion, which is far more personal an association than if she'd been a maid. Bridie has lost a good friend. And, as to your question, not yet, we're making progress on the case."

Not entirely true to my knowledge, but a reassurance Jamieson often used when questioned.

"We?" Janet asked, taking more interest in me.

"I'm part of the investigative team, and I would like to ask you a few questions."

A shadow crossed her face. "So this isn't a social call."

"No."

Janet replaced her coffee cup in the saucer with a clank and raised a thickly penciled eyebrow. "I suppose you want to go over every detail regarding that silly disagreement I had with the woman."

I managed to keep my expression neutral, and I nodded as though that were exactly what I wanted to discuss. Which it was, now that I knew there was a point to be discussed.

"It isn't anything worth wasting taxpayers' money over," she continued. "Really nothing at all. Except now she's dead, and I assume you have to follow up on every single little thing."

"Tell me your version," I said, as though I'd heard another side of the story already.

Janet scowled. "I fully expected to be welcomed into Bridie's home," she said. "I'd introduced myself as a Dougal by e-mailing the distillery's contact number well in advance. I gave my arrival date and approximate time of day that I thought I'd be there. That hired woman wanted me to go through her instead of dealing directly with Bridie as was my right. I'm a Dougal, maybe not a blood relative, but my marriage should count for something."

She paused as Jeannie came by and refilled our cups. This time she skipped the eye roll on her way out.

I added cream to my coffee and said, "How many Dougals would you estimate live in Scotland?"

"I couldn't say. Quite a few, I imagine."

"And in the States?"

"Many, would be my guess. America has been a popular destination for my husband's relatives since the first ship set sail, and goodness knows the Dougals like to multiply. Do you have a point?"

"So every single Dougal, no matter how remote, how little the other Dougals might be aware of them, all should be treated as family, free to pop in on each other at will?"

I'd meant it as a point of contention, but Janet chose to take my comment as affirmation of her position on the matter.

She nodded enthusiastically. "We all should be treated like family, considering we *are* family. That's the point I was trying to make. The least Bridie could have done was given me a place to stay. Instead that dead woman . . ."

"Henrietta. Her name was Henrietta McCloud."

"Yes, her. She booked me into this inn, not that it isn't

nice, but well, not a single soul even offered to pay for my lodging. Then this Henrietta wouldn't allow me to speak to Bridie to voice my complaint. It's a miracle that I found out about the whisky tasting in advance."

Ah, yes, now I remembered. Janet had been a party crasher.

"How exactly did you learn of the tasting?"

"That relative of the dead woman's was in here and I overheard him. He was her nephew, I believe."

"Gordon Martin?"

"That's the one. Did I mention that I'm rather a connoisseur of fine whisky? When my husband was alive, we toured distilleries from the New York Catskills to Bourbon County in Kentucky, from Tennessee to Montana and Washington. Anyway, I gave Henrietta McCloud a piece of my mind."

"Go on," I said, sounding just like the inspector.

"I phoned yesterday afternoon to request detailed directions to the distillery. When she gave them, she was extremely vague as though she hoped I'd lose my way. I told her exactly how thoughtless she'd been from the moment I arrived in this village."

"And?"

"And then she called me an ugly American!"

Janet Dougal *was* an ugly American. She gave the rest of us a bad name worldwide, with her superiority complex and her sense of entitlement. Janet hadn't even bothered to learn the most basic social protocols before arriving in Scotland, and she certainly wasn't learning by example as a normally conscientious person would.

"Did you actually meet Henrietta, face to face?"

She shook her head. "All of our communications were

by telephone. I didn't even meet Bridie until last night, and I can't say she was any more welcoming, although she said she'd call on me for lunch soon. But that was only after I pressed. By the way, I'm holding her to that offer."

"When did you arrive in Glenkillen?"

"Last Thursday, two days before the tasting. And I'm scheduled to leave this weekend. Now this! Who knows when I'll be allowed to go." She shuddered. "I find Scotland cold in all respects. The climate as well as the people."

As Janet complained about one thing after another Scotland-related, I realized I didn't have any sort of timeline leading up to and culminating in Henrietta's death. When had it taken place? She'd been murdered either in the afternoon (since I'd seen her in the late morning) or in the early evening before the tasting. The thought that it might have occurred during the tasting was unacceptable to me. No one could be that brash and bold, could they? No, the risk was way too high.

"One last question for now," I said. "Where were you yesterday afternoon?"

"Ah, of course. If I'd known that the woman was going to get herself killed, I would have been more public with my movements, but I'm afraid I spent the entire afternoon before the tasting in my room."

"Can anyone vouch for that?"

Janet found my question highly amusing. "If you want to know if I was finding out what's under one of those man skirts, the sad truth of the matter is that I was completely alone."

And I didn't need to wonder why! I pitied her poor deceased husband for all the years he'd had to tolerate her.

Janet leaned back and cocked her head to one side. "Have you worked closely with Inspector Jamieson?"

"Yes, as his special constable." I wasn't about to explain my volunteer status. "Special" conveyed a certain superior status to someone not familiar with the actual definition. And Janet fell into the clueless category. "I've worked with him on prior cases."

"He seems like a nice man."

I shrugged, eager to be on my way rather than indulge in small talk.

"Is he single?" she asked, coyly.

Ah. She was interested in him. "He's a widower."

She smiled as though she were thrilled with his status.

I wished her a good day and made my way back to the reception area, highly amused by Janet Dougal's interest in the inspector. He, though, most certainly would not find anything humorous about it.

Jeannie was on the telephone booking a reservation. When she hung up, I inquired about Patricia Martin.

"No sign o' her yet," Jeannie told me. "But it's early and she might not be one o' those early birds tae catch the worm."

I jotted a message to Patricia along with my cell phone number and handed it to Jeannie. "Give this to her, please."

"Aye. And good luck with uncoverin' the devil that did this. We'll all rest easier then."

Outside, I raised my coat collar against the cold, crisp air. Janet Dougal had volunteered plenty of information, although determining if it was useful was another matter. Janet had had an altercation with the dead woman, however much she tried to downplay it, and she lacked witnesses to support her whereabouts.

After interviewing the unpleasant woman, all I wanted to do was prove her innocent and send her back across the Atlantic Ocean. The less I had to deal with her, the better. She grated on my nerves. And I wasn't the only one who disliked being around her. From Janet's own account, Henrietta and Bridie had felt the same way.

I decided there were only two ways to steer clear of her. One was to quickly eliminate her as a suspect. The other, if evidence against her strengthened, was to hand her over to the inspector. And I liked him too much to wish that on him.

When I walked past the pub on the way to my car, Sean Stevens pulled up beside me and rolled down the window of his red Renault. "It's monkeys outside," he called to me. "What are ye doin' strollin' along like it's summertime?"

"Monkeys?" I paused in spite of the cold. This was a new expression.

"It's common enough here. It means it's freezin' cold!"

"I thought you were assigned to watch over Bridie Dougal."

"Look who's checkin' up on me like she's the big boss." Sean had on an attitude today, not that unusual when he worked a case. Sean treated Vicki well and I respected him for that, but he was a completely different man during an investigation when he puffed up with self-importance. Then his testosterone kicked in. "If ye must know," he went on, "I'm fact checkin' with the hairdresser down the street a ways. Bridie claims she was having her hair done in the late afternoon, and her whereabouts needs tae be verified. And it's a fine time since she's visitin' with her son."

"Bridie definitely had her hair done," I told him, remembering that her hair had been styled professionally for the tasting.

"Well, thank ye very much. Now I don't have tae bother the hairdresser. And that's sarcasm if ye missed it comin' by."

What was wrong with everyone this morning? A bunch of crabs. By now I was hopping from one foot to the other, trying to keep warm.

"I only wanted to share information," I explained, wondering why I bothered.

"Okay then, but ye better be gettin' inside me car before yer ears turn black and fall off."

So we sat in his car. I turned up the heater while I told him about my conversation with Janet Dougal.

"Bridie tried tae avoid her," he said. "And had managed up tae a point. Then she had tae deal with her at the tasting, but only briefly as the hostess retired early."

"Janet Dougal is a piece of work. She hadn't even been invited to the tasting, but she went anyway. She's lucky Bridie didn't throw her out. By the way, have we narrowed down the time of death?"

"Not by much. Bridie says she didn't see Henrietta after the back o' four. Her hair appointment was fer half past."

I didn't want to ask what back of four meant, but I could guess. I interpreted it my own way—the last time she saw her companion was shortly before four. The tasting had begun at seven, and I was convinced she'd already been dead when the gathering began while we were sipping fine whisky. Was Bridie the last one to see Henrietta alive? Or had another family member seen her after that?

I needed to speak with Patricia to find out if she'd been

in touch with her sister in the afternoon. The inspector would be asking me about that interview with Patricia the next time we spoke, and I really didn't want to have to tell him that I hadn't pinned down the sister. In a few minutes, after this conversation with Sean, I decided I should go back to the Whistling Inn and demand to see her even if it meant barging into her room. I shouldn't be waiting on her convenience.

Sean continued, "I need tae establish that the hair appointment was kept. Ye never know who we're dealing with."

"I doubt that Bridie Dougal is capable of killing anyone," I pointed out. "She's an old woman. Besides, Henrietta was her longtime companion. What reason would she have to murder her caregiver?"

"Aye, we agree on that, we do, but ye know the inspector. He's a cautious one and doesn't skip over steps in an investigation like this one. He's thorough."

Which was certainly true. No stone unturned by Inspector Jamieson.

Reluctantly, I got out of the warm car to go back to the inn. But before I could get from the sidewalk into the warmth of the reception room, my cell phone rang.

It was the inspector.

"Get yerself over tae the hospital," he ordered. "It's Katie Taylor."

"The young caterer?"

"Aye. She's been injured, and it wasn't an accident."

"I'll be right there."

CHAPTER 9

The inspector and a dark-haired woman were in the critical care waiting room. He introduced her as Gayle Brown. I guessed Gayle to be approximately the same age as Katie, midtwenties, and fashionably dressed, a special talent during these snowy months, one I've never been able to achieve. I tend to look as shapeless as a polar bear once I bundle up. But Gayle wore her form-fitting white jacket with class. She also was visibly worried about her friend, the smeared mascara under her eyes an indication that she'd been crying.

"Gayle was aboot to run out tae pack a small bag fer Katie," he explained to me. The fact that both of them were still in their outerwear meant the inspector had phoned me as soon as he learned about Katie. "Katie was staying with Gayle when it occurred. She'd made arrangements prior tae the tasting due tae the bad weather. Then o' course, after the murder, she was prepared tae stay there until we completed our interviews."

We? I felt privileged.

"Can ye tell us once more what happened?" the inspector asked Gayle with a gentle tone. "Constable Elliott should hear what ye have tae say."

I was rather amazed by his uncharacteristic inclusive attitude. Usually my boss handles situations single-handedly unless the task is too large for him to deal with alone. This time, he'd included me when he didn't necessarily have to.

Gayle shifted her attention to me. Neither Katie's friend nor the inspector suggested that we sit down. A moment later I found out why. Gayle paced while she spoke, only a few steps, then a turn, a few steps, then a turn. It was obvious she was highly agitated.

"I help out at the bakery in the wee hours o' each morning over at A Taste of Scotland, so I wasn't at home when the break-in occurred. Although I can hardly call it a forced entry, since I hadn't locked up and all the person had tae do was waltz right in. This is all my fault."

She began crying. I could sympathize. I'd felt exactly the same way when Henrietta was murdered. I'd blamed myself. We waited patiently. I handed her a tissue from a box on a coffee table.

"If only I'd thought tae lock the door, but how could I have known," she said, wiping her eyes. "Anyhow, I finished up with some lovely lemon burst meringues and the regular trays o' morning rolls . . . families like tae stop off fer take-aways on Sunday mornings."

"It's a top-crust bakery," the inspector said, but I could tell he was anxious to talk about the incident rather than A Taste of Scotland's reputation and products. "Go on."

"When I returned home from the bakery, it was pitch-black inside, not a single light on, which wasn't out o' the ordinary bein' earlier than Katie gets up. Except there was Katie, lyin' on the floor near the fire stove, with a poker tossed down beside her."

"What time was this?" I asked.

"Not long ago. About eight. I came home a wee bit earlier than usual. I didn't sleep well and so decided tae start bakin' earlier. I have a key tae get in tae the shop, ye see, so it doesn't matter what time I get there as long as I finish before it opens."

"I suspect that she's been hit over the head with the fire poker," the inspector added. "She musta startled the intruder."

Ginny nodded. "I couldn't wake her, and called an ambulance. She has tae be all right, she just has tae."

The inspector and I exchanged glances. Mine was questioning, wanting to inquire into Katie's prognosis, but reluctant to do so in front of her friend. His return look showed real concern.

"In the end, your actions might be responsible for saving her life," I told Gayle, sure she would grasp for any straws of reassurance to exonerate her from the heavy burden of blame.

"And how do ye see that?" she asked, and I could see the hope in her eyes.

"By getting there when you did," I said, punting. "If you had stayed at the baker the usual length of time instead of going home early and calling for prompt medical attention, it might have been too late by the time help arrived."

Gayle hadn't considered that. I could tell it had a positive impact. "I might have heard something when I came in," she said, speaking hesitantly, "now that I'm thinking back on it."

"Go on," the inspector said, pressing her in the calm professional tone I'd come to recognize and recently found myself imitating. "Anything you can remember is useful."

"At the rear o' the house. I mighta heard a sound, like the back door closing." She thought hard while we waited, then shook her head. "But I can't be sure."

"Was anything taken?" I asked, thinking perhaps it was a robbery gone wrong. The thief could have been familiar with Gayle's morning routine and expected an easy in and out, not anticipating a guest staying at the house.

"I rushed tae hospital, not stayin' tae check my belongings," she answered. "My personal effects don't matter at all in the scheme o' things. But I do vaguely remember seein' the telly where it usually is. It's an old thing. Nothing struck me as out o' place except the poker. Besides, I don't have much in the way o' valuables."

"What do the doctors say about her condition?" I asked, looking from Katie's friend to the inspector.

"They aren't sayin' other than they are doin' scans and such," Gayle answered. "And will speak further with the family once they arrive."

"I couldn't get more out o' them, either," the inspector offered.

Not surprising. From my experience dealing with doctors when my mother was gravely ill with MS, they don't like to express any opinion one way or the other unless they're forced to do so by a persistent family member. And then only if pinned right up against the wall. The medical world is more gray than black or white. Anything is possible.

"I've notified her family," Inspector Jamieson told us.

"They'll be here as soon as possible. They live in one o' the villages a ways out, although the roads are goin' tae be icy and snow covered. That will slow them down a bit."

"I'll be back as soon as I can," Gayle said. "I want tae get a few o' Katie's things fer her."

"We'll leave ye tae yer task then," the inspector said to her.

Gayle set off to gather personal items for Katie's overnight bag.

Once she was out of sight, he added more detailed information. "I've been through the house and nothin' seems tae be obviously missing. Sure money or jewelry might have been taken, but if it was, there's no sign o' a hurried search. No drawers or closets left open. As Gayle told us, other than the lass and fireplace poker on the floor, nothin' was out o' order."

"If the intruder wasn't expecting anyone to be in the house and suddenly came upon Katie, that might account for the fact that nothing is missing. She interrupted."

"Aye, it's possible that it's as simple as that."

I peered into his serious blue eyes. "But you aren't buying it?"

"I don't know what tae believe at this point. It happened too close in time tae the murder tae discount a connection. Especially since Katie Taylor was in the tasting room last night. Whether there's a common thread here or no, I can't say as yet."

"You questioned Katie along with the other guests. What did she say?"

"The lass didn't know a reason fer what happened tae

Henrietta. Other than her hirin' Katie tae cater at the tasting, she'd never heard o' Henrietta McCloud before that. The only connection between the two o' them is Tainwick."

"Tainwick?"

"Aye, the both o' them are from the same town. Although Henrietta left years ago, before Katie was even born."

Tainwick. That name again. Where had I heard it before? Of course, Patricia had mentioned it at the tasting when we'd briefly spoken of the sisters' pasts. But even then it had a familiar ring to it.

A moment later I thought I'd figured it out. I enjoy studying maps, and I pull out a map of the Highlands whenever I get a chance. There seem to be thousands of small villages, all with unusual names. In fact, I'm pretty sure I'd seen Wick on the map. And a Tullich. I wouldn't be surprised if there was one named Tain. Or maybe I actually saw Tainwick on the map and that was where my familiarity with it came from.

The inspector interrupted my wandering mind by saying, "Noo that I'm thinkin' o' that bit o' information, that both o' them have a Tainwick background, I better stay here and question Katie Taylor's family members. It's not much o' a clue, but it's not like we have any others at the moment. Have ye uncovered anything o' importance this morn?"

I filled him in on my conversation with Janet Dougal earlier in the morning, omitting the personal tidbit regarding her expressed interest in his marital status. If she intended to pursue him, he'd find out soon enough on his own. I could imagine his dismay at that revelation. He wasn't exactly fond of her. "Space cadet," as he'd referred to her, was hardly a term of endearment.

"She continued to claim that her spat with Henrietta

was insignificant," I finished. "Barely worth mentioning, in her opinion."

"I have a feeling that woman would butt heads with a goat over a single bit o' hay in a haystack. Bridie doesn't have any good tae say about this distant relative o' hers, and I find the woman more than a bit over the top as well. What's that little smirk on yer lips fer?"

"Nothing. I'm not smirking!" But I must have been. I just couldn't get over the image of Janet Dougal chasing Jamieson far and wide over the snow-covered hills of Glenkillen. I attempted to straighten my expression appropriately.

After a piercing gaze, he abandoned the possibility of an explanation and asked, "Ye haven't mentioned Patricia Martin. What's on with her?"

That was exactly the right question to wipe the smirk off my face. So much for staying one step ahead of him. I'd really tried and would have succeeded if not for Katie's attack. I'd been on my way back into the inn when the news of Katie reached me. "I was about to find out when you called me away to come here."

"It's probably my own fault that ye haven't managed tae pin her down. After all, I strapped ye with yer fellow American, and she took up all yer time."

"Please don't stereotype me. That woman is *not* typical in any way."

"We'll see." A light in his eyes danced. "The jury's still out on that one."

CHAPTER 10

"I gave her yer message, I did," Jeannie told me when I returned to the inn and firmly insisted on speaking with Patricia Martin in person. "She was on her way out, saying she was goin' tae visit Bridie Dougal tae see how she was coping. And in spite o' me insistin' that she take care o' yer business first, she went right out the door."

"You did what you could," I reassured her. Inwardly, I groaned. There was more than one reason I was disappointed that Patricia had slipped away. First, she'd disregarded my request, which most likely wouldn't have happened if it had been the inspector making the same demand. She wasn't taking me seriously and that was annoying. But it was her destination that bothered me the most. I wasn't ready for another encounter with Bridie, one in which she was sure to bring up the side of my family I wanted nothing to do with.

Just don't let her get me off alone, I warned myself, my

thoughts turning to my father in spite of my efforts to ignore his existence.

Based on the short conversation with Bridie the morning of the murder, she hadn't been in contact with my biological father since my grandfather's funeral over thirty years ago. So he'd gone into hiding someplace far removed from his past acquaintances and their disapproval. He probably obtained some sort of Scottish divorce and remarried and has a new family that he actually cares about. But if he needed my mother's signature, which I wasn't sure about, only positive he hadn't made the request of her, he could be living with someone without the benefit of marriage. And if he'd passed on, my last wish for him was that he had suffered as much as or more than my mother.

I took a few deep breaths and talked myself down from a volcano of erupting bitterness and disappointment that had been my constant companions as long as I could remember, dating back to my earliest memories of my mother's diagnosis of MS, to the moment I realized he wasn't ever coming back.

Sitting in my car outside the inn, the heater turned up full blast, I wondered (not for the first time) if Ami Pederson had had ulterior motives when she'd suggested a Scottish Highlands setting for the series. As a longtime friend, she'd been perfectly aware of my history and my father's abandonment. What if she considered this one of her brilliantly executed subplots? Ami had pushed and prodded until she got her way. As always.

If my suspicions were correct about her motives, she'd been right about one thing, though. The setting was perfect for a romantic novel. But she'd been wrong if she had thought my trip to Scotland would reunite me with any members of the Elliott clan.

Why did I have to run into these issues now? I'd managed to avoid hearing a single word about my ancestors for the months I'd been in the Highlands. I'd barely thought about them at all. And now, less than two weeks before I was scheduled to depart, I found myself dealing with a clan chieftain who had known my grandfather and father. And on top of that, I was working a murder that put me in an orbit around Bridie. Like the pull of gravity, I was trapped in some sort of magnetic attraction and I couldn't break away.

Which brought me back to the problem of questioning Patricia Martin and steering clear of Bridie Dougal. Bridie was a delightful person, one I would have enjoyed keeping company with, if not for her affiliation with a certain part of my past I'd buried long ago and wished to remain buried while she intended to dig it up.

Maybe if I remained in the car outside the inn long enough, Patricia would return. To while away some time, I dug around in the glove compartment and pulled out a road map I'd purchased my first week in Glenkillen. I unfolded it, spread it out across the steering wheel, and began a search for Tainwick. I found Glenkillen and Loch Ness and began reading the names of villages north of the lake.

There it was, not more than a thirty- or forty-minute drive when roads were in good shape. I spent ten or fifteen minutes studying the map, before realizing I could be sitting in the Peugeot for a long time. Replacing the map, I had an afterthought.

I should have offered to hang around at the hospital and let the inspector chase down Henrietta's sister. Sitting and waiting was more special constable–like anyway.

Thinking that was an excellent idea, I tried calling Jamieson's cell phone. He didn't pick up. Coverage inside the hospital was probably limited. I could drive over there. Then I went on to reason that it would be awkward showing up at Bridie's home to interview Patricia. That wouldn't be very professional. What had I been thinking? Besides, wasn't Sean out at the Dougal home? Why couldn't he interview Patricia?

I called Sean's cell phone. He answered promptly. "Constable Stevens," he stated with pride. "Servin' the residents o' Glenkillen. To whom might I be speakin' with?"

"I know you have Caller ID," I pointed out.

"It's habit, is all. What can I do fer ye?"

"Patricia Martin is supposedly visiting Bridie."

"Aye, she arrived a ways back. Got away from ye, did she?"

I ignored that. Or tried to. I was about to ask Sean to speak with her. But after that flip remark, it didn't seem like such a good idea. Actually, she *had* slipped under my radar. And wasn't she my responsibility, not Sean's?

"Make sure she doesn't leave," I said instead. "I'm on my way."

"Okay, then. I'll cuff her if she tries tae escape."

"Please don't do that."

"I was only jokin' with ye. No need fer ye tae get testy. Did yer sense o' humor get away from ye, too?"

I hung up without comment. Apparently my sense of humor really had flown out the window.

The drive to the distillery took only a few minutes. It was hard to believe it had only been yesterday morning that I first came here and met Henrietta and Bridie. It felt like ages ago, eons since I'd pulled Henrietta McCloud out of that tub full of whisky.

Sean greeted me at the door. "They're having tea and want ye tae join them."

"You told them I was on my way?" I'd wanted a certain element of surprise, not an organized tea party.

"Don't worry. I'll back ye up."

Back me up?

I was confident I could handle the two women but couldn't come up with an excuse to extricate myself from Sean. Besides, he might be my buffer against any personal references and discussion of the Elliott clan. So I nodded in agreement. We'd go in as a team.

"Eden," Bridie called out when I entered the room. "Come join us. Sit here next tae me and have a cuppa."

I glanced around, searching for Henrietta's Scottish Fold cat, before I took the indicated seat. Bridie tuned into my thoughts and said, "Snookie is in Henrietta's room, waiting fer her tae return. It pains me to see the poor thing, so trusting and me knowing she's never coming back."

Patricia, sitting erect, her long legs crossed, gave me a head-to-toe appraisal before saying, "Constable Stevens tells me you are a volunteer constable."

I glanced at Sean, who had stopped just inside the doorway as though guarding against intruders or unexpected problems. Actually, *he* was part of the problem. What a blabbermouth!

"Yes, that's right. I'm a special constable." I sat down

and accepted a cup of tea from Bridie, my heart going out to Snookie, wondering what would happen to her. I supposed she'd remain with Bridie.

"We have special constables in Edinburgh as well," Patricia said. "I keep up on those sort o' things since my husband, Connor, is up for re-election in May. This will be his second term as a member of the Scottish Parliament, but he's made quite a name for himself in a short period o' time. Because of his position, I don't express my personal views in public, of course, but privately I can't say I agree with allowing ordinary citizens the full rights o' our police force."

I reminded myself that when I first heard about these volunteers, I'd reacted exactly the same way. There was a time I would have agreed with her. Private citizens with police powers wasn't typical in the world I was used to. But would it be common practice in the States someday? I highly doubted it. Trying to explain the reasoning behind the unusual volunteer policy to Patricia was going to be challenging. Especially after the condescending tone she had affected.

I was about to make the effort, but our gracious host headed off any possible difference of opinion that might lead to an unpleasant disagreement. "Come in and join us," Bridie called out, addressing Sean.

I could tell he'd taken offense to Patricia's comment regarding special volunteers by his coloring. He was several shades redder than normal as he reluctantly sat down in the only available chair next to Henrietta's sister and said, "Many o' the special constables are cut o' the same cloth as the others on the force."

"I don't doubt it," Bridie said, hastily.

I looked at Patricia. "I have a few routine questions to ask you," I said, deciding we could debate that issue another time. "We can proceed in a more private setting if you wish."

"I have nothing to say that can't be said in front o' others."

Bridie cut in. "The last I saw o' my dear Henrietta was about four o'clock yesterday afternoon, several hours before the whisky tasting. That's when I left fer the hairdresser." She carefully handed a cup of tea to Sean, who gave me a slight nod, implying that her whereabouts had been verified.

"Your appointment was in the center of the village. How did you get there?" I asked, assuming that at her advanced age and with the road conditions treacherous that day, someone surely would have driven her to Glenkillen.

"Archie took me and waited at the pub"—Bridie's voice began to quiver—"and brought me back around half past five. We didn't see Henrietta on our return, so I automatically assumed she'd decided to remain in her room. That wasn't unusual fer her. She hasn't been well."

Bridie gave a little gasp of anguish and buried her face in a handkerchief.

"I woulda got around tae askin' that very question aboot her transportation," Sean assured me, giving himself away. He hadn't even asked that? Sean had been assigned to Bridie. For now, she was his only job. Shouldn't he have been more thorough? At the moment, I could understand the inspector's ongoing frustration with his trainee.

"About her illness . . . Patricia . . ." I said, steering the questions and answers over to Henrietta's sister. "Besides Bridie, who knew about Henrietta's prognosis? I imagine Gordon did."

"Yes, my son knew. And my husband, of course."

"I didn't tell another soul," Bridie added, then, after a pause, amended her statement. "Other than the local vet, who happened to be here when Henrietta had a wee bit o' a fainting spell. Even Archie and Florence were kept in the dark. Henrietta insisted and made us promise, didn't she, Patricia?"

Henrietta's sister nodded. "It was a secret only a few of us shared."

"Secrets have a way o' getting out," Sean said. "Like they have a life o' their own."

Sean was right. Secrets are hard to keep.

"Perhaps, but we did our best," Bridie continued, "In any case, Archie and Florence weren't informed, at least not by me. Henrietta couldn't abide by the thought o' any o' us taking pity on her. And she refused to let me hire someone tae help her with the more strenuous household chores. Her efficiency was slipping, but I pretended not tae notice. It woulda hurt her tae the quick if I'd brought in others tae keep up. She was a proud woman, determined tae continue with her duties."

"She *was* stubborn," Patricia agreed. At the tasting, Henrietta's sister had expressed frustration with Bridie, but hopefully she now understood that the old woman really cared about her companion's well-being. The truth had been that Bridie couldn't slow her down.

"Do either of you know of any reason why someone would kill Henrietta?" I asked. "Did anyone hold a grudge against her that you were aware of?"

"She rarely left the house," Bridie said, "only tae run the occasionally personal errand. Florence always takes care of my own purchases and the household supplies. And Henrietta didn't have any friends tae speak of, although in the past I encouraged her tae have a life o' her own. She always claimed my family was enough fer her. And her sister and nephew were important tae her. She adored ye, Patricia."

Tears gleamed in Patricia's eyes as I addressed the next question to her. "When did you last see her?"

"Friday morning," she said without hesitation. "And since you will certainly ask, she appeared to be exactly the same as always. We spoke of the upcoming tasting and its preparation, and when I attempted to address her condition, she refused to discuss it. Typical Henrietta."

"So she wasn't upset about anything? Had no personal issues of concern other than her health? She didn't give you any indication that might be associated with prior circumstances leading to her death?"

Patricia shrugged, helplessly. "No, nothing at all. My sister never was very social, even less so as she aged. We were exact opposites in that regard."

"Did Henrietta have any psychological issues?" I asked, delicately.

"What do you mean?" Patricia's tone changed.

"She spent her life in virtual seclusion," I said. "She'd basically withdrawn from society. That could mean a number of things. She might have had a social anxiety disorder. I wonder why is all."

"It was her personality. There doesn't need to be a reason."

I dropped that line of questioning. "And you didn't speak with her on Saturday?"

"I assumed she'd be busy with the upcoming tasting and that I would spend time with her that evening. But as you know, she didn't leave her room, didn't pick up the phone when I rang her." Here, she paused to consider other options. "Or . . . perhaps . . . she was already . . ."

Sean, who'd exhibited remarkable restraint until now, piped up and agreed. "Most likely she had passed tae the great beyond by then."

Which caused the two women to break down together. I waited an appropriate amount of time, then said to Patricia, "I'd like to discuss your sister's past with you. Perhaps there is something there."

"What do you want to know?" Patricia straightened, dabbed under her eyes, and pulled herself together somewhat.

"Anything you can tell me about failed romantic relationships, any private matters that have been hidden away."

Henrietta's sister looked disgusted. Her lips curled in distaste. "It's obvious to me that you and this officer"—her eyes shifted to Sean—"and that inspector don't have a single shred of useful evidence to work with, and so you are grasping at straws, trying to make this Henrietta's fault."

I didn't respond immediately, startled by her outburst. A moment later she went on. "Instead of attempting to dredge up nonexistent dirty laundry, I would expect you to be focusing on the present situation and who might have committed this horrific crime."

Patricia's pain over her sister's death was expressing itself in anger directed at me. I shouldn't be surprised. She had to be an emotional mess, and I was an intrusion she was forced to deal with against her will.

"I'm sorry to have to put you through this," I told her, "but it's important." Then I turned to Bridie. "Tell me about the rest of your afternoon once you arrived back home." That translated as a request for an appropriate alibi. Not that I expected the chieftain to need one, but it was a lead-in to Patricia Martin's whereabouts.

"Archie went off tae make sure everything was in order fer the tasting. I wanted tae rest a spell, but I couldn't lie down after visitin' the hairdresser, so I sat in a chair in my room with my feet up, reading a book fer half an hour. Then I dressed fer the evening. Oh, and I should mention that today I had that little family meeting that was postponed after what happened. Archie is relieved that I've decided not to sell and that the business will remain in the hands of our family."

"That's good news for all of you."

"'Tis."

"And yerself?" Sean asked, his attention turned to Patricia. "Where were ye between four in the afternoon and yer arrival at the tasting?"

"In my room at the inn," came the pat reply, delivered in a clipped manner.

Terrific. Janet, Bridie, and Patricia were all in their rooms.

"Do you have someone who can vouch for you during those hours?" I asked.

"I was alone, of course. Who could possibly have been with me? My husband wasn't able to join me as he had to be in Edinburgh with his constituents. And I resent the implication that I need an alibi! This is my sister we are talking about!"

Wonderful. Just dandy. Three women under suspicion had been in their rooms, with no one to confirm or deny their claims.

"Welcome," the inspector would have said, "tae the wonderful world of crime solving."

I could just hear him.

CHAPTER 11

"Tae recap," the inspector said as we ate a late lunch of fish and chips at my favorite table at the Kilt & Thistle, "ye accused the sister o' blabbin' tae others aboot Henrietta's cancer."

"I'm pretty sure Sean was the one who alluded to that," I said defensively, before popping what I'd call a thick-cut French fry in the States into my mouth, after seasoning it with salt and vinegar.

"And then ye challenged her sister's mental state." The inspector dipped his hearty potato wedge into chippy sauce, a mix of vinegar and brown sauce.

"Well, there could be a psychological reason that Henrietta chose to become some sort of hermit," I argued.

"I'm surprised that ye didn't accuse the victim o' hiding out from her own criminal activity."

"That's absurd," I said, detecting a hint of humor in his tone.

"And ye couldn't have made a fast friend when ye told Patricia Martin ye wanted tae air the family's dirty laundry."

"I said nothing of the sort!"

The inspector chuckled and dug into his meal.

Reflecting on the interview, I said, "I didn't accomplish much, did I? Aside from alienating Patricia."

"On the contrary, you confirmed that she hadn't seen Henrietta around the time o' her death. And ye established the lack of one more alibi tae join the pile o' others without them."

That didn't sound like much progress to me. I wish I'd mentioned Katie Taylor and Tainwick to Patricia. I'd intended to, except things got quite heated before I had the opportunity. I wasn't used to taking heat, and even though I'd remained cool on the surface, I'd come away with a few wounds to lick.

"It wasn't easy questioning Patricia," I told him, using one of the excuses I'd concocted to make myself feel slightly better. "Bridie kept jumping in."

"The old hen is used tae the limelight," he agreed. "While ye were havin' tea, I've been following up on the victim's brother-in-law. Connor Martin was campaigning in Edinburgh on the afternoon o' the murder."

Jamieson was a man of many surprises. I wouldn't have thought of following up on Patricia's husband, at least so soon. Martin wasn't at the tasting, and he hadn't been in town at the time of his sister-in-law's murder. At best, his whereabouts would have been an afterthought, if I were in charge. A good reason to defer to the experienced inspector.

"Where was he after that? In the early evening?" I asked, joining in. "Could he have driven to Glenkillen? And, more importantly, what would have been his motive?"

"It's over a three-hour drive. He's not our killer, but I hadn't thought he was. The only reason I pursued any line o' questioning with him was because he phoned me, all blustery, aboot solving his sister-in-law's murder promptly, as though I'm not in any kind o' hurry without him having tae pester me. I imagine Connor is most worried aboot his own aspirations and how something like this on his wife's side o' the family could affect him politically. He said he wanted tae come tae handle the situation, but his wife talked him out o' it. Then he tried tae strong-arm me intae releasin' his wife tae go home. Anyhoo, he's in the clear."

"A murder for hire?" I suggested. Then, when the inspector frowned, I muttered, "Playing devil's advocate." It was farfetched, but my personal opinion is that no theory should be discounted, no matter how unlikely, without at least a cursory glance.

But I'd misunderstood the frown. The inspector seemed to be actually considering that. "Those things have a way o' surfacing," he said. "Especially if the employer is in the public eye. He'd have tae be mad as a hatter tae arrange fer murder. Connor Martin is known fer his integrity. And he isn't afraid tae take responsibility in times where it's needed. Besides not havin' a motive."

I sighed after considering the scope of our problem. "It's going to take forever to establish alibis for every single person who is related to someone who was at the distillery that afternoon."

"Aye, process o' elimination. It's how we plod along."

"And who else have you eliminated as a suspect?"

"No one, and that's the unfortunate truth. The postmortem examination is underway. It's doesn't take much detecting on my part tae foresee the ruling as a drowning. Only it won't be one o' misadventure."

I must have looked bewildered because he said, "Accidental drowning. It won't be ruled an accident, not considering the circumstances. And I've already been informed by the coroner regarding an approximate time—he won't be able tae narrow it down as much as we'd like."

"So we're on our own," I said, finishing the entire plate of fish and chips. "Bridie is sure she last saw Henrietta around four, but has anyone else been able to substantiate that one way or the other?"

"Are ye suggestin' she might be mistaken aboot the time? Granted, she's gettin' up there in years."

I shook my head, confident in the old woman's mental faculties. "Bridie seems extremely sharp to me. If she says four, we can believe her. I was out there that morning myself, as you know, and had time to assess Bridie. She's amazing in her awareness." I paused then, remembering that scene, how she'd blindsided me with mention of the Elliott family. I hadn't shared that topic of conversation with the inspector and wondered if she had. I hoped not. "What I meant to ask was if anyone else saw Henrietta after four."

"No one's come forward," the inspector said. "Let's assume fer now that the murder occurred after four o'clock and before seven when the guests gathered in the tasting room. I forgot tae mention when ye inquired aboot the suspect list a moment ago that ye've been eliminated in spite o' yer ability tae hover in the vicinity o' disaster."

I did a Jeannie-worthy eye roll as he continued, "And fer the sake o' argument, let's add Bridie Dougal tae the list of those who didn't murder Henrietta McCloud. See? We're makin' headway. And one o' the guests wants tae have a chat with me that might shed new light. Although I'm not holding my breath."

"Janet Dougal?"

"Aye. She wants tae have a chat with me privately. The request was on my voice message first thing this morn."

"I'll bet she does." *And light isn't what she's hoping to shed*, I thought.

"And what is that supposed tae mean?"

"Nothing, other than it would be nice if she had something constructive to add."

After a piercing stare, he presented me with the most interesting news so far. "Henrietta was in Bridie's will."

"Don't you mean Bridie was in Henrietta's will?"

"I meant what I said. Henrietta didn't have a will or any real possessions tae leave behind other than a few family treasures that Patricia will claim. But if she'd lived, she'd have been well taken care o'."

After a moment's thought I said, "She was loyal to her employer for a lot of years, and Bridie strikes me as a generous woman. I'd be more surprised if her longtime companion had been left out. What were the terms of the will?"

"Once Bridie was gone, Henrietta was tae stay in the house and be cared for through a trust until her own passing."

"Did Archie know?" I asked, sensing a possible family conflict.

"Aye, Bridie updated her will this past summer, before Henrietta's diagnosis, and she told her family all about the change. At the time, the old girl assumed that Henrietta would still have a long life tae enjoy—twenty years or more, barring some unexpected illness."

"Like terminal cancer."

"It's a sad situation, it is. Archie and Florence Dougal weren't too happy when Bridie presented them with that arrangement, thinkin' they would move intae the family home once Bridie was buried."

"Bridie will probably outlive us all."

"Aye, isn't that the truth."

I remembered that Archie and Florence had their own home in the village, and mentioned it.

"They do," the inspector said. "But the daughter-in-law had her sights set on playing lady o' the manor and didn't get on well with Henrietta."

"I don't see a motive for murder, considering Henrietta wouldn't live to enjoy the house. Oh . . ." It was becoming clear. "Except they didn't know she was dying."

Jamieson nodded. "Bridie's son and daughter-in-law weren't apprised o' the victim's condition. And neither o' them has a solid alibi. They were flitting here and there. According to him, he was seeing that the whisky was properly selected. And the wife was busy with the table settings and getting herself ready."

"That certainly makes for interesting speculation."

"That it does."

I pondered this new information. Archie and Florence had a motive. They wanted their mother's house and her companion gone. And they both had plenty of opportunity to slip into the warehouse and fill a washback with whisky. One thing we knew for sure—this was premeditated.

Someone had put a lot of thought and planning into her murder.

We sat for a few minutes, quietly contemplating, sipping tea. I was going to miss these shared moments at the pub, hashing over possibilities with the inspector. I especially enjoyed times like these, when our conversations ended and each of us sat in reflection, at ease without the need for spoken words.

"How is Katie doing?" I finally broke the stillness to ask.

"Aboot the same. The doc says the next twenty-four hours are critical. Her parents have arrived and are optimistic that she'll make a full recovery. When I questioned them about Tainwick, neither was acquainted with Henrietta McCloud nor her sister Patricia. They weren't even familiar with the McCloud name, saying none are living in the area, at least that they are aware o'. I did a bit o' investigating, and what they say is true. Whatever McClouds were there in the past, they've moved on since."

"So, if the murder and attack are connected, it isn't through Tainwick."

"Other than a common place o' birth, there isn't another link at present."

We fell silent again.

The assault on the caterer was most likely a robbery gone wrong. It certainly appeared that way. Unless Katie had seen something at the tasting she shouldn't have, something that didn't impress her as important at the time, but had worried the killer enough to go after the young woman.

"Do you have Katie under protection?" I asked.

"The medical team has been advised against allowing any visitors other than the parents and Gayle, who, by the way, is stayin' with her boyfriend temporarily in case whoever did this returns to her house. She didn't seem too put out by the arrangement, though. I suspect she'll enjoy a few days cozying up tae her beau."

"I was thinking Katie could use additional security."

"We think alike, we do." He frowned in concentration, then brightened as an idea struck. "I believe we've found another job fer our Sean."

"I thought he was protecting Bridie."

"Bridie dismissed him without my consent, claiming he has better things tae do than babysit her."

"I hate to see her all alone in that big house."

"Ye're looking at me as though ye think I have a say in the matter. She's a tough old bird, used tae having her own way. Besides, even if it turns out that her own son murdered the house companion, he isn't about to harm his mother."

I was forced to agree. "The obstacle of contention has been removed."

"Both of his problems have been eliminated. Henrietta is gone. And he's been assured that the family business will remain in the family for at least another generation. Archie will groom his son tae take the reins after him."

"I really hope the murderer isn't Bridie's son."

"It would kill Bridie faster than advanced age is goin' tae."

He used his cell phone to call Sean and assign him to the hospital to guard Katie. "And don't leave her side until I relieve ye," he warned. "Plan tae spend every night until she's released intae the care o' her parents. And don't let on that we're concerned over her safety. Tell the parents it's routine."

I'd heard that before. I was quickly learning that routine was anything but routine.

When the inspector departed and I was alone at the table, I dug my laptop out of a tote to touch base with Ami and was surprised to discover that she hadn't left any messages for me. It was odd for her to go off and forget about me. Didn't she want to hear about the whisky tasting? In her own words, she'd been excited about it. Not that I had anything earth-shattering to report about my personal life. Leith and I hadn't shared anything more than a hug. And that was only because of the murder.

Missing her, I sent off a short synopsis of yesterday's main event, starting the action at the tasting, with a brief description of the food and differing flavors of each sample of whisky based on age. I even included a description of my date and his innate ability to wear a kilt to its best advantage. Then I went on to share the ending with her—the horror of finding Henrietta, drowned in a vat of whisky, and the subsequent investigation into her death after the abrupt end to what should have been a great evening.

Sometimes a reply to an e-mail to her comes zooming right back at me. Ami is addicted to her computer and the Internet, especially to social media, spending many hours every day writing her historical romances on her home computer and then communicating with her fans.

This time, though, all was silent.

I could have really used a word or two of comfort from my friend.

Where was she when I needed her?

CHAPTER 12

Leith Cameron found me, still at the same pub table, staring at my laptop, hoping for a new message in my inbox. While I waited, my mind had been processing all the information I'd learned regarding Henrietta's murder, with special attention to the lack of alibis and newly discovered possibilities for motives within the Dougal family.

"I thought I'd find ye here," he said, giving me a crooked, boyish grin as he slid into the chair closest to me. "I had tae leave Kelly in the Land Rover, so we have tae be double-quick, or she'll complain aboot the cold."

I returned his smile. "Double-quick?"

"I've come tae collect you. Tae offer my special brand o' service."

I arched a brow. "Are you propositioning me?" I teased. Our relationship has been casual and prone to a friendly innuendo now and then, such as the one I sent zinging his way now. This handsome man could make me smile in the most trying of times.

"Aye," he said, grinning widely. Then he explained. "I'm offerin' tae be yer bodyguard fer a private viewing o' the warehouse. I thought ye might be interested, considering yer lofty status as one o' our finest crime fighters."

"That's a stretch," I said with a laugh. But was I interested? Absolutely. "I'm not sure that's possible until the inspector—"

"He approved my suggestion not more than half an hour ago. I was over at the distillery, payin' my respects tae Gordon Martin, when the inspector came by."

The inspector must have finished searching for clues. There wouldn't be anything left to find, because Jamieson was thorough, but I still wanted to see it from the vantage point of an observer rather than as the unwilling participant I'd been during the discovery of the body. "Yes, I want to see it."

"Mind ye, it won't be a social event, considerin' the circumstances. A tour o' the distillery can be set up fer a later date when this is behind us. But Gordon is willing tae share a wee bit o' his own opinion as tae how it mighta happened."

"He's already spoken with Jamieson about these opinions of his, right?" No way was I going to step on my boss's toes.

"O' course. But ye never know. It might be helpful tae have ye do a walk through as well."

I quickly gathered my belongings, bundled up in my quilted coat, and followed Leith to his vehicle, where the border collie was patiently waiting in the backseat. As soon as she spotted me, she stood up and began to wag her tail.

We reunited after I slid into the front seat, with plenty of hugs, pats, and licks.

"I told ye a porkie," Leith said, after he'd gotten in behind the wheel. "Kelly likes this sort o' weather just fine. She's got a thick winter coat and doesn't mind nearly as much as we do."

"I'm used to you stretching the truth."

He grinned and started the Land Rover, and we pulled away from the village center. A few minutes later we parked in the distillery's lot; reassured Kelly that we wouldn't be long, though she didn't seem concerned about waiting in the SUV; and walked into the tasting room, where we found Gordon Martin.

"I'm so sorry for your loss," I told him, all the emotions of the previous evening washing over me.

He nodded solemnly and said, "Anything I can do to help find my aunt's killer, I'll do, starting with my own theory and how I think the manner o' her death mighta come about."

We walked through the warehouse to the back and paused next to the tub where we'd discovered Henrietta's body. I vividly recalled those first moments when I'd tried to pull the body out.

"The final stage in the process o' maturing whisky takes place in this room," Gordon explained, giving me some background. "Tae be considered whisky, the casks must remain sealed fer a minimum o' three years, but many lie aging in the wood fer eight, ten, twelve, even as long as fifteen years, during which time a small amount evaporates."

Leith piped up. "Which is called the angel's share."

"I like that," I said.

Gordon continued, and I noticed his face was drawn with grief and exhaustion. "Our objective is tae produce consistent flavors each time. That's my most important job."

"Consistency is an art form," Leith added. "And Gordon is the best."

Gordon flushed at the compliment but plowed on without acknowledging his own expertise. "A distinctive flavor and bouquet is attributed tae the essential oils in the barley and a pure source o' water, along with the origin o' the casks. Even our climate influences the flavor. I play only a small part in the final product."

"I know that the source of your casks is a business secret," I said, "but are they made specially for you?"

Gordon shook his head. "Ours are shipped from a bourbon producer in the States. Casks can only be used once for bourbon, but they can be used over again fer our whisky. So the bourbon producer is happy and we are happy tae take the casks."

While I found everything I'd just learning fascinating, and wished I'd taken time for a tour earlier in my Highland visit, the murder was foremost in my mind. I eyed the tub where Henrietta had drowned and said, "Tell me, Gordon, what do you think went on here prior to your aunt's death?"

"Someone pulled the empty washback over to this cask," Gordon said, and then I remembered that he'd called it that last night. Washback. He'd said something about it being a vat used to ferment whisky prior to maturing. This one was made of wood, still filled almost to the brim with whisky as it had been when we discovered it last night.

"Do you mind?" I asked. Without waiting for his reply, I

walked over to one of the empty ones and gave it a push. It didn't budge. Then I tugged at it instead, pulling it toward me. Step by step, I managed to drag it a bit at a time. A few inches more, having my answer, I stopped.

"Heavy," I announced. "But I could have moved it over underneath the cask if I'd been determined."

Gordon selected a wooden hammer from a nearby shelf. "This isn't the exact one used to open this particular cask," he said. "I brought it along for demonstration purposes. The mallets in this room were taken away by the police fer examination."

He went on to point out what he referred to as a keystone near the rim of the cask. "That area is thin enough tae punch out with this mallet once we want tae tap it fer the whisky inside." He showed us what was certain to have taken place prior to Henrietta's murder. "The washback was placed there, just so, then the hole was punched, and the whisky allowed tae pour out intae the washback."

"Wouldn't someone who worked here have noticed that sort of activity?" I asked. "It had to have been arranged in advance."

"This warehouse isn't frequented much, other than tae bring in another batch tae age. It has its visitors during tours, but we don't do much in the way o' during the winter months. Sometimes we'll have a private tour, but none recently. Especially not yesterday with the private tasting planned. Someone must have known that and taken advantage o' the opportunity."

I gazed at the vat filled with whisky.

"This was extremely well thought out," I muttered. "Someone set this up prior to the tasting fully intending to lure the victim . . ." I paused, realizing whom I was talking with. Henrietta's nephew. Did I really have to go into graphic details?

"Don't try tae spare my feelings," Gordon said.

"I don't want to cause you any more pain," I said, not sure that was possible.

"The only way tae relieve what my family and I are going through is with the capture o' the monster who did this tae my aunt. Someone drew her in here, overpowered her, and held her head under until she drowned."

"She musta been in a weakened state anyway and easy to overcome," Leith said. "Last I saw her, she had lost a lot o' weight. She was thin as a groat." Then to me, "It's out and about that she had cancer. I'm not at all surprised. Seeing her waste away, I knew she wasn't well."

"Gordon," I said, "think back. Did she say or do anything that might be significant to the investigation? Any change in her mood? Was she more anxious than usual?"

"I've been goin' over and over the days leading up tae her death, askin' meself those same questions." He gave me a helpless shrug. "But nothin' comes tae mind."

"She was dying," I prodded. "How was she handling that news?"

"Aunt Henrietta wasn't a complainer even at times when she had all the reason tae gripe. She kept going on as usual, regardless o' the circumstances. Once we found out about the cancer, my mum tried to convince her tae accompany her back tae Edinburgh where she could be cared fer properly. She refused tae budge."

"We should all be as determined tae carry on when our time comes," Leith added. "There's something tae be said aboot passing on in familiar surroundings, not away from the comfort o' yer own home."

Then Gordon frowned. "Sometimes she would make a comment or two regarding her past. I think she had regrets."

"I imagine that's a normal reaction," Leith said. "We all have things we'd change if given a second chance."

I glanced at Leith. He'd expressed a truism, one well worth remembering. If I could have a do-over, what sort of man would I choose now that I was older and wiser? One more like myself? Someone prone to introspection and more sensitive to the needs of others? Next time, if there even was a next time, I'd put more value on kindness.

I wondered what Leith would have done differently. He'd produced a daughter but hadn't been able to establish a lasting love relationship with the mother of his child. Based on his devotion to Fia, she definitely wasn't one of his regrets, though.

And what about Henrietta McCloud? Did she regret her choices? Apparently so.

"What did she say that made you think she regretted past actions?" I asked Gordon.

"A few weeks ago we had lunch together. She got a faraway look in her eyes and looked about tae cry. When I asked her what was the matter, she wiped her eyes and said something tae the effect of, 'If only I'd been a better person. I dinnae deserve tae have a happy life filled with bairns like I'd always dreamed o'. I don't even deserve tae have a nephew like yerself, Gordon, ye're like a son tae me, and every day I give thanks fer havin' ye in my life.'"

I didn't find her ruminations particularly unusual. My mother, when dying, had uttered similar sentiments. "If onlys" and "why hadn't Is" are probably very common when one is facing the end of life. But my mother had let go of unresolved issues from her past and accepted what was. Henrietta hadn't had the chance for that reconciliation. She'd been robbed of that possibility, not by an inner malignancy but by an external one.

"Then last week," Gordon continued, "I heard her mumbling something about setting things right, and it seemed like whatever decision she made had lifted a heavy weight from her shoulders. She wasn't exactly happy, but I thought she'd come tae terms with her lot."

"Any idea what she meant by setting things right?"

"None. I asked what that was all aboot, but she said tae never mind."

I continued to question Gordon about his aunt while Leith listened patiently. As far as her nephew knew, Henrietta minded her own business, attended church regularly, didn't gossip, and took care of Bridie's needs with loyalty and dedication. When I asked him how she got on with Archie and Florence Dougal, who were the only ones at the moment with legitimate motives, Gordon responded that their relationships remained courteous from the beginning until the end, if not exactly warm.

"They appreciated her attention tae Archie's mum," he said. "No one could fault her fer her care o' Bridie, that was fer sure."

"Your aunt came to live with Bridie when she was a young woman," I said. "I would have thought she and Archie would have developed an affection over the years. 'Courteous' seems an odd way to describe their relationship."

"I was thinkin' more o' his wife," Gordon said. "A cold

fish, that one. From the first time Archie brought her home tae meet his mum, Florence didn't warm tae Aunt Henrietta. But then she hasn't warmed much tae me, either."

Gordon's observation was the first concrete evidence I had that Archie's wife had an issue with the dead woman prior to the discovery that Bridie had revised her will. If Florence hadn't liked Henrietta from the very beginning, how would that have changed once Florence found out about Henrietta continuing to live in the house once Bridie was gone? It wouldn't have gone over well at all.

I rearranged the suspect list in my head, moving Florence Dougal ahead of her husband. Florence was about my height and carrying a bit more weight. If I could pull a heavy wooden tub across a warehouse floor, so could she. And she certainly knew her way around the distillery.

I thanked Gordon for his cooperation and watched him leave through a doorway leading into the other areas of the distillery. When Leith and I reentered the tasting room on our way out, Bridie was waiting for us. She had Henrietta's Scottish Fold in her arms and a catlike grin on her face.

"Snookie needs a new home," she announced, her eyes riveted on me. "Some nice and cozy cottage away from all this sadness and that lonely bedroom. She doesn't understand that her best friend isn't coming back. And she's taken quite a liking tae you."

"Leith," I said, ever hopeful, avoiding the old woman's eyes. "Kelly might enjoy a playmate."

"Ye're the one in the hot seat, not me," he replied.

"I can't keep her here," Bridie said, pleading. "It's too much fer me to care fer her, what with having enough work taking care o' myself now. Henrietta used tae look after me like I was royalty. She spoiled me, she did. And besides, what do I know about a cat!"

"I couldn't possibly," I stammered. "I'm only in Scotland temporarily. I'm leaving in two weeks, and . . . you'll hire another companion, right? The new employee can take care of Snookie."

"Maybe some time in the future I'll have another, but not when Henrietta's death is so fresh in my mind. I don't care about a bit o' dust. But a cat! I couldn't possibly cope."

"Why don't ye give it a go, Eden," Leith suggested when he should have been staying out of the conversation, especially if he wasn't going to volunteer. "It might be good fer both o' ye. And if need be, I'll find the beast a new home when the time comes."

"I'd hate to disrupt Snookie twice," I said, but I noticed that my tone wasn't nearly as firm as I intended it to be. "Once she adjusts to the cottage, it will be much more difficult to . . ."

"I gathered a few o' her things." The slyster interrupted my babbling. "She doesn't need much. A log o' her health and vet visits, and all the supplies tae keep the both o' ye in fine form until well intae next week."

"Then it's settled," Leith said.

They were ganging up on me.

"I don't know the first thing about caring for a cat," I said.

But it was too late. Snookie had been transferred into my arms. Her ears were down flat against her head, and since that was one of her characteristics, I couldn't tell how she felt about all this. Didn't regular cats plaster their ears to their heads when they were upset? And swish their tails? Snookie's tail wasn't swishing. Oh no, was she purring?

"It's the easiest thing on earth," Bridie, the woman who claimed she knew nothing about this cat, explained. "Brush her a bit, feed her when she's hungry, and make her feel loved. Ye can put her in that little crate right by the door. She'll travel in more comfort that way, and there's her bag beside it."

I really needed to say no, there was absolutely, positively no way I wanted to get roped into this. I tried to dredge up a firm negative. Instead I squeaked, "But . . . what about Vicki's Westies? They'll fight with Snookie."

That was lame. Coco and Pepper didn't fight with Jasper. They wanted to play with him. Although the barn cat was above all that and refused to give them the time of day. "And we already have a cat," I croaked.

Before I knew what was happening, Snookie was in the carrying crate. Leith raised it by the handle. He handed me her bag of personal belongings.

Then he led me, dazed and confused, out of the house and into the cold.

Kelly watched our approach from the Land Rover, her tail wagging.

The cat meowed.

I groaned.

CHAPTER 13

"What a cutie," Vicki said, her eyes instantly taking in the new addition to the household. A moment earlier, she had entered my cottage with a tote over her shoulder and balancing a slow cooker between both hands. She'd expertly knocked on the door with an elbow. Expecting her, I'd opened the door to delightful aromas wafting from the pot and realized I was starving. Touring a crime scene will do that, make me crave life-sustaining nourishment.

"A boy or a girl?" she asked.

"Snookie is a female."

"Where did she come from? Did you rescue her from a snowdrift? Poor, sweet little kitty."

Vicki placed the slow cooker on my counter while I explained how I'd inherited Snookie in spite of my resistance, which had been futile. The Scottish Fold had already checked out every nook and cranny of the cottage and was now sitting on one of the upholstered chairs: legs and tail sprawled out in front of her, front paws resting on her belly exactly like the position of a traditional Buddha statue. She acted like she owned the place already.

"I can't possibly keep her," I said. "I'm leaving in less than two weeks! Not that I want to go, you know that, but I'm being forced out by rules and regulations. And having a fur ball for a roommate will only make it harder to leave than it already is going to be."

Vicki gravitated to the cat and sank to her knees on the side of the chair to get a better view. They stared at each other, and then Snookie stretched forward, sniffed, and gave Vicki a lick on the nose.

"You've been officially accepted," I guessed.

"How could you even consider giving her up? I travel all the time with Coco and Pepper. You could take her back to Chicago with you."

"To where? I gave up my mother's apartment, remember? I don't have a home any longer." Then I remembered another problem with that idea. "And Ami, who is my last resort for temporary asylum, is allergic to cats."

"Don't worry, everything will work out."

I humphed. Fat chance. "Everything might work out for you and Sean. And for Snookie eventually, and for all the other critters here at the farm. But not for me, it won't."

I didn't mention that Ami had been strangely quiet lately, not deluging me with e-mails as she usually did. So even my friend across the pond might be abandoning me to my fate as a Chicago homeless person. No home decorated for the holidays awaited my return. No warm fire to share with good friends beckoned from afar. I pictured myself struggling to ward off stiff winter winds at Christmas time, huddling over sidewalk grates, and standing in long lines waiting for free bowls of soup.

"Look at you," Vicki said lightly with a grin as she returned to the kitchen, seeing some sort of invisible humor that was escaping me. "You're a sight with that big pout. Sit down and eat. A little comfort food will put you back on the right track."

She placed dinner in front of me. It was a hearty winter stew and she'd artfully sculpted a border of mashed potatoes around the edge of the plate. "What is it?"

"Inky Pinky. Don't you remember that I promised to make it for you, and now's the perfect time what with winter settling in. The ingredients are simple—leftover roast beef, carrots, and onions warmed up in gravy with a splash of vinegar, salt, and pepper."

"It's wonderful," I exclaimed after tasting a forkful, feeling better already. "Sorry for the whining, but I'm frustrated."

"You've had to listen to plenty of complaining from me over the last months. Returning the favor is the least I can do." She spotted my knitting effort where I'd left the work in progress on the other end of the counter. "I see the Merry Mittens are coming along nicely."

"Just don't look too closely," I warned her.

"I'm looking very closely at your life since you arrived, since we met. You're learning to knit. You have a cute kitty to warm your lap and logs burning in the fireplace. And speaking of sizzling, you have a hot man to show you a good time. From my point of view you lead a charmed life."

"You sound like Ami."

"She and I are smart women."

"And as to a hot man, if you're referring to Leith Cameron and our so-called date that ended in murder . . . well, that didn't go off exactly as planned."

"You still have two weeks," the matchmaker said. "A lot can be accomplished if you put your mind to it."

It was time for a subject change. "I thought Sean was joining us."

Vicki paused with a forkful of Inky Pinky in midair. "He was. Until the inspector put him on another special assignment."

"He's watching over Katie Taylor. She's the young woman who catered the whisky tasting and was attacked in her friend's home early the next morning. That assault might not be related to the murder, but Jamieson felt it was wise to give her extra protection for a short while. Even if it's unrelated, she may have gotten a good look at her attacker before he was scared away by her friend, and the guy might be lurking around."

"I hope not."

"The inspector is being cautious."

"Sean said she woke up."

"That's great news. Has she talked about the attack?"

Vicki shook her head and said, "She can't remember a thing about it. Sean says the doc thinks that's common after a head injury. No one knows if she'll ever remember."

"Not such good news. Well, hopefully she'll recover quickly and the doctor will release her to go back to Tainwick with her parents."

I'd barely finished my sentence when Vicki jerked suddenly as though she'd been zapped by a surge of electricity.

She dropped her fork to the floor. It clanged sharply. Recovering, she reached down and retrieved it, and when she sat upright again, her face was flushed. "Tainwick? Did you say Tainwick?"

"Why? Do you know of it?" I asked, puzzled by her reaction.

Vicki didn't respond immediately. She rose, tossed the fork into the sink, and got a clean one. When she replied, she'd recovered her normal coloring. "Ah, sure, of course I do. It's not far from Glenkillen, a little north of Loch Ness."

"Is there something unusual about the place? The first time I heard reference to it, I thought the name seemed familiar. What about it?"

"It's just a small village like ours. Nothing special about it at all."

"Then why were you so startled that you dropped your fork?"

"Me? I wasn't startled at all, just clumsy. What gave you that idea?" Vicki sat back down and concentrated on eating.

What had made me think that? The startled expression on my friend's face when I mentioned Tainwick? The dropped fork? The evasive eyes? All of these things? Or was I overreacting after a day filled with all kinds of suspicions? Probably. It had been one of the longest in memory, beginning at this very table with Charlotte's visit, then a lengthy conversation with Janet Dougal at the inn, followed by a call to the hospital, then Bridie's house, and the distillery. No wonder I was seeing things where they didn't exist.

Vicki wasn't involved in the investigation in any way,

hadn't been present at the scene of the crime, didn't have any stake in the murder other than the fact that Sean was involved. She had absolutely no reason to react suspiciously.

I decided to test her anyway. "Henrietta McCloud was also from Tainwick," I announced with a bit of theatrical flair. "Her sister told me they lived there growing up."

But Vicki simply shrugged. "We all have to be from someplace. That's as good a place as any."

"Don't you find that odd?" I pressed on. "The murder victim *and* one of the guests from that evening viciously attacked?"

"What does the inspector say?" She was calm and met my eyes.

"Not much. In fact, he's considering dismissing it as coincidence after interviewing her parents and not finding a connection."

"Well, there's your answer."

"He tends to store things away when he can't make sense of them, but that doesn't mean he's forgotten."

"He's good at what he does. And with you by his side, and my Sean, the killer doesn't stand a chance of getting away." She smiled.

I decided I'd imagined Vicky's reaction after all.

While we finished our meals, I went on to tell her a little about my trip to the distillery with Leith. Vicki was back to her old playful self because she said, "You two were meant for each other. If only one or the other of you would realize it and do something to move it to the next level."

"I'm not so sure. His focus is on raising his daughter and earning a good wage so he can educate her."

"He's a young man with a lot of energy. He should be able to manage a woman, too. I bet he could manage you just fine."

I didn't bother trying to explain. I'd tried before. Leith had been very clear from the beginning. He wasn't into the dating scene. Fia's well-being was his primary concern, as it should be.

"Want another helping?" Vicki offered.

"Yes, but I'm stuffed."

"I've brought a few seasonal decorations to make the cottage sparkle," Vicki said after we'd rinsed and put away our plates. She dug through the tote she'd had slung over her shoulder when she arrived. "I decorated my house this afternoon. Let's do yours now."

Was everyone in this place delusional but me? "I have to leave before Christmas," I reminded her. "I don't feel very festive at the moment."

"Posh," Vicki said. "We'll fix that."

So we spent the rest of the evening decorating while Snookie looked on. It didn't take much to transform the cottage. A glass bowl filled with tiny multicolored ornaments as the table centerpiece. Cascading strands of silver and white gift bows dangling from strings in front of the window gave the illusion of falling snow. We wrapped birch logs in twinkling lights and framed them with votives and strung fragrant evergreen garland on every available ledge.

Bright white lights, candlesticks, red and gold, silver and green. Vicki's talent for holiday décor gave my world a soft glow, however temporary.

Afterward we sipped hot mulled wine before the fire while real snowflakes began to fall outside. We even decided to introduce Snookie to Coco and Pepper. Vicki trudged through the newly fallen snow and returned with the Westies. The trio got on famously. Somewhere in Snookie's past she'd been used to dealing with dogs. That was a relief, one less worry.

Later that night in my bedroom, I tried to coax Snookie into the room without success. I left the door ajar in case she decided to join me later and realized that several hours had passed without a single thought of Henrietta's murder. Even the looming departure date had been glossed over earlier and forgotten in the spirit of friendship and camaraderie.

I slept like a log.

Chapter 14

I awoke Monday morning delighted to find Snookie curled up in the space between the headboard and my pillow. She opened her eyes, rolled onto her back, yawned, and stretched. I grinned, which isn't usually part of my morning routine. Not that I'm cranky first thing like the inspector is, but I'm not overly gleeful, either. Grins and smiles are mostly reserved for special moments that come after several cups of coffee and a hot shower, and with a sufficient reason to do so.

I stroked the Scottish Fold, and she rewarded me with a soft purr of pleasure deep within her throat.

When was the last time I'd had a warm body in my bed? One so obviously pleased to be there?

It had been so long I couldn't remember.

I busied myself by feeding Snookie from a small tin of food in the bag Bridie had packed, took a long hot shower, and drank a second cup of coffee while admiring the fresh coat of snow outside and last night's holiday handiwork. Even without a tree, it set my mood to fine.

I decided to skip breakfast. I'd eaten an enormous amount yesterday, first clootie dumplings with clotted cream, then fish and chips, and finished the day with stew and mashed potatoes. Enough calories to last several days. I needed to cut back or I'd have to buy a new wardrobe, a size or two larger. Instead of eating, I added wood to the fire and sat down, picking up and opening the spiral notebook that Bridie had sent along with Snookie.

As the older woman had told me, it contained the cat's medical records, carefully documented visits with the vet for vaccines and checkups, all neatly recorded with dates and results. Charlotte Penn's notations and initials were on the most recent examinations. Apparently Snookie was a healthy, well-cared-for cat.

Two loose papers slid out and floated to the floor. I retrieved them.

The first was the document from the breeder that proved the Scottish Fold's purebred status. Not that it mattered to me. She could be a mix of fifteen different breeds, and it wouldn't mean a thing unless I intended to sell her or breed her, which I didn't. But perhaps this would be important to someone else. I tucked it back into the record book and studied the other, which was folded in half.

"Princess Hen" had been handwritten on it, whatever that meant. I unfolded it.

And another reminder of my past smacked me in the face. I felt my breath become labored while my pulse raced. I looked away, into the fire, composed myself, and then stared at the piece of paper.

A clan crest of a hand holding a cutlass had been sketched onto it. And below it in Latin—*Fortiter et Recte*, which I effortlessly translated as "Boldly and Rightly."

I recognized the Elliott crest instantly, of course.

I'd been so intent on evading any mention of the Elliotts, and had been successful until a few short days ago when Bridie Dougal had reeled me in with a cunning game. She'd wanted to get to know me solely based on my last name. The name I didn't want to maintain a connection with.

And now this! Another glaring reminder that escaping one's past is harder than it seems.

Snookie jumped onto my lap and settled as I tossed around possibilities and accusations. Was this another one of Bridie's tricks to pique my interest? She hadn't made a secret of her friendship with my grandfather and her wish to discuss my family, and I'd been just as open about my own feelings. But she'd apologized for upsetting me, and we hadn't spoken on the subject since. I didn't think this was intentional on her part.

I looked it over again. The paper was old, brittle, and yellowed, the ink faded. I wondered about the person who might have sketched it. My grandfather? Or Bridie? How it got inside Snookie's vet journal was easily explained. Henrietta probably found it on the floor ages ago, tucked it inside the notebook, and forgot about it.

As I held part of my own history in my hand, I experienced a feeling of extreme pain over my losses. Distant cousins were all that remained on my mother's side, and I knew little about them. Even less was known about my father's family. Both his parents were deceased, I knew that much. My father, Dennis Elliott, had been an only child, so there weren't any aunts or uncles to track down. Again I wondered if my father was alive. If he'd passed away, where was he buried? Was there a family burial plot? Where was my grandfather's gravesite?

If my father was alive, living in the Highlands, where was he hiding?

Apparently I was more curious than I cared to admit, even to myself. Sitting before the fire with Snookie on my lap, I gave myself permission to remember.

I'd been six years old when my mother had been diagnosed with MS. At the time, her illness didn't affect me unduly. The disease had been explained at my level of understanding, and the gradual but steady progression of her disabilities only impacted me later, in young adulthood, when I became her primary caregiver.

I remember being told that my grandfather had died, which didn't mean much to me back then, either. I'd never known him, and the miles between Illinois and Scotland were incomprehensible to a small child.

Anyway, my father flew far away in a plane to attend the funeral. I remember standing next to my mother, waving good-bye after he'd picked me up and hugged me.

Then he'd never returned.

My mother's letters went unanswered. I'd never seen her composing them, but when I was older, she told me she'd written many, sending them overseas. Now, for the first time, I had questions.

Who had those letters been addressed to? Had she known how to contact my father? What words had she written? Did she beg him to return? All those old, painful memories and disappointments, all the resentment flooded back. I was on the verge of tears.

Finding this crest and motto and suffering the feelings it invoked reminded me why I've spent years erasing my father, eliminating him from my world the same as he'd done to me. Recollection was painful. His actions only made me angry. And in the end, there wasn't anything I could do to reconcile those feelings of bitterness.

Quickly, I folded the drawing along its creases and returned it to the notebook. Tossing it aside, I stretched to pick up my laptop from the end table without disturbing Snookie, balanced it on the arm of the chair, and powered up.

I clicked on my inbox. Finally! An e-mail from Ami. Something to take my mind off myself and these pesky personal issues that had cropped up in my path like an endless, unavoidable patch of poison ivy.

"I'm so sorry your special evening turned out the way it did," Ami wrote. "How awful! At least you had a strong shoulder to lean on in the form of a hunky Scot. My suggestion, not that you've asked for it, but you know me, I can't resist, is to spend your remaining days in the Highlands writing steamy romantic scenes and acting them out authentically. Leave that horrible crime for the police to solve. Who knows? The invitation snafu might be the catalyst to kick your relationship with Leith Cameron into high gear. Go get him while the getting is good."

Leave it to Ami to turn a mistake like the invitation mess-up into an advantage. But why shouldn't I go after my dreams? Because I wasn't sure what they were. As much as I enjoyed Leith's company, I wasn't head-over-heels infatuated. Had I lost that schoolgirl ability to fall hard for a cute guy with a dynamic personality?

Leith had great qualities—he was self-assured without

a flashy ego, and he was fun and outgoing. He was caring, hardworking, and a wonderful father. The list went on and on. So why wasn't I chasing after this outstanding man? It wasn't as though a good one came along every day.

After mulling over Ami's note, I didn't respond to it. How could I explain in a way that she would understand?

Working this murder investigation was *exactly* what I needed right now to escape the demons in my head. Writing more emotionally charged scenes with the Scottish Highlands as a backdrop would only accentuate the feelings of loss I was going to be experiencing soon enough. Besides, having a fling with a man I most likely would never see again wasn't my style. And I was positive it wasn't his.

Reluctantly, I coaxed Snookie from my lap, closed my laptop, dressed for the wintry day, and left the cottage. I warmed up the Peugeot, found that Vicki wasn't in her house, and took time to cuddle with her Westies. Then I did the same with Jasper inside the barn before driving the short distance to Sheepish Expressions. I got out, leaving the car running, and spotted the red mail van pulling in from the main road. The Royal Mail delivered to the shop almost daily, since it stocked yarns and garments from vendors all across the Highlands. As items were purchased and went out the door on a routine basis, so new products and old standbys arrived. It was a virtual merry-go-round of activity.

The driver and I exchanged greetings. Today's delivery was especially large, as it tended to be on Mondays. I pitched in, offering to carry as much as I could.

"What *are* you doing?" Vicki shouted when she saw me standing at the front counter with various parcels stacked in front of me. I was idly sorting through the letters, not really expecting any to be for me. Since I'd been in Scotland, I'd had exactly zero personal snail mail, what with the expense and time to reach me and the ease of e-mail.

Vicki snatched the letters out of my hands and protectively clutched them to her chest.

For a moment, I gaped at her. She certainly hadn't been herself recently. "Kirstine needs to get better ASAP and get back to work," I advised after considering my friend's change in behavior. "Because covering for her without a break is making you squirrelly. You're acting strange."

"I'm perfectly fine," she snapped.

A close and personal visit from Sean would also do the trick. I'd have to see if I could get him relieved from his security duty for this evening, even though that meant I'd have to stand in for him. But if it would improve Vicki's mood, I was willing. Even better, Katie might be released and depart with her parents, freeing both of us.

"Okay, then, I'm on my way to Glenkillen. Do you need anything?"

Vicki took a deep breath and forced a weak smile. "I'm fine, really. And Kirstine is coming in this afternoon to relieve me. She's feeling much better. Once I get back to spinning and knitting at home, I'll be much happier."

Which I realized was true. Vicki was in her element when she was spinning yarn from the farm's wool and creating patterns for her knitting students and yarn-of-the-month members.

"And I'll see what I can do about giving Sean a break," I offered.

"That would be wonderful."

"If he shows up later and I don't, feed Snookie for me."

"Sure. Where are you off to right now?"

"Two guests from the tasting are staying at the inn," I told her. "Both of them maintain that they were in their rooms the afternoon of the murder. They claim they were there until they left for the tasting. Neither has anyone to substantiate those alibis. I'm going to try to prove or disprove their claims."

"How in the world are you going to do that?"

"I have absolutely no idea."

And I didn't.

But as I drove away from the farm, I realized that Janet Dougal and Patricia Martin weren't really today's primary goals. They were simply housekeeping. Someone else without an alibi had entered my radar range. Someone with a motive.

But first things first. I'd follow up on alibis for Janet and Patricia, at least as far as I could go.

After that, I'd set my sights on Florence Dougal.

CHAPTER 15

When I arrived, Inspector Jamieson's Honda CR-V was parked outside the Whistling Inn. Its horizontal yellow stripes framed by blue and black checkers were unmistakably his. After entering the inn, I exchanged small talk with Jeannie at the front desk and once again admired the inn's festive decorations. Then she directed me to the breakfast room, where the inspector sat at a table with Janet and Florence Dougal. From the looks of things, they had just finished eating.

This was an amazing stroke of luck, considering that Bridie's daughter-in-law had been in my thoughts on the drive over. I wouldn't have to track down Florence now because she'd been delivered right into my lap.

As I joined them, I remembered that these two women had seemed to get along well at the tasting. I recalled my astonishment that evening when I noticed that Janet had managed to make a friend, considering her brash personality and how she had rubbed the other guests, including me, the wrong way. Right now, she was on her best behavior, sitting a bit too close to the inspector, invading his personal space, turned more than slightly his way, an intently concentrated expression on her face.

The inspector was visibly relieved to see me. He rose quickly, almost tipping the chair in his haste to offer me his seat. Accepting it, I suggested he bring over another. He muttered something about leaving soon anyway.

"The centerpiece is gorgeous," I said, admiring the bouquet of holly, ivy, and mistletoe trussed up with ribbons, an arrangement worthy of Vicki.

"Holly is native tae Scotland," Florence informed us. "Except for the most remote parts o' the Highlands. And ivy is very common, o' course."

"I didn't know that!" Janet said. "You are such a wealth of Scottish trivia."

"It comes from a lifetime o' living here."

"I best be off," the inspector said from behind me.

"Why the hurry?" Janet protested. "You should stay and grill us for more information. We've hardly begun."

"I have a busy day before me." Jamieson had caught on quickly to her scheme.

As if on cue, Janet rose. "I'll show you out then," she said.

He glanced at me and said, "We'll be in communication a wee bit later. I'm off tae the hospital tae check in on Katie Taylor."

"A sad affair," Florence added. "It's all about the village that some cad musta been passing through and seen an opportunity."

"What a coincidence," Janet exclaimed, catching a glimpse of herself in a decorative mirror on the wall and preening. "I was about to go to the hospital myself. I was shocked when I heard what happened to the poor girl and want to show my support. May I impose upon you for a ride, Inspector? My rental car is acting up."

Jamieson grimaced when he realized his mistake. Amused, I waited to see how he might extricate himself from her clutches, but she had more experience in the fine art of web casting than he had in evading the net. Besides, I felt sure she could have countered any defenses he presented.

"All right then," he told her. "Get yer coat. I'll be waitin' in my vehicle fer ye."

Florence removed the napkin from her lap and placed it on the table, a sure sign that she expected to leave also.

"If you have a moment or two," I said to her. "I'd like to speak with you."

"That's a good idea," the inspector agreed, addressing Florence. "Ye should go over the facts as ye know them with Constable Elliott. She's got a keen eye and will assist in speeding up the investigation once she is apprised of all the facts. Ye need tae fully cooperate with her."

I shot him an expression of gratitude for having faith in me. Then I watched him sweep out of the room with Janet right behind him, her hustling form reminiscent of Sean's dogged determination when chasing after the inspector.

Over tea, and while I nibbled at toast spread with marmalade, Florence calmly answered an assortment of personal history questions that I politely presented as social etiquette, carefully avoiding any tones associated with an interrogation.

She'd been married to Archie for thirty-one years, having met at a social function at the same Edinburgh business school that their son, Hewie, attended now. As soon as Archie graduated, they married. Hewie was an only child, and although they had hoped for more, it was not to be. Her husband had been intrigued by the family business from the time he could walk. He'd explored every corner of the distillery, and his aspirations to one day run the business were cemented early on.

"Although he's had some conflicts with his mother," she added. "If they don't see eye to eye on the best course, Bridie overrules him every time."

"What about your son? Does Hewie want to follow in his father's footsteps?"

Florence continued with an affirmative. He shared those aspirations. Hewie had been disappointed that he couldn't jump right in, but his parents had insisted that he get a proper education before taking over the reins one day.

While Florence spoke of her husband's and son's hopes and dreams, I studied her. She must have been pretty at one time, but weight gain and the creases of a perpetual frown had marred that beauty. I wondered if she'd had any dreams of her own, and if they had come true.

"You seem to have struck up a friendship with Janet," I said at one point, which brought the conversation around to the present situation.

"We share a common bond. We married into a tight-knit family. Both of us will always be considered outsiders. Neither o' us is exactly welcome as far as my mother-in-law is concerned. Bridie barely tolerates me. The least she could do is pretend."

Bridie hadn't given any clues as to her opinion of her daughter-in-law one way or another, so I had no basis to judge that—other than the terms of the will, giving Harriet a home for life in a house that some might think should have gone to Bridie's son and wife. "I'm sure that's not true," I said anyway to comfort her.

"It's spot on," Florence insisted. "And she hasn't gone out o' her way to embrace her American relative, either. Janet traveled a long way to meet us. She deserves better treatment. And Bridie soured Henrietta against me from the beginning. And the way Bridie carries on! She causes as much trouble as she possibly can—sitting in that big house, plotting against us. Her latest little trick was tae make us think she was selling out. It was a ruse o' course. It always is."

"Are you saying that you didn't believe her from the start?"

Florence shook her head. "Not fer a single moment. Archie neither. Bridie wants Archie tae be dependent on her, but he's a strong man and won't bend tae her will. But when I phoned Hewie as I do weekly and told him what she was considering, that upset him, it did."

I ventured into the territory of Bridie's undated will. "If Henrietta had survived Bridie, she would have been allowed to stay in the house."

"Another way o' sticking it tae me. Bridie knew I had my eye on being the mistress o' the place. Tae leave it tae her housekeeper is a slap in the face."

"She was providing for Henrietta, if anything should happen to her." Not to mention that Bridie was ninety and that possibility existed. "Henrietta wasn't actually inheriting the house."

"She might as well've been."

"Couldn't you have moved in also? The house is large enough."

"And subject myself tae her barbs on a daily basis without the ability tae let her go fer showing disrespect? I think not."

I was surprised at Florence's bitterness and went on to say, "Others I've spoken with describe Henrietta as unassuming, saying she tended to her own business, was rarely seen and then not often heard. Are you saying she could be petty and vindictive?"

"Ha. That woman was as spiteful as they come. Do more digging and the real Henrietta McCloud will float tae the surface like a rotten fish. She was skating on thin ice even with her own family toward the end."

Skating on thin ice?

I felt a chill because the warning note discovered by Henrietta had used that same phrase. Something about skating on thin ice. That the plans for Saturday night needed to be canceled. A warning not to be taken lightly, according to the author who penned the note, or else.

"What did you just say?" I asked, watching her closely, my voice sounding colder than intended even to my ears.

Florence bit her lip. I took that to mean she'd let something slip and realized it. "What I meant," she said, trying to explain herself, "is that Henrietta didn't get on with anybody other than Bridie. She even argued with her own sister, who only wanted what was best fer her."

"Are you aware that a threat was made prior to the tasting on Saturday night?"

"Tae whom?"

"That isn't clear. Bridie assumed it was meant for her, but it may have been intended for Henrietta."

"I don't know anything about a threat tae anybody."

"You just used the same phrase."

Florence was beginning to look unsettled, her tone turning as frosty as mine. "And what phrase are ye referrin' tae?"

"'Skating on thin ice.'"

I went silent, waiting.

"It's a common enough expression. And wha' with the icy weather outside, it came tae mind. Ye aren't accusing me o' anything, are ye?"

"I'm simply stating a fact." I wasn't sure where to go from here. "The expression implies that a person is doing something dangerous to their health. Are you the one who sent that note?"

"I don't know a thing about any note."

"Florence, when was the last time you saw Henrietta McCloud alive?"

"I resent yer implication!"

She was on her feet, the chair she'd been sitting in shoved back, teetering on the edge of crashing to the floor, an expression of barely suppressed rage on her unfriendly face. Several diners on the opposite side of the breakfast room glanced our way.

"These are routine questions," I told her, lowering my voice a few octaves. "Everyone at the tasting the night Henrietta was murdered has to answer that same question. So I'm asking you again. When was the last time you saw her alive?"

Instead of offering a response, as she should have, Florence Dougal whirled and stomped out of the room.

Well, that certainly didn't go well. Florence had quite the temper.

As I stared at the festive table arrangement with the ivy, ribbons, and evergreen holly, a Scottish expression came to mind that I was almost positive would apply to Florence.

She never lies but when the holly's green.

Nothing she'd said rang true.

I immediately phoned the inspector and told him what had transpired. When I stacked everything up, I felt more and more convinced that Florence was hiding something. I summed it up. "Florence had a lot to lose if Henrietta lived and a lot to gain with her out of the picture. And she hadn't known about the cancer or that her problem would have gone away soon enough."

"Ye sound a wee bit worked up," the inspector said.

I carried on, without acknowledging his comment. "She's an unpleasant woman who thinks everyone is against her, which they probably are, since she's so disagreeable. She also claims she didn't believe Bridie was going to sell out, but that is certainly arguable. She also mentioned her son, Hewie, and told me he was upset at the prospect of losing his future inheritance. *And* people become very protective when their children are concerned. *And* she used the exact same idiom the sender of that note used!"

"Ye think she sent the warning tae which one o' the women exactly? Bridie or Henrietta?"

Good question. I was still working out the finer points. "That isn't clear at the moment. Bridie probably. Or both of them. And she refused to answer when I questioned her about the last time she saw Henrietta alive."

"Is that how ye broached it? Like that?"

"Yes. How else should I have worded the question?"

"And she got riled up, did she?" The inspector asked.

I paused to consider the approach I'd used with Florence. Okay, it could have been smoother. Bold and brash worked much better in the States. Here, I needed to learn to tiptoe.

Our conversation had gone along fine until she'd used the exact same expression as written in the warning. Then I'd lost my cool. And then she had.

Jamieson never allowed his emotions to get away from him. Sometimes I wondered if he had any. But of course he did. They were buried under perfectly proper professionalism. The exact opposite of my current demeanor. With discomfort, I realized that if he and I played bad cop, good cop, I'd be the bad cop!

"Still with Janet Dougal?" I asked, changing the topic while I considered how I might have done things differently so future interviews were less volatile.

"She's in the waiting room. No one is allowed intae the girl's room, and if I'd had my wits about me, I would have used doctor's orders tae my advantage and wouldn't be committed tae puttin' that woman back in my vehicle. Right now, I'm in the hallway, waiting fer the doc tae finish up. As good a time tae rid myself o' my passenger as any other."

"I could have done a better job with Florence," I admitted aloud.

"Sometimes a suspect overreacts with anger tae cover up," the inspector said. "She had no business refusing tae cooperate with a member o' my team. I intend tae back ye up."

Which made me feel slightly better. "Florence was in and out of the tasting room throughout the day," I said. "With plenty of opportunity. She could be our killer."

"Aye," he said, sounding tired. "Ye managed tae get some new information before ye had her flying out o' the inn. The fact that her son was concerned about Bridie sellin' the company is worth a follow-up. But," he added quickly, "I'll handle him. And as tae the information she refused tae supply ye with, she claimed yesterday that she never laid eyes on Henrietta that entire day. At the present time, we have no way o' confirming the truth o' that. I'd say she's the one skatin' on thin ice at present."

"Very funny."

As we disconnected, I thought I heard him chuckle.

CHAPTER 16

I didn't want to place too much stock in Florence's analysis of Henrietta McCloud's unsavory character, mainly because Bridie's daughter-in-law could have been describing herself rather than the house companion. But I decided I should at least spend a short time pursuing her claim, as frivolous as it probably would turn out to be.

According to Florence, Henrietta McCloud was a spiteful woman. She'd implied that Henrietta had a mean streak and was capable of acting out. My first impulse was to disregard anything coming from Archie's wife, but then I remembered what Gordon had told me. Henrietta's nephew had said she'd expressed unspecified regrets, had wanted to make things right. If she wanted to make amends, with whom? And why? And did she get that chance before she was killed?

The only people who knew Henrietta's full history were her sister, Patricia; Bridie; and Gordon. And all three of them were considered suspects. Not at the top of the list, but suspects just the same. No one from that night had been eliminated.

Did that mean I should also take Gordon's observations with a grain of salt? He might be lying. Florence could be lying. Any of them might be. How was I supposed to wade through all the information they offered and sort truth from fiction? That was the hard part.

Briefly, I wondered if forensics was uncovering anything useful. Would damning evidence come to light in the next day or two? A fingerprint on the side of the washback would be the perfect solution. But if the killer knew the warehouse wouldn't be used that day, there would have been plenty of time to wipe away any traces of evidence. And didn't those of us who tried to save her touch the washback? I had. Leith and Gordon certainly did. Who else had?

While I was pondering which of Saturday's guests to bother next, I decided I'd better adopt the inspector's method of eliminating one at a time. Jeannie came over to clear away the plates.

"Two of your guests claim they were in their rooms all afternoon on Saturday," I said. "I'm hoping to substantiate their assertions."

"Ye're referrin' tae Janet Dougal and Patricia Martin, I've no doubt."

Sometimes I tended to underestimate Jeannie.

"Don't look so shocked," she said, reading my thoughts. "Ye're an investigator, investigating a crime, and those two are on yer short list. I didn't see either o' them until aboot six thirty or so when they came down tae go tae the tastin'."

"How did they get out to the distillery?"

"They both have rental cars, but there had been the

snowstorm so Gordon Martin came round tae fetch them. Although it was a bit awkward noo that I'm rememberin' it."

"Awkward?"

"Janet rushed over tae Patricia, who was mindin' her own business waitin' in the lobby, and told her that she was tae ride with her out tae the tasting. Patricia said she didn't know anything aboot that and who was she anyway tae be making such demands. Janet was cheeky, actin' like she expected service, sayin' she'd planned tae drive herself but the weather had turned bad and she was afraid o' the roads.

"When Gordon came in tae collect his mum, he didn't know aboot it, either. But Janet wouldn't let up, and what could they do but take her along and sort it out later. That's a pushy one, that."

Yes, she was. Janet would do pretty much anything to get what she wanted. With her attention focused on pursuing the inspector, I pitied him.

Then I asked, "How well did you know Henrietta McCloud?"

"By sight only. She rarely came intae the village. She kept tae herself."

"I've heard that she had a nasty side, that she could cause her share of trouble."

Jeannie snorted. "If she did, I woulda heard, and I didn't. Who'd say such a thing?"

"Scuttlebutt only," I said evasively.

A few minutes later I wandered over to the Kilt & Thistle Pub. Outside, the owners' redheaded twin boys, Reece and Ross, were lobbing snowballs at each other. Since I spent so much time in the pub, we were on friendly terms. A snowball caught me in the back, and suspecting it wasn't an accident, I joined in for a few lobs of my own before scooting inside.

Dale, the proprietor, took one look at the evidence on my coat and tried to apologize.

"They're just being boys," I assured him.

"Their mum is taking them sledding in a bit. A few climbs up the likes o' those hills will wear them down some."

Still determined to eat lightly today, I ordered more tea while presenting the same questions about Henrietta to several of the regular customers, and with the same results. The dead woman hadn't been around town much, but when she was, she was polite, respectful, and proper.

I wondered how much more evidence we'd need to arrest Florence Dougal for the murder of Henrietta McCloud. It was amazing how much proof was required in these cases. Just because she had a motive, the means, and plenty of opportunity didn't mean we'd get a warrant. My boss was probably working on the finer details right now.

Something concrete like fingerprints, DNA, a witness, or a confession would be required to proceed. Most likely a witness to the murder would have come forward by now. We'd have to wait and hope for fingerprint or DNA evidence. On that front, I wasn't nearly as positive. And a confession was the least likely.

At loose ends and not feeling very productive, I decided to relieve Sean of his security duty. I drove over, and armed with my laptop to help while away the hours, I found Vicki's main man in a small waiting area across the hall from Katie's room where it was easy to keep an eye on her door. Sean was eating bakery from a plate on a counter and drinking coffee from a disposable cup. Life as a body-guard wasn't all that rough.

"Are Katie's parents here?" I asked, as I watched a nurse wearing a navy blue tunic and navy trousers enter Katie's room with a stethoscope around her neck.

"No, some bossy head nurse came by early this morning and scolded them fer botherin' the girl. 'She needs her rest,' says that one, and she's not tae be disobeyed. The parents haff been by her side since they were called, even though Tainwick isn't that far off, and now she's out o' the woods and tae go home tomorrow, they went off like they were ordered." Sean finished a cinnamon roll and helped himself to another. "That nurse is a real battle-axe, if ye ask me."

"Anything new on your end?" I asked. "Have you heard anything?"

"Nothin'. What brings ye by? I was hopin' ye'd haff news that I've been let off this hospital floor or that a murderer is in custody. Or that a robber's been apprehended. Something tae give me a free day."

"Not anything nearly as big as a criminal in custody." I went on to tell him that Vicki missed him terribly and that he was free to leave for the farm. "I'll fill in for you until Katie is released tomorrow."

"That would be swell," he said with a big grin. "I'll be back in a crack if ye need me, but this assignment is one tae put ye tae sleep. Don't count on seein' any action. Have ye informed the inspector o' your decision?"

"No, but I will shortly."

"All right then. Would ye like tae borrow my baton tae reassure yerself?"

He turned to display the black club resting in a holster

on his side. As far as I knew, this was a new addition to his wardrobe.

"No, thank you, I'll be fine." I couldn't see myself using a baton on anybody. The pepper spray I carried would do the trick in a dangerous situation. Besides, I didn't expect one.

With that, Sean made a dash for the elevator, almost colliding with the nurse exiting Katie's room. A few minutes later, I peeked into my charge's room and found her asleep. I settled at a table in the waiting room, facing the hallway and her room, powered up my laptop, and considered working on *Hooked on You*, something I'd determined to avoid for the short term. Now here I was—back to writing. Or rather, thinking about writing.

The biggest problem with taking a few days off from the novel is that I lose forward momentum and have to backtrack, refreshing my memory, which hasn't been serving me as well as it should. I was past the dreaded middle, where it's so easy to let up on the conflict, which can be a death knell if the reader's interest wanes. That's the reason for plenty of additional sexual tension and several turning points throughout to keep the reader guessing. At the current stage, it was up to me to give Jessica and Daniel some final dark moments before a joyful resolution. That was the beauty of romance novels. They always had happy endings.

If all went as planned, I'd have the first draft finished by the end of the year and then a long winter in Chicago to make revisions.

The thought of Chicago reminded me of Ami. E-mails had been few and far between with both of us busy. Briefly I considered sending one to her, except not much had happened since my last update. She already knew about the tasting and the murder. With no new developments to report, and not much in the way of progress on the novel, what could I say of interest? Then I remembered that I hadn't responded to her last e-mail.

Procrastinating, which was a particular talent of mine, I reread it and paused at Ami's reference to the invitation confusion. That really had been a mess, a minor one considering the larger picture that night, but at the time it had seemed huge. Then to discover it had been a big manipulation by Bridie Dougal . . .

Something about Ami's e-mail bothered me. I went back and reread the one I'd sent that prompted her reply.

Nowhere had I mentioned the invitation mix-up.

So how had she known? Unless she was communicating with someone on this side of the pond. Leith? Certainly not. Jamieson? I couldn't imagine those two becoming pen pals. Vicki, then. Which struck me as very strange, especially since neither of them had mentioned their communications to me.

Should I say something to Vicki? But if she wanted me to know, wouldn't she have told me? Did this explain her reaction when I'd popped in unannounced? Had I almost caught her passing e-mails behind my back?

The immature little girl who resides inside me struggled not to be hurt at the thought that my two best friends were getting close. But they didn't tell me. Didn't they want to include me anymore?

The big girl in the room popped up and snorted, giving the floor to the woman, who wisely decided to let it go. For now. There had to be a logical explanation.

The clanging of metal food trays and squeaking of approaching wheels brought me back to the present moment. I caught a flash of navy blue, the standard hospital uniform, and soon after rose to check on Katie. She was sitting up with a tray in front of her. When she spotted me, she smiled.

"I thought I'd check on you," I said, not mentioning that we'd been keeping tabs on her round the clock.

"I can go home in the morn."

"I heard and that's great news. Well, eat your meal. I'll stop in again later."

"No, please. I'm not very hungry. Keep me company."

"Only if you eat while we talk. I had something earlier," I lied. Unless I counted the toast at the inn. The few pieces of remaining bakery in the waiting room were going to have to hold me over until morning unless I hit up some vending machines later or made a run for the snack shop. I hadn't thought this through very carefully. A change of clothes would have been smart. And a small overnight bag.

"My parents are coming in the morning tae collect me," Katie said. "That head nurse shooed them off, so they went back tae Tainwick fer the night."

"They must be relieved. Do you remember what happened?"

Ignoring her food tray, Katie told me what she knew about the assault, which wasn't much other than she'd heard a sound and gone to investigate, and that was the last she remembered until she woke up here. It only confirmed the small amount of information I already had acquired from her friend Gayle.

"The night o' the tasting, Bridie Dougal suggested that you and I get together," Katie said, picking at her food after my insistence, pushing it around with her fork. One of the hospital staff in the navy blue uniform was straightening up in the bathroom as we talked, proving that there was no such thing as privacy in a hospital. Or any real rest.

"She did, did she, and why is that?" I said with a light laugh. "And just so you're aware, she's a bit of a trouble-maker."

Katie laughed along. "I gathered that. High drama and all. When we were deciding on the menu for the tasting, I realized what a character she is. When I told her about the book I hoped tae write one day, using actual stories from the Highlands, she thought you might be inspiration for me. You're actually published!"

"Not yet." I went on to explain about my work and gave her a tentative timeline for publication. "Next summer," I said. "But what I do and what you are thinking of doing are very different types of writing. I doubt that I'd be helpful."

"But they both involve research."

"Yes," I agreed, "and every story is a mystery, in a way."

"Mysteries are what got me started. When I was research-ing my own family, then went on with some of the local families, I discovered that almost all the histories had gaps, unknowns, mysterious things that were never resolved. It fueled my imagination."

"A vivid imagination is a great gift," I said. "I'd like to talk more about your ideas, but right now you need to rest."

"Perhaps sometime soon. You could give me yer opinion."

"Maybe," I said, knowing that most likely we wouldn't meet again in the short time I had left. Katie would return to Tainwick to recuperate, and I'd continue to work the murder case with the inspector.

"I don't remember yer name," Katie said. "I've been trying, but I just can't. Maybe it's because o' the blow tae my head."

Thinking back to the tasting, I wasn't sure I'd thought to offer it. "Eden," I said.

"I'm glad ye visited me, Eden."

CHAPTER 17

Settled on a comfortable sofa in the small waiting room right across the hall from the patient's room, fortified with a sweet roll and a cup of tea from the service counter, I thought about Katie's research and how this latest murder was one of those mysterious events that she might end up writing about, especially if we didn't solve the case—although I was confident that we would with Inspector Jamieson at the helm. Still, Henrietta McCloud could very likely make an appearance of some sort in the young woman's future work.

I was the only one in this particular waiting room. The inspector had arranged to keep other visitors away from Katie's area. I considered turning on the television for company. But someone from the staff offered me a pillow and blanket, which I gratefully accepted, and I promptly decided I was sleepy. Glancing at the clock on the wall, I realized that it was only midafternoon, but in these winter months when dark descends as early as three thirty, nights are extremely long. This one coming up might prove to be my longest ever.

I'd given up one of my precious last days for this. What I should have done was let Sean and Vicki suffer through another twenty-four hours without each other. In the morning Katie would leave. Sean and Vicki would have lots of tomorrows in their future together. The generosity I'd felt earlier drained away, leaving me annoyed.

And sleepy.

But what good is a security guard who isn't conscious? Which made me wonder how Sean did it, so I called him.

"And tae whom do I have the pleasure o' speakin'?" he asked.

"You didn't stay awake through the whole night, did you?" I said, without preamble. Sean knew exactly to whom he was speaking.

"Course not. I wouldn't be human if I had, would I?"

I wanted to point out that that was part of the job, staying alert for trouble. But how could one person accomplish that without backup relief?

Sean explained, "During the day when there's a lot o' activity, if ye need some shut-eye, ye tell the head nurse that ye are takin' a bit o' a snooze, and they aren't tae let anybody near the room who doesn't belong."

"Shouldn't I move into her room in that case?"

"No, no, no, that would alert her tae the fact that the powers that be are worried about her safety."

"Which we are."

"Tae a small degree, is all. The patient needs tae stay calm. Havin' police protection in her room won't help that, now will it?" After a brief pause, he remembered the most important part of the equation. "As tae the nighttime, I forgot tae inform ye earlier that her room is tricked."

"Tricked?"

"Aye, once the door is closed." He paused to ask, "Is it closed right noo?"

"Yes."

"Okay, then, if anybody were tae enter, it alerts the nurse desk and somebody will come runnin'. They can turn it off anytime they want tae check on her."

"Thanks, that's helpful."

I hung up, miffed with Sean. What if I'd peeked in? It would have triggered the alarm. Although I was relieved that the "trick" was in place. That meant I could get some decent rest without worrying.

This gig was turning out to be a gravy job. Or rather it would be if I were actually being paid like Sean was. I'd have to speak with the inspector about hazard pay. I grinned at that and was reminded that I hadn't phoned him about the switch with Sean. At the moment, it didn't seem as important as a few minutes to rest my eyes.

Arranging myself in a comfortable position, I felt myself starting to float in fluffy dreamy clouds, sinking into the pillow, my breathing evening out.

I wasn't sure how much time passed before I was startled awake. My eyes popped open. Someone had turned off the overhead lights in the waiting room and had closed the door partway. A beam of light shone on the floor from the hall lights. What time was it? How long had I been asleep?

Instantly my mind flashed to Katie, worried until I remembered about the tricked door and the alarm system at the nurses' desk. I sat up suddenly and sensed a rush of motion over my left shoulder. Something slammed into the pillow where my head had been resting moments before.

It happened so fast, in such a whoosh of movement. From the corner of my eye, before I had time to turn and face my attacker, I sensed something descending again. I raised my arm to deflect any blows as I slid from the sofa to the floor. A rush of air told me I'd been quick enough, but barely.

I found my voice long enough to shout, "Get away from me!"

I screamed. Then tried to remember where I'd stashed the pepper spray. But my mind was blank.

Later I would chastise myself for reacting by squealing instead of swinging. But reflexes kicked in and my survival instincts were in high gear. So I went on screaming, keeping my arm raised, and swiveled on the floor to face my attacker. All I saw was a dark shadow moving away, caught a glimpse of white shoes and navy trousers before the person who had intended to harm me was out the door.

I rose to my feet and scrambled through a pocket for the pepper spray, intending to give chase. But by the time I reached the door and had protection in hand, the hallway was deserted, except for several nurses and aides I didn't recognize hurrying toward me.

The night shift had swung into action.

I turned my head in the opposite direction and caught the tail end of an exit door swinging shut. But by then, the help I'd shouted for was surrounding me, questioning my motives, wrestling the spray out of my hand, and standing firmly between me and the exit door. No one was sure if I was the source of the shouts for help or if I was the cause, and they weren't about to let me go off without explaining myself.

By the time I managed to convince them that I was the victim of an assault, pursuit was too late. Which probably worked out for the best.

What had I planned on doing if I caught up? Pound the first person I encountered wearing a navy blue hospital uniform? And with what? With the baton I wasn't carrying? Or maybe I would have shot off a round of pepper spray only to discover I'd zapped the wrong person, and experience the wrath of Jamieson descending on me?

Once I convinced Katie's night nurse that I was on the same side, I opened Katie's door, hearing a buzzer sounding down the hall. The nurse gave me a scowl before heading toward the desk to turn it off.

"What's going on?" I heard Katie's sleepy voice. "Who's there?"

"Everything okay in here?" I affected a bit of a Scottish accent and kept hidden in the shadows, not wanting to alarm her.

"Aye, but, I thought I heard screaming."

"A bad dream, probably. Do you need anything?"

"No."

Katie was safe. That was the most important thing.

I would have phoned the inspector next, but hospital security had arrived, and I was informed that he was already on his way. He found me at a little after seven o'clock in the semidark of the waiting room with my eyes peeled on Katie's room and the canister of pepper spray in my hand.

"A bit o' excitement?" he said, taking a seat beside me, his eyes serious, concerned.

"My life flashed before my eyes."

"A surgical hammer was found in the stairwell. Now, ye better start at the beginnin'."

I told him what I knew.

"It was either a member of the hospital staff," I said, finishing, "or someone dressed to play the part."

"It wouldn't be difficult tae dress appropriately in navy tae pass yerself off as a member o' the medical community," he agreed.

"I never expected it."

"Ye can put away the pepper spray. Ye won't be needin' it. As soon as the call came in, I ordered hospital security tae check the premises; that's when they found the hammer but no sign of an intruder. It would take a halfwit to still be lurkin' aboot. I'm supposing we won't find prints on the weapon."

"I think I remember a glimpse of a glove, so probably not, but I can't be sure. It happened so fast."

"Ye're safe now."

"Why attack me?" I said aloud, voicing the question that had plagued me since the encounter. "Why not go right into Katie's room? Whoever this was probably wasn't aware of the door alarm. Even if this individual did know, it would have been a simple matter to disable it disguised as one of the staff. Why go after me?"

The inspector frowned. "What are ye doin' here any-hoo? Ye should be snug in yer own cottage and Constable Stevens should be in this room."

"I decided to spell Sean so he could be with Vicki." A thought occurred to me. "Do you think those hammer blows were meant for him?"

"Anybody with eyes in their head could have told the difference between the two o' ye, able tae get a good look while lurkin' in the room while ye were sleepin'."

A good point. And creepy to think about. If I hadn't awoken when I did, I could be dead.

"Noo I'd like to know," he continued, sharper now. "Who approved this change o' orders? I must be goin' dotty, because I don't recall it coming from me."

"I apologize," I said, meaning it. If I'd kept my nose out of it, I wouldn't have been alone in the waiting room and none of this would have happened. "I wasn't thinking that it was a big deal."

"And now 'tis a big deal."

"But why would anyone go after me? Katie's supposed to be the one needing protection."

"Have ye noticed anything unusual lately in yer goin' aboot?"

"Like someone watching me or following me? No."

"Who knew ye were comin' here tae take over fer Sean?"

I thought about that. "No one, other than Vicki. I hinted at it this morning."

"Someone found out. But ye haven't been on guard fer that sort o' thing, either, have ye?"

Why would I have? The inspector and Sean didn't go around looking over their shoulders, afraid that evil lurked in every shadow, waiting to pounce. I shuddered at the thought of someone preying on me. Biding their time. Waiting for the perfect moment to strike.

"What have ye done, Eden Elliott," he said, "tae cause someone tae take this kind o' risk tae take ye out o' the picture once and fer all? If that hammer had—"

He didn't have to finish; we both were aware of how close I'd come. All I could do was shake my head in utter confusion.

Henrietta McCloud was dead, Katie Taylor had been attacked, and now it had been my turn.

We were interrupted by the entrance of Sean. And he wasn't happy that his romantic interlude had been cut short. "Leave ye with a simple task," he said to me, "and what comes o' it? More trouble, that's wha', and me havin' tae pick up the pieces."

"Are ye aware o' what transpired here, Constable Stevens?" the inspector asked.

"Not yet, since ye didn't elaborate when ye ordered me tae appear. I imagine the special constable isn't likin' the duty and is requesting her leave."

We filled him in. Sean grew noticeably quieter.

"Ye're officially relieved o' duty, Special Constable Elliott," Sean said, showing a humbler side than usual. "Or maybe we've been standin' guard over the wrong woman!"

"I can finish out here tonight," I said.

"Ye're finished," Sean insisted. "I wouldn't leave ye alone. Vicki would have me head on a platter and serve me up!"

The inspector and I exchanged glances. He gave me a wink. In spite of my underlying fear, I found comfort in that simple show of support.

CHAPTER 18

Morning's first light brought with it more new snow that had fallen during the night, a light dusting that left the scenery outside my window glistening as the sun rose over the hills. The fire had gone out sometime in the very early morning, and without that warmth to counter the chill in the air, I stayed in bed longer than usual, enjoying the warmth of my comforter and Snookie's body beside me.

The fact that I'd been able to sleep amazed me. But after going over the scene in the waiting room again and again, I wasn't any closer to understanding why it had happened, other than that it had to have something to do with the murder investigation.

And it had been more than a warning note written out. Much more. What had I learned to cause that violent reaction? Or was I on the verge of a discovery?

Eventually, I forced myself out of my cocoon, restarted the fire, put on coffee, fed Snookie, ate a hot bowl of porridge, and prepared for a new day. I refused to allow myself to continue to dwell on yesterday evening's assault. Instead I concentrated on the murder case, rationalizing that only by solving the case would I find out why I'd been targeted at the hospital.

Sitting beside the fire with my cup of coffee, I phoned Bridie Dougal. When she answered, I identified myself and spent a few minutes talking of the weather forecast, which called for a cold front bringing more wintry conditions and more of those colorful warnings. Bridie seemed delighted with the possibility of going from the yellow of aware, through amber to prepare, and touching on red, which meant prepare for the worst. When she ran out of weather topics, I got around to the real reason for my call.

"There's been some mention of an unpleasant side to Henrietta," I said. "And I'm hoping you can clear that up for me one way or the other."

"People love tae cause mischief," Bridie, a bit on the impish side herself, said. "Henrietta's old ways o' dealing with life, why that's fiddler's news."

Another expression I was familiar with after almost half a year in the Highlands. Bridie was telling me that was old news.

"Go on," I encouraged.

"Henrietta was a much different person when she came tae work fer me. Her father was a drunk, the mother a sad sack, beaten down from years o' abuse. A neighbor of hers appealed to me after learning that I was looking fer home help and asked me tae take her in, see if she might work out. That first year she needed tae heal from such a cruel home life."

"That was kind of you."

"It wasn't kind so much as selfish. I enjoyed her fussing over me. Henrietta seemed happy with her lot, and stayed, as ye know. She had a lot o' anger built up and it took time fer her tae let it go, but she managed eventually."

"What about her sister?"

"Patricia was makin' her own life in Edinburgh. Henrietta said she'd rather be on the dole than takin' advantage of her sister and comin' between her and her husband by intruding. Especially with a new family started."

I thought about that before saying, "Could something in Henrietta's past have anything to do with her murder?"

"Ye mean her past catchin' up tae her?" Bridie paused, then said, "That was a long time ago. Over thirty years at least. What sort o' person would wait that long tae exact revenge?"

A point I'd considered. "I was hoping you'd have some idea. Someone with incredible patience?"

"I can't help ye there, Eden. Henrietta ran away from a bad childhood, but she was never any trouble tae me, never had anybody unsavory coming around callin' on her, either. Why don't ye stop by fer tea," she interjected. "It's about time we discussed yer Scottish family. I have lots o' history tae share with ye."

"I'm afraid I won't have time for social calls until Henrietta's murder is solved and we have her killer in custody," I said firmly.

"I can make up some lovely finger sandwiches. Ye still have tae eat, don't ye?"

"Soon, perhaps." I wasn't about to get into a debate with the old girl, because I wouldn't win, so I wrapped up our conversation with, "If you think of anything that might be helpful, please call me. And could I please have your son's private number? I'd like to touch base with him."

Touch base. That had a nice personal ring to it. Bridie didn't hesitate to comply.

When Archie answered, I identified myself as Constable Elliott, and his attitude remained respectful and helpful. "What can I do fer you?"

"Were you aware of a threatening note that was received by Henrietta and assumed to be directed at your mother?" I asked.

"After the fact, I was. Was it intended fer Henrietta, the poor old girl? Did you get tae the bottom o' it?"

"Not yet, but we will," I replied with more confidence than I felt. "Your mother's initial thought was that it might have something to do with her plan to sell the distillery and her announcement that she had something to discuss with the family members after the tasting."

"She thought one o' us sent it?"

"Only at first. After Henrietta's murder, she changed her mind. Now she believes the warning was intended for her companion."

"And since Henrietta died a violent death, that assumption is valid, wouldn't ye say?"

"Perhaps." I remembered clearly my conversation with Florence. She hadn't thought Bridie was serious about selling out. Neither had her husband, Archie, according to his wife. They'd assumed that Bridie had been bluffing. "Did you believe your mother intended to sell the distillery?" I asked, following up on Florence's claims.

"We all presumed she meant it," he said, surprising me.

"Mother can be impulsive, rashly deciding important issues without consulting her family. It's exactly something she might pull out o' her hat. I spend half my time keeping her in check."

Which was exactly the opposite of what Florence had told me.

"And your son? Was Hewie worried?"

"He's away at university and doesn't get involved in family politics."

I thanked him for his time and disconnected.

Florence had lied about her family's reaction. She and her husband believed Bridie was capable of selling out; her son, who she said had been concerned, wasn't one bit, according to his dad; and Florence had uttered the same phrase used in the threatening note—"skating on thin ice."

Interesting information, but confusing as well. If Florence had sent the note to Bridie, what in the world did that have to do with Henrietta's murder? Had the housekeeper figured out that Florence was involved in the threat and so been killed to keep her quiet? Was that what she'd wanted to tell me after the tasting? To report Florence for threatening Bridie? In my view, that wasn't much of a motive for murder. But getting rid of Henrietta before she could occupy the family home as grand dame was.

Florence's dream was being threatened by the housekeeper. And if Bridie followed through with her intention to sell the distillery, Florence's husband's livelihood and their son's future were at stake.

Granted, there would be cash from the sale, but that would be deposited in Bridie's bank account, and Florence's dreams would be shattered by her mother-in-law. Thus, the warning shot across the bow?

The issue of the distillery had been successfully resolved, whether a result of the note or a change of heart on Bridie's part. The only remaining roadblock to Florence's final destination had been Henrietta.

For good reason, Florence was at the very top of my suspect list. Had she been the one who had dressed in hospital garb and crept in to attack me? Had she figured out that I was on to her after my reaction to her comment about skating on thin ice? That certainly had been a major slip of the tongue on her part.

Florence Dougal was about to learn that I don't give up easily. If the old Eden's life had been threatened, she might have turned tail and headed for the hills. But the one who was awakening in the Scottish Highlands wasn't such a pushover. Was I a force to be reckoned with? I hoped so.

Still, while sitting before the fire with my coffee and Snookie, I couldn't help thinking that something about this case wasn't right. I sensed that important pieces were missing. And it started with last night's intruder. An attack on me wouldn't stop the investigation. Actually I was the weakest link. The inspector would get to the truth with or without me. And the assailant didn't have any guarantees that the inspector didn't know everything I'd learned. It was a risky move.

After careful consideration, I was confident that I hadn't been targeted for death because I was getting too close to pinpointing the killer. So . . . then . . . why?

Maybe more than one thing was going on here, and I was failing to recognize it.

I thought about that possibility in a personal context, harking back to my mother's illness and the effort it took to finally get a proper diagnosis.

Multiple sclerosis isn't easy to identify. There isn't one simple test. So before my mother's diagnosis, the doctors went about ruling out genetic disorders, brain tumors, infections, inflammatory diseases, and nutritional deficiencies. To make matters worse, she had an underlying condition that masked the real problem. Unbeknownst to all of us, she'd been suffering from depression. Once the depression was addressed, and those other possibilities ruled out, the MS was discovered.

More than one thing had been going on in her body, and for a long time we failed to recognize that fact.

Was the same thing happening here?

My eyes came to rest on Snookie's health records. Inside the notebook, folded neatly in half with "Princess Hen" written on it, was an aging sketch of the Elliott crest with the motto skillfully and beautifully penned beneath the crest.

Once this case was solved, I'd have to remember to give the drawing to Bridie, as I was certain it belonged to her.

My phone rang, startling me. It was the inspector.

"I'm on my way to question a certain American compatriot o' yers, and handcuffs are a distinct possibility," he said.

"Janet Dougal?" Where had this come from?

"And I'd appreciate backup," he continued.

"Why?" I asked, thrown off by the suddenness of his decision. Obviously he was arresting her. Why Janet?

"Why?" he roared, predictably as cranky as always first thing in the morning. "Because the woman is after me, that's why, and if I have tae deal with her on my own, she's goin' tae think she has a chance and won't take what I'm chargin' her with seriously. It's been bad enough up till now, bein' stalked, I was, and I'll have tae use handcuffs if ye aren't there. Havin' ye at my side will hopefully keep her at the proper distance."

"*What* is going on?"

"Just meet me at the Whistling Inn."

And the line went dead.

CHAPTER 19

Janet Dougal didn't stand a snowball's chance of escaping once she opened the door to her room.

"Ye're tae come with us," the inspector demanded by way of a greeting. "Constable Elliott will stay with ye while ye change intae something more appropriate. I'll be waiting in the breakfast room."

The smile on her face faded. "Is something the matter?" she called after his retreating back. Then to me, "He isn't at his best in the morning, is he?"

An astute observation on her part. I've been on the receiving end of his snarly morning disposition several times, and it wasn't pleasant, even when he wasn't gunning for me as he was Janet.

"Let's not annoy him further," I suggested, glad that she'd already applied her heavy-handed makeup before-hand. Otherwise we would have taken much longer than it ended up taking. And since the man she'd set her sights on was involved, she hurried without any prodding from me.

"What's the fuss about?" she asked as she changed.

The inspector hadn't taken time to fill me in either on the phone or a few minutes ago in the reception area downstairs, so I was almost as clueless as Janet. "He'll explain himself in due course," I assured her.

We entered the breakfast room ten minutes later, the only ones there. Tea was already laid out for a party of three, with the inspector sitting quietly before one of the servings. Jeannie brought a basket of toast as we joined him.

I wasn't particularly hungry in a physical sense after the big bowl of porridge I'd eaten earlier. My craving was for an end to the suspense that had been building inside me ever since the inspector's summons. I still didn't know what was going on, although I had my suspicions.

Oblivious to the tension in the air, Janet dove for the basket of toast, withdrew several halves, buttered them lavishly, and was spreading them with marmalade when the inspector chose that moment to enlighten us.

"I'm aboot tae ask ye some hard questions," he said to her. "And I expect nothing less than completely honest answers."

"Of course," Janet said, as though she wouldn't even think of any other option, her smile warm and reassuring.

"I believe ye had more than a few words with Henrietta McCloud."

"I told both of ye about that incident," she said, intent on preparing the toast.

"Aye, but ye failed tae mention a second encounter the very same afternoon that the victim was murdered."

I hadn't seen that coming, mainly because Janet had insisted she'd been in her room during the time in question, and I hadn't found anyone to say otherwise. Apparently, the inspector had. I wondered who had come forward with this revelation.

Janet glanced up, startled. "And who offered up that pile of rubbish?" she demanded.

"Let's just say I have a firsthand account. Ye were seen drivin' away from the inn in that car ye've been renting at approximately four o'clock that afternoon."

"What if I did?" Janet gave him her most dazzling smile. "That's hardly proof of anything."

"Except ye were also placed at Bridie Dougal's house shortly afterwards."

Janet's smile slid sideways and the piece of toast fell from her fingers. "It's time to come clean, then."

"It's past time," I told her, growing more agitated, irritated that the woman had lied about her whereabouts from the beginning. More lies. A pile of lies, if I added hers to Florence's.

"Henrietta McCloud rang me up," she explained nonchalantly, as though it hardly mattered. Although this time she remembered the dead woman's name.

"What time was this?" the inspector interrupted to ask.

"Roughly around three that afternoon, if I had to guess. She suggested that I come right over to have an early supper with Bridie before the tasting, that she was in fact looking forward to it, and that I couldn't possibly say no. *About time Bridie Dougal treated me properly*, is what I thought at the time. So I drove out there, expecting to be warmly welcomed.

"Instead, Henrietta answered the doorbell, opened the

door only partway, as though I was some sort of unwanted salesperson. She refused to let me in, claiming I hadn't been expected at all. Well, of course we had words *again*, I told her what I thought *again*, and I ended up driving back to the inn to wait for the appropriate time to go to the tasting. Actually thrown out, as it were. That woman was playing some sort of nasty game with me!"

"Ye killed her then before ye left?" The inspector's blue eyes were piercing like daggers.

"No! How could you possibly think that? Henrietta was very much alive. I'm the one who might have suffered a collapse of some sort after that shabby treatment. But you can see why I covered it up once the woman was found dead in a whisky barrel. I would have been the main suspect!"

I refrained from verbalizing the retort on my lips.

"I did a bit o' research with the assistance o' authorities in the States," the inspector informed her, "using their database. Not only do ye have a working knowledge o' distilleries, by yer own admission, havin' made a hobby o' touring them, and could have easily tapped the cask and emptied the contents intae the washback, but it appears that ye also have a criminal record."

"The problem with the United States," Janet said with a huff, after a brief moment to think about that, "is that old records aren't purged after a certain amount of time, which would only be fair. A person does one little thing wrong, and it follows her for the rest of her life."

What she claimed was true, a problem with the system, at least from an ordinary citizen's point of view. I've witnessed plenty of situations where people were denied employment because of black marks in their distant pasts. But from law enforcement's prospective, it was a huge benefit, as I was discovering now.

Inspector Jamieson leaned in and lowered his voice even though the room was empty of any other diners. "Ye were charged with assault on two different occasions, both o' them occurring in the last year. I'd hardly call *that* a small spot on the linen that has followed ye fer years. Restrainin' orders were required tae protect yer victims."

Janet snorted. "Victims? Hardly. That silly tramp didn't deserve him, but he was blind to that fact. And yes, they both requested restraining orders, but she put him up to it. I'm over that infatuation now and can hardly believe I had feelings for him." Her voice softened as she went on, "He isn't like you, not nearly as intelligent and interesting."

The inspector grimaced, and there were a few moments of awkward silence all around before he continued, "I'm afraid I have no choice but tae detain ye fer further questioning in the murder o' Henrietta McCloud. Ye have a history o' violence, the knowledge tae have arranged the crime scene as we found it, and a witness that places ye there during that time frame. Do ye have anything tae say in yer defense?"

"I can see why it doesn't look good from your point of view," she admitted. "Especially when you lay it out like that, in such a cold fashion. I want an attorney, and that's all I have to say."

Janet might be done, but I wasn't quite through.

"Not only are you facing murder charges, but you attacked me at the hospital last night," I said, and it wasn't a question. I'd never have thought she had it in her. "And before that you assaulted Katie Taylor. More charges will be pending, I assure you."

"Katie who?"

"The caterer."

"That's preposterous," Janet said, still blustery, but there were cracks in her composure. "I don't know what you're talking about. I don't know this person and I haven't set foot in the local hospital. And when I left Henrietta McCloud, she was alive. Inspector, you aren't really arresting me, are you?"

"Ye need tae come along quietly," he said.

"I won't!"

"Ye most certainly will," I heard from the doorway, and glanced up to see Sean strutting our way, hitching up his trousers in a display of authority. "I can take on the responsibility o' this one, as I should, considerin' my newly appointed position."

Jamieson was visibly relieved to pawn her off. "Take the suspect away, and I'll be along shortly."

"I don't have a proper vehicle fer transportin' suspects," Sean told him, producing a pair of handcuffs from his belt. "I'm still drivin' that ratty old Renault when I should be travelin' in a beat car o' me own."

The inspector sighed. "Fer right now, ye'll drive what ye have."

"You can't handcuff me," Janet said, rising from the table, staring at the handcuffs, the seriousness of the matter finally dawning. "I'm an American citizen."

"And a Dougal at that," the inspector added.

"That's right! And I have immunity," she insisted. "Based on my nationality."

"Sean, see that herself's immunity remains intact and watch out, she's got a record o' aggression."

After a few more verbal indignations from Janet, Sean managed to convince her that it was in her best interest to go along without creating a scene, and he escorted her from the room.

"Who finally decided to come forward with information?" I wanted to know the minute we were alone.

"The bit aboot seein' her drive off from the inn came from an anonymous tip-off, called in early this morning. The part about a witness tae her arrival at Bridie's house, well, that was a fabrication on my part."

I feigned surprise at such underhanded tactics. I'd have done the same if I'd thought of it. "You trapped her!"

"Her confession was a surprise, I must admit. I'd already found out aboot her past assaults on that poor man in the States, before the call came in."

"No idea who saw her driving away from the inn?"

"Somebody who shoulda come forward immediately, but better late than never. It was the catalyst that got me goin'."

"Don't you need that witness?"

"Not with Janet Dougal admittin' she went out tae the house."

"So you actually arrested Janet for Henrietta's murder."

"She hasn't been charged yet, but it's appearin' likely that she will be."

I shook my head in wonder. "I never gave her a second thought."

"A number o' factors came intae play. It was a stroke o' luck."

What could I add? Janet hadn't even been a consideration as far as I was concerned. I'd had a one-track mind. I'd been after Florence Dougal. It was hard to let go of her perfectly wonderful motive and instead accept that Henrietta had been killed by a kook simply because she had slighted her one too many times.

"And all along I thought you and Janet were an item," I said with a grin.

"There's room in that jail cell fer one more," the inspector warned.

I picked up a piece of cold, dry toast and nibbled on it.

The inspector rose and said, "I best be on my way."

"To put the screws to her, I imagine," I said, with a straight face.

The inspector didn't dignify my comment with an answer. He turned on his heels and disappeared after passing Patricia Martin with a terse greeting.

She entered the room and said, "I saw Janet Dougal being escorted away by that constable. What's goin' on?"

"I can't say yet."

"The police have arrested her for my sister's murder, haven't they?"

And without waiting for a reply, she was gone, chasing after Jamieson.

CHAPTER 20

I stepped out of the inn onto the sidewalk and raised the collar of my quilted coat against a gust of icy wind from the north. I didn't feel any particular sense of relief now that Janet was in police custody. Maybe it was too soon for my brain to process, the reality that this woman was capable of murder not having set in yet. Whatever the case, I should have been glad that Henrietta's murder was cleared up, and those of us involved could go back to living our lives. I'd been completely off the right track with Florence Dougal, but I told myself I wasn't exactly an expert in crime solving and should forgive myself if I chased after a red herring or two. No one had been hurt by my singular focus on the wrong suspect, and the inspector had done what he does best—solve crimes.

Still, I was more than a little embarrassed by my mistake. Maybe the fine art of crime fighting wasn't my forte. It had been an interesting side job, though, as rewarding as entertaining readers with romance and intrigue.

My role as special constable was more passive than active for the time being, so what should I do? This day and the next several could be rearranged to suit myself. I didn't feel like writing at the pub even though I knew I should. Yet the warmth of the fire at the Kilt & Thistle drew me in, and I took a table as close to the fireplace as possible after greeting several regulars. Dale was at his post behind the bar as usual. "I'll order something in a little while," I told him as I slung off my coat and hung it on the back of a chair.

I still felt certain that more than one thing had been going on. Janet might have murdered Henrietta McCloud, but what about that threatening note? How did it fit with the American woman, and did it necessarily have to? I leaned back and stared into the fire. If (as I was starting to suspect) the warning found in the mail didn't involve the murder, the timing of its arrival couldn't have been worse. And so I'd allowed it to become the focus. It had overly influenced me. I had a lot to learn.

My cell phone rang.

"Herself is still proclaimin' her innocence," Jamieson said from the other end of the line. "Nothin' surprisin' aboot that. I have enough tae hold her fer now, during which I'll clear up a few unresolved details tae make murder charges stick."

"This feels anticlimactic, like there should be more."

"I know just what ye mean. Real life isn't like one o' yer books, though, and I have tae remind myself o' that every time. There's always some unfinished business. It isn't all tidied up in the end with wrapping paper and a nice bow."

"What if Janet was set up? Someone could have lured her out there intending to cast blame on her."

"Every convicted felon says that from behind bars. I thought of it myself, and might have believed it as a possibility if not fer the rest. The restraining orders against her didn't help her case."

"No, they wouldn't have."

"The Martins are pleased as punch. Patricia Martin was like a bloodhound once she set eyes on the situation. I left her tae speculate, but she's a sharp one and has figured out what's on, and so that pressure is off."

Of course, Patricia and her political husband had been vocal about wrapping up the case as soon as possible to deter more attention than necessary.

"The Edinburgh papers have been following the investigation?" I asked.

"As have all the other rag sheets, with a lot o' silly speculation."

"Anything more I can do?" And how did I feel about that? Did I want to continue to work to put Janet behind bars?

But that wasn't in my future because the inspector said, "Nothing that our Sean can't handle. The weight o' proper evidence is my burden tae bear noo."

I had complete faith in the inspector's abilities. And in spite of his comments about real life's untidy bows, by the time he was through, the ribbon would be tied perfectly.

The last thing he said before disconnecting was, "Why don't ye take some time tae enjoy yer last days in Glenkillen? Ye've been a big help. I couldn't have done it without ye."

A big help? Yeah, right. The man was a solitary investigator. I might have been a big help if he'd kept me informed. As it was, I hadn't been even close to the truth. Maybe I should do as he suggested and just enjoy.

There's something soothing about a roaring fire. It's almost hypnotic and I found myself staring blindly into the flames, wondering what to do with the time I had left.

Ten short days. Seven hours of daylight each day times ten days equals seventy hours of light from the sun. Not much time in the scheme of things. What should I do with it? Chucking my writing was tempting. Or I could reverse my schedule and write in the evenings from my cottage. If I put my mind to it, I could still have that first draft of *Hooked on You* completed by the end of the year. Without any further duties as a special constable, I could also spend as much time as possible with the friends I'd made.

Like Dale and Marg, who had served me many times in this pub. And all the other shop owners I'd met around town—those from the bookstore, the inn, the whisky shop, the bakery—I wanted to visit all of them at least once more before leaving.

Then there were the most important people in my life these past six months. Vicki, who had been a wonderful and supportive ally since our meeting on that fateful inbound plane from London. And Charlotte and her many visits to the farm to care for the animals, always finding time in her busy schedule for a chat at the kitchen table. And what about Sean, blustering a bit and a tad self-important, but with a good heart and good intentions?

And the animals on the MacBride farm—Coco and Pepper, and Jasper the barn cat, and now Snookie.

And of course, Inspector Jamieson, appearing in my new life shortly after arrival, not always under the best circumstances, but his dry sense of humor and wit were calming forces in the darkest of times. And the inspector had been the one who had introduced me to some of the Kilt & Thistle's more interesting culinary delicacies. I'd eaten haggis, thanks to his encouragement.

An image of Leith Cameron's handsome countenance appeared in the flames from the fire. He'd been the knight in shining armor who, along with Kelly, had rescued me from the side of the road all those months ago when the rental car I'd leased had broken down. I could still see the lazy grin and his easy self-confidence from that experience. It was hard to believe that he and I had attended the whisky tasting only this past Saturday. Three days ago. Finding Henrietta's dead body would stay fresh in my mind forever.

Then I realized that I hadn't heard from Leith, and I was used to some sort of contact almost daily. We'd gone together to the warehouse on Sunday to speak with Gordon, but yesterday had passed without a call from him or a surprise drop-in. Would I see him today? Should I call him? But what would I say? That I was free, maybe invite him to dinner? Actually cook him a meal in the cottage and afterward . . .

Afterward what?

I could hear Ami on the sidelines, cheerleading, encouraging me loud and clear, the same refrain she'd been singing since I arrived in the Scottish Highlands. Let yourself go. Experience life to the fullest. Ditch all those old-fashioned inhibitions. Quit "shoulding" yourself.

"'Should' is officially banned from your vocabulary," Ami had said that day in the Chicago airport. "So is 'shouldn't.' Throw out those archaic words and begin anew. How many of us have an opportunity for a fresh start like you're getting?"

I'd smiled, knowing what came next.

And it had. "Introduce a few new phrases into your vocabulary, like . . . 'Yes, take me!'" she'd exclaimed with dramatic flair. "And . . . 'More! More!'"

"Stop it," I'd ordered her, laughing.

Much to Ami's chagrin, I hadn't followed what she referred to as her "sage advice." But my characters had.

And she hadn't been completely wrong. I'd had a fresh start. After listing those I considered as friends, I realized my world had expanded by leaps and bounds, if not necessarily in the direction she'd envisioned.

I heard a crackle and a pop and a spark leapt from the fireplace, bringing me back to the present. The logs had been nearly consumed and most of the flames had died down to burning embers. Dale appeared at the hearth with an armload of firewood. He tossed a few logs on, poked them around, and watched as they caught fire. Then he turned to me, wiping his hands on an apron tied around his waist, and said, "It's all aboot the pub how the inspector has arrested that American woman fer murderin' Henrietta McCloud. Before the talk goes out on the street and burns up the town wires faster than these pieces o' wood, I thought I'd confirm the facts with ye."

"She hasn't been charged with a crime," I told him, carefully choosing my words. "The inspector is questioning her."

"Well, that's hardly worth all the blarney going round. But we live in a wee village where nobody has a thing tae do except spread rumors without much care whether they're true or not. They want this one tae be real, though, tae relieve them o' the idea that it was one o' our own who killed Henrietta."

Which was understandable. It would be easier to accept a foreigner as a murderer over one of the locals. And one more reason to distrust outsiders.

"The other bit o' news is that ye aren't assistin' the inspector any longer, that ye are off as special volunteer."

What? That was news to me. The inspector had suggested I take the next few days off, but he'd said nothing about relieving me of duty.

My mouth snapped open to refute that, but I quickly closed it and reconsidered. *It's just gossip*, I told myself. *It's not like this came directly from the inspector.* Still . . . I felt a twinge of disappointment that the community had already dismissed me even before my boss had.

"I'm looking forward to a few days to explore," I told Dale, not confirming or denying what Jamieson would call local blather.

"Ye ready fer a cuppa, then, tae start ye off?"

"Yes, tea would be nice. And do you have any shortbread?"

"I'll see what I can do fer ye. I believe I can scrape up a biscuit or two."

By the time the tea arrived with an assortment of oatcake crackers and shortbreads, Sean had slipped in and taken a seat beside me. "It's lookin' like we have our criminal," he said, helping himself to a shortbread.

Sean glanced up as Dale placed a tea serving before me. "I'll have a pint," he said.

"You're on duty," I pointed out, not for the first time. "Nothing stronger than caffeine for you."

"I don't know how I survived without yer interference," he said, but nodded to Dale. Tea would have to do.

"The mystery o' the threatening note has been solved," he told me.

"Oh?" Another piece of the puzzle connected without me.

"'Twas Archie and Florence's boy, Hewie, away at college. One o' his classmates egged him on tae throw a scare intae his grandmum tae get her tae back off on sellin' the family business."

"It had nothing to do with Henrietta's murder." As I'd come to suspect.

Sean shook his head. "Florence Dougal is in hot water with the inspector fer covering it up. She found out aboot it right after it was sent and kept it hidden."

"Florence slipped up when she mentioned skating on thin ice," I said.

"Not much in the woman's head, if ye ask me opinion, tae make a foolish mistake like that. Once ye told the inspector aboot what she'd said, he was on tae her but good."

So it was finished. Hewie Dougal had pulled an ill-timed prank. Janet Dougal had tipped over the edge of reason and killed Henrietta. It was only a matter of time before we discovered why she'd attacked Katie and me. I couldn't fathom why. Unless she'd gone totally crazy and intended to murder everyone she thought had slighted her.

"Why are you here?" I asked next. "Vicki's at the farm."

"Ye're not always spot on, ye know? Fer yer information, she's on her way tae this very pub. So is Leith Cameron."

What a pleasant surprise, was my first reaction. I'd kill some time at a cozy table filled with my very favorite people. My fireside wish was coming true. "What's the occasion?"

"That's fer me tae know, and fer ye tae find out."

"Oh, good, I love intrigue."

But several minutes later, I could have eaten those words.

Leith strolled in first. He didn't take a seat as I anticipated but instead came to stand behind me, resting his hands on my shoulders. Before I could turn and peer up, ask him what was going on, sensing some drama about to take place, Vicki slid into the empty chair opposite Sean.

In my peripheral vision, I became aware that others at the pub had turned their attention our way.

"Go ahead, Sean," Vicki said.

"I'm hear tae officially relieve ye o' yer duty as special constable," he said, solemnly. "And I am requiring the return o' yer warrant card and any other equipment that is the property o' the Scottish government."

He'd said it so professionally, so coldly, that I was taken aback.

"It's routine," Vicki pointed out, not looking me in the eye.

"Really?" I said in disbelief, glancing from Sean to Vicki and back to Sean. Then I fumbled in my coat pocket and produced the card that I'd carried to identify myself as a part of the law enforcement team. Apparently my membership had expired.

"Anything else ye should be returnin'?" Sean said.

"That's all," I lied, refusing to give up the pepper spray I'd been approved to carry, wondering why my termination hadn't been handled privately. Although then I probably would have cried. Here, in the pub, I intended to keep a stiff upper lip.

Sean took the card and slid it into his shirt pocket. "Now ye can go back tae a regular life."

"Yes," I muttered.

I saw concern in Vicki's eyes as she leaned forward, speaking softly so only those at our table could hear, "Besides, it's time we found your father," she said.

CHAPTER 21

It was the last thing I expected, and more than I felt capable of handling. Especially from this gathering of friends. Instinctively, I attempted to rise, tears threatening to erupt, but Leith kept steady pressure on my shoulders.

"At least hear Vicki out," he said, his voice as firm as his grasp. Music started up in the background, not especially intrusive, just enough to give us some privacy. Those who had been following our interchange determined that their eavesdropping was at an end. They went back to their own drinks and settled down to their own business. But the damage had been done. I'd been publicly humiliated. By friends, no less.

All I wanted was an escape route, but I wasn't going anyplace surrounded by this determined bunch, so I nodded, as though I had a choice.

"Ye might call this an intervention," Sean announced to me.

"Sean." Vicki shot him a look that said she could handle things just fine on her own, that this was a delicate situation and he should step down.

He understood her because he stood up, hitched his trousers with importance, and said, "Now that my part here is finished, I best get back tae me station."

"What station is that?" I asked, wondering what errand the inspector had assigned to Sean and if it had to do with Henrietta's murder case.

"I'll see you later," Vicki said to him before he could respond. I had the impression she wasn't going to let him.

"Good luck tae ye all," Sean said, ignoring me.

"To explain, I need to go back to the beginning," Vicki said once he'd gone. "Which might take a while. If you promise to listen and not try to run off, Leith can sit down at the table and give his legs a rest."

"Fine," I said through gritted teeth, not one bit fine.

But Leith removed his hands from my shoulders and sat down across from me. I glared at each of them in turn, expressing my extreme displeasure with them.

"It begins with Ami Pederson," Vicki said, "and why you really came to Glenkillen in the first place."

"To do research on the Highlands," I told her even though she knew that perfectly well. "Ami had been to Glenkillen and liked it well enough to recommend it. She thought Glenkillen was the perfect setting."

"Yes, that's true, but there was more to it than that."

"And how would you know?" I said, sounding childish, even to myself. "You weren't part of my conversations with Ami."

"I know this because she and I began communicating through e-mails a few months ago, in October. We were, and are, concerned about you."

So the two of them had ganged up, for whatever reason, for my "own good," as they probably told each other to justify the deception. The thought that my two friends had plotted behind my back made me feel defensive and manipulated. I crossed my arms and waited for whatever was to come with a closed mind. My expression must have been thunderous because Vicki looked over at Leith, her face expressing doubt.

It's way too late, I thought, deciding our friendship was teetering on the brink.

Leith, as though reading my mind, winked at me. What was that? Some sort of reassurance?

"Don't make light of this," I warned him before pointedly looking away.

"You and Ami have been such good friends for so long," Vicki continued, "that she knows all about your history, and she came up with the idea to send you here, specifically to Glenkillen, not only to research the Highlands for the series you're writing, but with the hope that you'd reconcile with your father's family. With the Elliotts."

"Are you telling me that some of them are here in Glenkillen? You knew this and didn't tell me?" My best friends had turned on me. Now I understood Vicki's furtive behavior recently.

Vicki shook her head. "No, not in Glenkillen, but close by in a village called Applefary. A few Elliotts still live in that area, and Ami wanted you to at least meet them. In fact, so do I. You came all this way, from the US to Scotland,

and I think it's appropriate that you visit your ancestral home."

"And what about *him*?" I was determined to see this through without breaking down or showing my crazy side, since I was perfectly aware that I had issues when it came to my father. Ones that I'd happily refused to acknowledge. Just the way I liked them. Buried out of sight.

If it had only been Vicki with me and in a far less public arena, I most certainly would have vented and shown my dark side. She had no business dredging up what I didn't want dredged up. But with Leith sitting directly across from me, with those beautiful blues gazing at me, I tried to appear as normal as possible under the circumstances. Was that why he was here? So I wouldn't feel comfortable letting it all loose?

"I did a lot of digging and haven't been able to locate Dennis Elliott." Vicki refused to hold my gaze, and that made me think there was more to come.

"And?" I pressed. "What else?"

"I've been putting a lot of effort into finding your father, without a single lead. It's like he disappeared off the map. I haven't been able to place him on a flight back to the States, either."

"Because he didn't go back, that's why you can't find his departure," I said, exasperated. "If you really want to know where he is, why don't you ask the Elliotts you located in Applewhatever?"

"Applefary. I thought that would be crossing the line." As though she hadn't already crossed it. "We could visit them together, though, and ask those questions."

"What's so surprising about his disappearance? It isn't

exactly sudden. He left us for good. Why come back to the States when he could hide out here? He abandoned my mother to deal with her MS without his support. He left me, a six-year-old kid. What part of 'I don't want anything to do with him' do you not understand?

"Besides," I said, pointing out the obvious. "These Elliotts probably don't know where he is, either. He's hiding someplace where no one will ever find him!"

My voice squeaked. I'm sure my face was the color of a tomato. So much for appearing normal and well adjusted in front of Leith. Vicki didn't know what to say.

It was Leith's turn. "It was a terrible thing he did, and nobody expects ye tae forgive him or tae forget. It's only that yer own mum is gone and it doesn't appear as though ye have any family left in the States tae fall back on. Everybody should have some family tae call their own, and here ye are only a few steps from some o' yours and ye refuse tae acknowledge them. It's like blamin' the whole lot o' Germans fer Hitler's actions. There, is that a powerful enough analogy tae compare yer father tae Hitler?"

"Close," I said, sure that I was pouting.

"If ye go back without so much as a wee peek, you'll regret it one day."

I was angry with all of them. Leith for being the voice of reason. Sean and the inspector for the cold manner in which they'd stripped me of my constable position. Ami and Vicki for colluding behind my back. I even resented Bridie Dougal for starting all this by knowing my grandfather and wanting to share her memories.

I took a deep breath to calm myself. One part of me still wanted to resist. The other part argued that my friends couldn't all be wrong. Yet they hadn't lived my life, either, hadn't walked in my shoes.

Silence descended on our table. I listened to the background music; from the melody I could tell it was one of the standard Scottish ballads—a dramatic story of war, love, and betrayal.

"I still have ten days left," I said, mentally counting my remaining days in Scotland. December twenty-second was approaching quickly.

"And you have no other obligations," Vicki pointed out, brightening as she sensed my capitulation. "Instead of investigating crime, you can investigate your family. And I'll help you, be right there with you, that is if you want me to."

"And I'm offerin' my *services* as well," Leith said with a teasing double meaning.

"Maybe tomorrow," I told them. Tomorrow was another day. Putting them off would give me time to sleep on it. And if necessary, concoct more reasons to get out of it.

"What's wrong with today?" Vicki countered, guessing my intention.

"You drive a hard bargain," I told her. "And you're pushing your luck, I might add."

"The day is still young," Leith said, siding against me, which was becoming the norm.

"What do you two have in mind?" I asked, resigned.

"We'll start with Bridie Dougal," Vicki answered. "Since she knew your grandfather personally."

I narrowed my eyes. "And you knew that how?"

Vicki had the grace, which arrived way late in my opinion, to finally squirm with discomfort.

"Well?" I prodded.

"Bridie phoned me and told me about her own connection to the Elliott family, and we sort of came up with a plan."

"Did you now." I should have known Bridie was involved. The old woman was still scheming, manipulating everybody around her. She'd most likely go to her grave with a few unfinished maneuvers up her sleeve.

"We have an invitation from her for tea and sandwiches," Vicki announced. "In fact, we'll be a little late."

"Now?"

"Now."

It appeared that Bridie wasn't the only one who could engineer a coup. Vicki was a skilled operator also.

"I need to make a stop at the cottage," I said, thinking about the sketch of the Elliott crest and motto and how I might as well present it at the inquisition.

"Bridie lives between the village and the farm," Vicki reasoned. "We'd have to drive right past her house. And it's starting to snow. What's so important that it can't wait until another time?"

"I suppose it can wait."

"Do ye need more o' my help?" Leith said to Vicki.

"I can manage."

He turned to me. "I'm not much fer lady's teas," he explained with obvious relief. "I'll come by later tae see how ye're doin'."

A few minutes later as we left the Kilt & Thistle together, I could feel a roomful of eyes following us out the door.

Chapter 22

To say that my ego had been bruised by the confrontation at the pub would be an understatement. As I drove to the distillery with Vicki following behind, all I really wanted to do was crawl into a dark corner and lick my wounds. I'd been summarily dismissed from the police force without an explanation. The thing that hurt the most was the way it had been done. So publicly. And worse, the inspector didn't even make an appearance and handle the situation himself. I thought we'd been friends. I'd been wrong.

At least I had my own car in case I needed to make a quick getaway.

The setting of the Dougal manor house was as majestic as the first time I'd seen it, with snow covering the extensive exterior grounds like a fluffy blanket. I could only imagine how beautiful it would be in the spring and summer months.

The only difference today was that the lady of the house didn't greet Vicki and me at the door. Instead it was opened by Florence Dougal. And the greeting was hardly enthusiastic. I didn't blame Florence. We'd parted company on hostile terms. Not only that, I'd been blatantly obvious that I thought she was a major suspect. How wrong I'd been about that.

I'd made two bad judgment calls in a short period of time. First in suspecting Florence of murder, and second in believing that the inspector respected me.

Now, I made a show of reconciliation to the wronged woman by extending my hand and smiling brightly. The return handshake was limp and cold, but at least she shook my hand.

I introduced her to Vicki.

"You're expected," Florence said, and I was reminded that this had been Henrietta's role until her death.

Florence led us to the sitting room, where a round table decked out with a red, white, and gold tablecloth had been set for five. Bridie and Patricia Martin were already seated when we joined them, and I introduced Vicki to Patricia and Bridie, who already had a relationship of sorts with my friend via their phone conspiracy. Florence, after taking our coats, also joined us.

What was supposed to be an intimate cozy chat with Bridie about the Elliott clan had turned into an *Alice in Wonderland* tea party. Bridie was the Mad Hatter and I . . . well . . . I was the dormouse.

Why had I allowed myself to be talked into coming?

"I thought it would be nice to get as many of us together as possible," Bridie said, as Florence continued acting as maid-in-waiting by serving tea. I wondered how Bridie had coerced her daughter-in-law into the subservient role she'd assumed for this tea.

A three-tiered stand in the center of the table held finger sandwiches and bakery items. "Now that Henrietta's murderer has been apprehended, we can begin anew." The older woman's eyes seemed to watch all of us at once. "But first, let's enjoy our tea. Florence has graciously offered to assist."

Florence didn't seem one bit gracious.

We sipped strong tea from china teacups and nibbled on a variety of bite-sized sandwiches. Egg salad with cress, smoked salmon with cream cheese, and ham and mustard. We finished with freshly baked scones with clotted cream and jam, lemon macaroons, and raspberry tarts.

The conversation was light throughout the meal, carried mainly by Bridie, and focused on the food on the table and the weather outside. The only mention of anything of substance came from Patricia when she inquired about Katie Taylor's condition.

"Has she fully recovered?" she asked me.

"Sean Stevens says she's been released from the hospital," Vicki answered after an awkward pause. "And has gone on holiday with her parents, visiting relatives."

"I had so wanted her tae spend time with Eden," Bridie said. "She's done extensive research on many of the local families, including the Elliott family, ye know."

"I didn't," I said, surprised that it hadn't come up in my brief conversations with the young woman. Then I realized that I never told Katie my full name. She didn't know my last name was Elliott.

"A shame. I should have formally introduced the two of you, but I had so much on my mind that night. She's such a sweet girl. As sweet as these lemon macaroons. What do you think of them?" And talk turned back to the universally enjoyed topic of food.

When we were through, we retired to the other end of the room to relax on comfortable chairs arranged near a lit fireplace, where talk turned to more current affairs, in particular Janet Dougal.

"I recall thinking that woman was overly brash," Bridie said.

"Even for an American," Florence added, staring at me with implied meaning that didn't escape me.

Bridie went on as though she hadn't been interrupted. "But I never imagined she could commit murder over a slight disagreement. I blame myself fer hiding behind Henrietta, fer sending her out as a barrier to keep that dreadful woman away."

"She seemed nice enough tae me," Florence said. "The night o' the tasting I got tae know her a bit."

"Pushy," Patricia said, "and something about her gave me the impression that she was unbalanced. Eden, none of us are going to blame her actions on her nationality. We have our share of crazies in Scotland as well."

Henrietta's sister had softened considerably since our prior encounters. She'd been somewhat aloof at the tasting and after the death she'd seemed cold and distant, but today, perhaps since she'd had a few days to adjust to the loss of her sister and with Janet Dougal in custody, Patricia displayed a newfound social awareness and appeared to be appreciating her inclusion in our gathering.

"How did Janet manage to insinuate herself into the tasting group?" I asked, remembering Janet's laments about the snubs she'd received.

"I have absolutely no idea," Bridie said. "She overheard one of us, I expect. She appeared without an invitation."

"She forced her way into Gordon's car," Patricia said. "She'd been lying in wait and pounced."

"She was a relative," Florence added. "She *should* have been invited."

Bridie ignored Florence and went on. "Eden, you work closely with the inspector. What finally led to her downfall? What gave her away?"

Vicki glanced my way as though worried that I might actually answer. But I put her fears to rest quickly. "As far as I know, she hasn't been charged with a crime yet, and as to the finer details . . . I'm no longer a special constable and so am not privy to inside information."

I felt a small hole in my heart while saying that.

"Just as well," Bridie quipped. "I've been concerned about yer safety."

Vicki piped up and hastily added, "Eden is taking some time to enjoy the Highlands before she returns to the States."

"It's not as though she was ever in any real danger, Bridie," Florence said, and I suspected that disagreeing with her mother-in-law was an ongoing aspect of their relationship.

Bridie focused on Florence then. "Perhaps you could go about the rest o' yer day now that tea is finished. Thank you kindly fer all yer help."

Pointedly dismissed, Florence rose, lifted her chin, and left the room. I still hadn't been able to warm up to her. But did I have to? No, I decided, with the time I had left, I'd surround myself with pleasant people.

Bridie snorted, whether with glee or disgust was

debatable. "She thinks I'm punishing her fer the actions o' her son by making her wait on us." Then she giggled. "Perhaps I am takin' advantage o' her shame fer her actions, but she deserves it. Her son, Hewie, played a mean trick on me. Instead o' holding him accountable, she helped hide his indiscretion. And this during a police investigation."

"Bridie filled me in on the family drama," Patricia said.

"At least it's all straightened out now," Vicki said.

Bridie turned to me. "That musta been what Henrietta wanted tae speak with ye aboot. She musta known the scamp who was behind it and wanted tae share it with ye without my knowledge. She always was one tae protect me. But enough o' this."

"When are you returning to Edinburgh?" I asked Patricia.

"I'll stay a few more days to finish arrangements," she said. "Henrietta was a private woman and didn't want any sort of organized gathering. No funeral. No memorial."

"Henrietta wrote out her last wishes at my insistence," Bridie said. "When she was given such a short time tae live, I thought she should get her affairs in order. Before tea today, I turned over the sealed letter with her wishes tae Patricia."

Patricia nodded. "Henrietta wants her ashes spread in certain places that meant the most tae her."

We all went silent for a period of time as we reflected on the dead woman.

"I found something tucked inside Snookie's health record," I said, remembering to bring it up.

Bridie brightened. "And how is our little Snookie?"

"She's adjusting."

"I knew she would, with the right person, and I sensed ye were that person."

"Yes, well, we are getting on well. Anyway, inside Henrietta's records someone had sketched the Elliott crest and motto on a piece of paper."

Bridie smiled. *"Fortiter et Recte."*

"Do you remember the sketch?" I asked Bridie. "And who drew it?"

Bridie frowned in concentration. "Not offhand. Can you show it to me?"

If only I'd taken the time to drive to the cottage and get it. "No, but I'll bring it by as soon as possible."

"I best be off." Patricia rose. "It's still snowing. The roads will continue to worsen. And I've never been much o' a driver in bad weather."

After the appropriate good-byes, the three of us stayed to discuss the topic I'd come for.

It turned out that Bridie, clan chieftain of the Dougals, had a passion for the past. In fact, she dwelled there as comfortably and contently as she did in the present, if not more so. One of the characteristics of old age, I imagined, when the current days weren't nearly as interesting as those of old.

"The Elliotts were rustlers," she told us. "They raided in this area from the thirteenth century all the way into the sixteenth, and were well known fer going south of the border into England and stealing cattle."

"See how colorful your ancestors were!" Vicki said.

"Ye're the spitting image o' yer grandfather Roddy," Bridie said, "with yer ginger highlights and those eyes that ye can't tell fer sure if they're blue as the sky or green as grass.

Yer father took after his mum more than his da, but Dennis was a fine specimen o' a man, too, just as handsome, but in a dark, smolderin' sort o' way."

"Do you have any photos?" Vicki asked.

"Not a one. We had a fire years ago and lost many valuables."

Vicki didn't give up easily. "Tell us more."

"Eden, yer mum sat in the exact chair ye're in right this minute, before the fire as we are today. This was before ye were even a glimmer in her eye when they were still newlyweds. We exchanged a few letters early on, we did. She was a lovely girl."

Suddenly I recalled hearing about that visit. It had been a very long time ago. My mother had told me about the two of them paying a visit to Scotland to meet my father's family. At some point, though, we had stopped speaking of the past.

"They were so much in love," Bridie mused. "I refused tae believe the gossipmongers when they talked aboot what he'd done. Yer grandfather woulda had something tae say about that, if he'd been alive at the time. Roddy was a perfect gentleman and raised his son tae be one, too. I can't imagine what happened. I guess it's best that Roddy isn't here tae have tae deal with the shame o' it."

"Do you have any idea where Eden's father is living now?" Vicki asked, refusing to look my way, getting the elephant in the room out in the center.

Bridie appeared startled by the question. "What do ye mean?"

"Eden's father," Vicki prompted. "Dennis. We thought we might visit him."

Which wasn't even close to the truth. I hadn't agreed to

that! But it hardly mattered because Bridie piped up and said, "The last time I saw Dennis was thirty-two years ago at his father's funeral. He was leaving fer Chicago that same day. In fact, Dennis told me he was anxious tae get home tae his family."

My mouth dropped open. "That's impossible."

"He was in a hurry tae catch his plane," Bridie insisted.

I shook my head. "But he never came back."

"That can't be possible," Bridie went on, "It was many months after the funeral that I heard he'd abandoned yer mother in her time o' need and left her tae cope with her disease and with ye alone. I'm not even sure who told me. Ye know how gossip seems to have a life o' its own and nobody will admit tae startin' it. Yer grandparents weren't alive tae substantiate or deny the truth o' it. The Elliotts still remainin' in the area were distant relatives, scattered, and none that I knew well enough tae speak with on such a delicate matter."

"Are you saying, Bridie," Vicki said, "that all along you assumed Eden's father had gone back to the States and had left them sometime in the proceeding months?"

"Aye. Isn't that what happened?"

"And Eden, you assumed he stayed in the Highlands?"

"He did," I said.

"But I woulda heard," Bridie argued. "He went off, he did."

"Then," I said, suddenly caring very, very much, latching onto the fact that my father had told Bridie he was in a hurry to get home, "where the hell is he?"

CHAPTER 23

My friend and occasional tormentor sat across my kitchen table. We were eating leftover stew. Vicki's Inky Pinky was just as good tonight as it had been the first time she'd served it.

Outside, the night was deeply dark without a single star showing through the cloud cover. Holiday lights twinkled from the brightly strung logs and boughs scattered around my tiny cottage. Snookie was sound asleep in her favorite chair beside the fire. Coco and Pepper were curled up together on the floor so tightly entwined that it was difficult to know which body parts belonged to which dog.

It might have been an idyllic setting. Instead of feeling in a holiday spirit, I'd had plenty of time to think of theories on the slow drive back to the farm through heavily falling snow as I followed Vicki's car taillights, since they were all I could see.

Where had he gone? Had Dennis Elliott vanished into thin air somewhere over the Atlantic Ocean? But if there had been any plane crashes, my mother would have known; someone would have contacted us if the airplane he'd been on had gone down. Barring that tragic explanation (one easily dismissed), I was absolutely positive that my father had not returned to the States.

"I'll check every airline," Vicki said, intuitive as ever. Sometimes I think she can read minds. "To make sure."

"It might have been part of his plan," I said. "To throw off anyone looking for him."

"Right," Vicki said with a heavy dose of sarcasm. "A master plan to make those in Scotland think he was in the States and make you and your mother think he was in Scotland. And why would he go to all that trouble?"

I glanced at my friend. Her face was rather flushed, not at all her normal coloring. "He had another woman on the side," I said, "and wanted to begin an entirely new life. His father would have disowned him for leaving us, you heard Bridie. She was clear on that point. My grandfather was a gentleman and expected the same from his son. So, he had to have a plan."

Vicki was ready with a retort. "For one thing, his father had just died and wasn't around to judge him. For another, his name was blackened the minute he deserted you. So he had nothing to gain by disappearing after leaving the funeral."

I hated her voice of reason. "He probably went to Paris or London with *her.*"

"Then we'll find his name on a passenger manifest from around that time period. I need you to confirm for me the exact date of your grandfather's funeral."

"It must be somewhere in my mother's personal things in storage in the States." I played with my food and realized that Vicki was doing the same. Neither of us was particularly hungry after high tea at the Dougal estate.

"Bridie will remember the exact date. Your grandfather obviously meant a lot to her."

"You never give up, do you? Besides, he's probably dead by now."

Vicki rolled her eyes and said, "Ami says you've been spouting that for years. 'He's dead, so why bother?' But he'd still be relatively young, in his sixties. And for your information, Ami and I are bothering"—Vicki's words were slow and precise—"so you can stop being bothered."

"And how does that work exactly?"

"We find his trail, follow it to its conclusion, and then you can have some closure."

"And you think this is how I want to spend my last days in Glenkillen?"

When Vicki didn't respond, I went on, "Don't you have anything better to do than hang out here harassing me?" I meant those words, too, however unkind they sounded. All I wanted was for Vicki to go back to the main house so I could enjoy some much-needed alone time. I was a firm believer in personal space and quiet time, and my friends had been suffocatingly close today.

I'd been all friended out.

And if I didn't hear from Ami again until I flew into Chicago, it would be perfectly fine with me. The more I thought about slinking off, the better it sounded.

Vicki studied me before saying, "I don't have anything better to do than talk some sense into you."

I stared out the window at the falling snow. "Where's

Sean? Shouldn't you be cozying up to him? On a night like this you two should be together."

"He's busy."

Vicki didn't look particularly upset. Odd. Usually she whined when he was pulled away on duty in the evening. "What's he doing?"

"I can't say. I mean he can't say."

I was doing a slow burn from annoyed to infuriated, and for more reasons than just one. The Elliott family and my father weren't exactly my favorite topics, and I'd been pressured by sheer force of numbers to deal with those unpleasant things. Then I'd been kicked off the case for no apparent reason, pushed out of a loop I'd become accustomed to being part of, and it didn't feel so good. In fact, it felt awful.

Vicki, even more flushed than earlier, leaned her elbow on the table and dropped her head to her hand.

"Are you okay?" I asked, concern washing away the hostility.

"A bit hot and dizzy," she said. "I hope I'm not coming down with that nasty bug that Kirstine had."

"Let me walk you home. It's been a long day."

Vicki didn't protest, which caused more worry on my part. Usually she's a fiercely independent woman who takes care of herself and refuses any assistance of any kind, whether it's an offer to help at the shop or with something as simple as doing her dishes.

But tonight, after we bundled up against the howling wind, she hooked her arm in mine and we plowed through the gathering snow with the two Westies following in the path we created. I made sure she was safely inside with plenty of lights shining and her feet up on the sofa before leaving her alone.

Outside, I glanced up the path toward my home. White lights sparkled in the windows, invitingly, with the promise of a warm fire and gentle feline company. The cottage beckoned to me, but instead of returning, I turned in the opposite direction and trudged along the lane leading to Sheepish Expressions. The chilliness of evening was actually a welcome relief. It felt good to inhale the fresh windswept air and enjoy the darkness and the silence all around me. Completely quiet except for my own breath and the swish of my boots through the new snow.

Even without stars to guide me, I could make out the lane. I remembered an observation I'd made to Vicki recently during the amber weather alert. It really was like living in a snow globe, flakes cascading all around me.

Reaching Sheepish Expressions, I was about to turn back when something caught my eye, a flash out of the darkness of the parking lot. Something that didn't belong in the white and black of tonight's world, not part of the grayness between them, either.

From where I stood, I thought I could make out a large object, tucked back in the lot. My heart began to pick up several extra beats per second.

I wasn't sure what to do.

Should I investigate? Or hurry home and lock my door?

The inspector might have revoked my law enforcement license, but he couldn't do anything about my need to explore and rule out trouble. I took a few cautious steps into the shadows, hoping I hadn't been exposed if someone was out and about. But why would they be? The shop was closed. What reason would anyone have to be on the grounds?

Thoughts of robbery went through my head.

As I edged closer, I could see that the object of my attention was a vehicle covered in snow, and it looked abandoned for the night. I breathed a sigh of relief. Perhaps someone had visited the shop earlier in the day and had experienced car trouble. They probably had to leave it here until morning. That was a logical explanation.

Except, as I approached, I could see that the car's windshield wipers had been activated recently. The front windshield wasn't as thick with snow as the hood and roof were. There! Again! The wipers slowly arched across, the blades clearing the window.

Someone was inside the vehicle! But the interior was dark. I couldn't see inside.

I fumbled in the pocket of my coat, grateful when my gloved hand found the cylinder of pepper spray, the protection I'd refused to give up with my warrant card earlier in the day. That act of rebellion might turn out to be a stroke of extremely good fortune.

I'd have much preferred never needing to use it ever again.

Snow began falling faster, so heavy I could hardly see the vehicle from where I stood. My eyelashes were coated with the heavy stuff as I crept even closer, realizing there would be no chance of getting a plate number, or the make and model of the car. Not with all this snow.

I went over my options. This would be my last chance to take steps in reverse, hurry back up the lane, get inside, and call the police, let them come out and investigate.

I'd known from the start that I wouldn't do that, though.

So I removed my glove, flicked the spray nozzle on the pepper spray from the safety position to on, and continued moving forward, stopping only when I was close enough to the driver's side of the car that I could have reached out and touched it.

Prepared to defend myself if necessary, I rapped on the driver's window with my ungloved knuckles. Snow on the window had accumulated and was a good three inches thick. Because it was so wet and heavy it stuck where it landed. I could see the impression made by my knuckles.

As the window slid down under the weight of the snow, it fell away in sheets, giving me an opportunity to peer inside.

I recognized the occupant.

And almost fired a blast of pepper spray anyway.

It would have served him right.

"Would ye believe it if I told ye I was takin a wee nap?" Sean Stevens asked, looking totally busted.

"How could you do this to Vicki?" I shouted, my voice cutting sharply through the night silence. "Spying on her! What do you think? Some other guy is coming to visit her tonight? I wish that were true!"

I put the pepper spray back in my pocket where it wouldn't tempt me.

I bent down and packed snow between my hands.

Then I reached through the window and smashed it into Sean's sneaky little face.

CHAPTER 24

"Are ye some kinda nutter?" Sean sputtered from the driver's seat, his face awash in melting snow.

I turned and stormed away. The weather had nothing on my thunderous mood. I was my own red weather alert, and Sean should be running for shelter. Wait until Vicki heard this.

Instead he chased after me, yelling. "Ye have it all wrong, ye do. Will ye stop fer a bloody minute?"

The going was tougher than coming. The path my boots had created coming down the lane had already disappeared as I went up. The effort gave me time to cool off a little, down to about a roiling boil.

I whirled. "What a creepy thing to do to Vicki. She deserves better."

Sean's face was wet from the face wash, and the shoulders of his police jacket and the top of his cap were covered in snow. "I wasn't spyin' on Vicki."

"Then what were you doing?" This should be good. Let's see him worm his way out of this one.

"I was watchin' yerself. If ye weren't such a hothead, you'd have considered that possibility instead o' goin' off like a rocket tae the moon."

Oh. I hadn't thought about that. I'd just assumed the worst. Not that stalking me was any better. Was Sean telling the truth? If this was a lie to get out of a tough situation, Sean had concocted it in record time. He'd always been an open book in the past, wearing his thoughts and feelings on his sleeve for all to see.

Constable Steven might have often displayed signs of his own self-importance and could be a bit of a buffoon, but I'd never thought of him as deceptive or conniving, so there might be something legitimate about his claim.

"Me?" I squeaked. "You were watching me? Why?"

"Why don't ye come back tae my auto where it's warm and where we'll be out o' these forces o' nature. And we can talk."

So we trudged back. I slipped into the passenger seat, feeling more like I was inside an igloo than a snow globe. Within several seconds the windows steamed over. Not that it mattered. The world was white outside.

"Well?" I said, waiting for an explanation.

Sean squirmed, fiddling with the defroster buttons, turning them on. "I want tae tell ye, I really do, but I'm in a precarious position, in trainin' fer a real position as a police officer, and I have certain orders. Telling ye things I'm not at liberty tae divulge will violate those orders and put me at risk o' termination."

That was a distinct possibility. In the past, the inspector

had attempted to make the special constable redundant on at least one occasion that I was aware of. Though since Sean had gone for police training, Jamieson's threats had subsided, but they could easily be revisited with enough provocation.

"You've got me under surveillance," I said. "The inspector suspects me of something?"

"Now why would ye think that?"

"Because I just caught you spying on me? Because he had you publicly relieve me from my position as the new special constable? Because I haven't heard one word from him since well before that happened?"

The windshield wipers slid slowly across the front windshield. But the snow on the glass was too heavy. Not much cleared away. The wipers groaned and Sean turned them off.

"I don't know what he thinks I did." I paused to consider.

"No, no, no," Sean said. "The inspector has been busy buildin' a case fer murder, and it has nothin' tae do with yerself. Ye know how he gets and ye also know he's prone tae go off and forget about us. And sometimes he remembers us but still keeps us in the dark."

"That's true."

But in the past, he'd always kept me apprised, at least more so than he did Sean. We'd worked together well. Or so I'd thought.

I sat in silence, considering. "You can't tell me why you're out here without serious consequences," I said, "so I'll have to guess."

"Aye. Ye can do it," Sean said with obvious relief.

Okay, then what was going on? Why was Sean sitting in a car out in a snowstorm, watching the lane leading to my cottage, if he didn't have me under surveillance?

"You were spying on me, but why, if not because the inspector suspects me of something?"

"We better turn up the heat, it's getting cold in here, if ye catch me drift." Sean turned up the heat until it roared out of the vents.

Were we really going to play the childish game of Hide the Thimble? Hot, hot, cold.

"You weren't spying on me?"

"Cold, cold, cold."

"You're protecting me?" I guessed next.

"Ye're gettin' hot."

"What on earth are you protecting me from? Janet Dougal is in custody." I glanced sharply over. "She *is* in custody, right?"

"Aye, she's not goin' anywhere just now."

"Oh, geez, Sean, just tell me what's going on."

"I can't. I'm awfully sorry."

Again, I considered pepper-spraying him. Or at least threatening to. But I knew that his fear of Jamieson was greater than his fear of anything I could do to him.

"Ye're gettin' close."

I scowled. Sean was protecting me. From what?

"Does it have to do with Henrietta McCloud's murder?" I asked.

Sean had drawn his mouth into a thin grim line.

"Hot?" I asked. "Cold? Lukewarm?"

"Smokin' hot."

I thought back to the attack on me. Janet had a violent

past, so it had been easy to blame her for that, too, a reasonable assumption based on all the other facts. "Are you telling me that Janet wasn't the one who attacked me at the hospital?"

"It's gettin' scorchin' hot in here."

As if on cue, the engine died.

"Wha'?" Sean exclaimed. He attempted to start it up again without success.

"You're out of gas, aren't you?" I said in disbelief.

"It appears that might be the case. We're out o' petrol."

"We? This is hardly my problem."

"This wouldn'ta happened, I might add, if I had a proper beat car."

"All cars run out of gas if they aren't filled," I pointed out.

"Aye, but the gauge on this old junker isn't workin' properly."

If Jamieson found out about Sean's latest gaffe . . .

Suddenly I realized that I was in a position of power, and to my growing unease, I wasn't above using it.

"The inspector might be interested in knowing about this," I said with some menace in my voice.

"Ye wouldn't." His voice had a catch in it.

"What would he do if he found out that you ran out of gas while you were supposed to be ready for an attack on me? Or that I caught you out?"

"I don't want tae find out what he'd do."

"Then you need to tell me everything. We are through playing games."

"Ye aren't a very nice person."

Which made me pause for about one split second. "What's going on? All of it!"

So that was how I found out. If Sean hadn't run out of gas at that particular moment, I would have remained clueless. Instead I learned that Janet Dougal was in custody, but not for long.

"She's been detained only," Sean said with a tone of importance climbing into his voice. "Fer questioning. And the inspector has been authorized fer an extension from the regular twelve hours tae twenty-four. But time is running out, and he isn't one bit happy."

I understood the situation. According to the training manual I'd studied to qualify as special constable, Jamieson had twenty-four hours to prove a case against Janet or he had to release her. So the inspector would have to make a decision soon. Charge Janet with the murder of Henrietta McCloud. Or let her go. If he released her, he could charge her at a later date, but he couldn't detain her again.

"He doesn't have enough," I said.

"The inspector is all fer charging her fer the murder, and in my opinion he has enough tae do it. But he has somethin' he says he has tae follow up on first."

And that something turned out to involve me.

Apparently, Janet Dougal had a witness to prove that she couldn't have been the one who attacked me. Janet had admitted to being at the Dougal house right before the murder, and she made a statement that she'd confronted Henrietta.

"But she didn't try tae wallop ye with a surgical hammer," Sean said.

I turned this new information over in my mind. It wasn't likely that there were two violent individuals running around loose—one who drowned Henrietta and one who struck women in the head with hard objects. If I were in the inspector's shoes, I'd be hesitating, too.

"Who's her alibi?" I asked.

"Jeannie Morris from the inn. Seems that later in the afternoon the day o' the incident, Her Highness had decided she wanted tae upgrade her room. Sayin' it wasn't her fault she had tae remain in the village and that she needed some o' the comforts o' home. She threatened tae go public with information that would deter guests from checkin' in if she didn't get the biggest suite."

"How was she going to do that?"

"She was goin' tae go tae the pub at a busy hour and say the inn had bedbugs."

What a piece of work. I wouldn't be sorry to see her led away in chains.

"So Jeannie had tae help her move tae a different room, and even served her an early supper in her room tae shut her trap. And all that while yerself . . ."

". . . While I was fending off a surgical hammer."

"Aye. The inspector was fully ready tae go ahead with charges against Janet until that came tae light. As a precaution, he ordered me tae keep an eye on ye while he goes about firmin' up evidence against Janet and tryin' tae figure out this new twist in the plot." He glanced at me. "As ye writers like tae say."

Jamieson had been known to send Sean on wild-goose chases before, simply to keep him at a distance. But it wasn't like him to stick the trainee out in the middle of nowhere in a snowstorm. Besides, without this assignment, Sean would have been at Vicki's house, as far from the inspector as he was at the moment.

Therefore, after careful analysis, I decided that Sean's assignment to protect me had a ring of truth to it.

The inspector should have confided in me. I could do a much better job of protecting me than Sean could. The stalled-out vehicle and the constable without adequate transportation was a perfect example. If someone had turned in from the main road intent on harming me, what could Sean have done about it? Not much. He'd have been too busy trying not to freeze to death.

"That's why the inspector terminated my position," I muttered to myself, seeing clearly now; understanding dawned and relief washed over me. "He wanted it done where everybody in town would know about it immediately. Because whoever attacked me is still out there! It was all for show, intended for the attacker, to send a message that I wasn't a threat any longer."

"Ye're spot on. He musta disliked doin' it tae ye, but it was fer yer own good. And I'm here noo out in a blizzard just in case the message sent wasn't received."

"I still don't know why somebody came after me."

"Ye aren't the only one who's confused. Even the inspector doesn't have any idea."

"He's going to let Janet go today, isn't he?" I said. The inspector didn't rely on guesswork and intuition. He was thorough, and this one anomaly had him stumped. I could see why.

"Aye," Sean said. "Ye threw a wrench in the works, ye did."

The case was still wide open. I felt adrenaline pumping and a growing desire to get back on the case, one way or another. Good-bye Elliott family genealogy. Hello Henrietta McCloud murder investigation.

It wasn't until this moment that I realized how desperately I still wanted to stay away from my father's past. With Janet released, I could shelve my personal issues once again. Forget about my clan affiliation.

"Vicki knows all this, doesn't she?"

Sean nodded. "Aye. She's helpin' watch over ye by stayin' close by. So she understands why I can't be with her tonight."

I opened the car door and said, "Come on. There are gas cans in the barn and I'm pretty sure we'll find a full one."

"Nobody needs tae know, then?"

"What happened tonight is between the two of us. Just you and me. But I have one more condition you have to agree to if you want my continuing silence."

"Ye're a mean one." Sean grimaced. "I hate tae ask, but what is that condition?"

"It's easy. Tell Vicki to back off with the Elliott family quest. She's been putting me under a lot of pressure. The saga of my father can wait."

He'd been out of my life for over thirty years. He could stay that way.

As we trudged up the lane headed for the barn, Sean said, "I'll see what I can do, but Vicki is stubborn."

"She'll listen to you."

"We didn't get away with our scheme fer long. The inspector was worried ye might catch on."

"He doesn't need to know that I did."

What he didn't know wouldn't hurt him. I was tired of everyone thinking they knew what was best for me and making arrangements that affected me without my input. I might not have the credentials any longer, but that wouldn't stop me from poking around. But I'd have to be careful.

"Once you gas up your car," I told Sean, pointing out a full can of gas, "drive it up and put it in the barn. Vicki needs you. I think she's coming down with something. You're off security duty for the night. Nobody in his right mind would be out during a storm like this anyway."

I watched Sean walk down the lane, then went back to my cottage, where Snookie was waiting for me.

CHAPTER 25

Early Wednesday morning started out much like the last several days had, with dying cinders in the fireplace bringing chilly air into the cottage, a warm cat dozing beside my pillow, and a winter wonderland scene outside the festively decorated windows. I rose to my regular routine, noting that the paths hadn't been shoveled yet. Nor had the driveway leading to the lane. This storm had outperformed even John's ability to keep up with it.

I'd be housebound, or rather farmbound, for at least part of the day.

Leith Cameron called to ask how I was faring.

"Middlin'," he said about his own situation once I assured him that I was in fine shape. "I dislike bein' shut in."

Not surprising coming from this outdoorsy man. Whether fishing or raising fields of barley for the distillery, Leith usually could be found somewhere in the great outdoors. "I'm going tae have tae get a snowmobile if this keeps up. I don't remember ever havin' so much snow this early in December."

"Vicki said the same thing." Everything in the Highlands had seemed to be an anomaly since my arrival.

"How are ye coping with civilian life?" he asked next.

"I'm frustrated."

"I fer one am relieved," Leith said. "It was a dangerous way o' life. A perfect example is what happened tae ye while on guard duty at hospital."

"So you heard about that incident."

"Incident! Ha. Ye can't downplay it with me. Somebody wanted tae stop ye and was willing tae go tae extreme measures tae do so. Now that ye're out o' that job, we'll all breathe easier."

After a few more minutes of conversation, we hung up and I paused to consider why the attacker wanted to stop me. From doing what? That was the million-dollar question. I wasn't sure whether to be encouraged that I must be on the right track or afraid. One thing I was absolutely certain of was that I'd be much more careful in the future.

I bundled up, went outside, and made my way through the dark to the main house. Lights were on and Sean was in the kitchen.

"Vicki's still in bed," he told me. "She's down fer the count."

Coco and Pepper bounded from the back of the house and warmly greeted me. "I'll let the dogs out, then."

The Westies were overwhelmed by the depth of the snow and had to stay inside my footprints. We went to the barn. I turned on lights, and fed and played with Jasper. Again I entreated him. "Please come and stay with me," I said to the stubborn feline. "At least for a day or two. Take a mini-vacation."

Jasper had grown an incredibly thick undercoat and looked more like a miniature bear than a tomcat. As though he understood the request and wanted me to know that he rejected my overtures, he bounded up the barn steps and settled comfortably overhead.

"Suit yourself," I told him. "Come on, you two."

When I let Coco and Pepper back inside the house, Sean wasn't in the kitchen any longer. I knew he'd take care of all Vicki's needs. She was in good hands.

Back inside the cottage, I puttered in the kitchen, then decided to see if I had an Internet connection. Maybe Ami had sent an e-mail since last I'd checked, something casual, since she might not be aware that I was angry with her for interfering in my personal life. Behind my back, at that! Talking about me with Vicki. Plotting, scheming, manipulating. There was that word again. "Manipulating." It was one of my least favorite traits in others, yet everyone around me seemed to be indulging in it.

I wasn't able to establish a connection. Not surprising with all the snow and cloud cover.

Outside, John had arrived and was plowing the lane. Soon the path to the cottage would also be clear. But what of the roads? They had to be passable or John wouldn't have made it out here. But how passable was debatable. With my level of expertise on the winding narrow Highland roads, plus driving on the opposite side, I probably shouldn't risk driving until later when the gritters had another go. Where did I need to go anyway?

Settling into my favorite chair near the fire, with Snookie spread across my lap as usual, I spent a long time staring into the fire, thinking about what I'd learned from

Sean. If we assumed that the attack on me at the hospital had to be connected to Henrietta's murder and the investigation, we were almost back to square one. Janet Dougal had a lot of potential, but the alibi she'd established for the attack was problematic for those trying to build a solid case against her.

Katie Taylor had been attacked right after the murder. What did she have to do with anything? Maybe nothing. Maybe the attack on her at her friend's house was an amazing coincidence. Or not.

What did Henrietta have in common with Katie? A hometown. Tainwick. Not much there. What did Henrietta have in common with me? Or more precisely—what did her murder have to do with me? I was part of the investigation team. But so were the inspector and Sean.

Any possible threads broke down when I reviewed the three of us together—Katie, Henrietta, me. I couldn't see a link, other than the tasting that Henrietta had organized but hadn't attended.

I called Bridie at the first sign of daylight. "Did you survive the snowstorm without any outages?" I asked when she answered.

"It's lovely, isn't it? Easy fer me tae say, I can watch all day from inside. We're Scots. This is only a bit o' an inconvenience. Most o' the workers are at the distillery already, includin' Gordon and Archie."

"I'm snowed in for the time being," I told her.

"Then it's a time tae do some o' that writing, eh."

While we chatted, I idly withdrew the Elliott clan sketch from between the pages of Snookie's health records and glanced again at the inscription on the folded sheet. "Princess Hen."

"It's a fine day for getting some writing done," I agreed, meaning it. If I had to be snowed in, that was exactly what I should be doing. "Bridie, about that sketch of the Elliott crest and motto . . ."

"I still want tae see it, and I've been rackin' my brain about it since we talked. I don't remember anythin' like that being in my possession. But seein' it might jog this old goat's memory."

I laughed. "I'll try to get out later today. Would that be all right?"

"Aye, fer tea then. Three-ish."

"I'll be there."

"But ye also have more tae do than comin' round here tae entertain the likes o' me. Ye need tae go tae Applefary and soon."

Vicki and Bridie have one-track minds.

"Would ye like me tae come along?" she offered, and I heard hope in her voice. "We could make a day o' it, go round tae some o' yer cousins; no matter how distant, they'll welcome ye, they will."

"I don't know," I said, stalling. "The murder case is top priority."

"But ye aren't part o' the investigation any longer, and the inspector has a suspect in custody. Are ye sayin' Janet Dougal didn't kill Henrietta and the case is reopened?"

Bridie wasn't an old goat. She was a wise bird! All the more reason to be careful in my word choices when dealing with her.

"The case isn't closed until a verdict of guilty is reached," I said.

"It isn't yer problem. Unless ye've been reinstated . . ."

"Uh, not exactly."

"Then once the roads are clear and dry, we'll take a little road trip. Why, we might even go a little past Applefary intae Tainwick."

Tainwick? That name again. "Why Tainwick?" I asked, hesitant, not sure I wanted to find out.

"Because, my dear girl, that's where yer grandfather is buried. At the graveyard there. Applefary doesn't haff its own."

I'd just been searching for connections between Henrietta, Katie, and myself. If I was prone to wild speculation, this was the link I'd been searching for only moments before phoning Bridie. It wasn't much, but it was all I had.

After careful consideration, I ended the call and summarily dismissed it.

Or tried to.

Until I remembered Vicki's reaction when I'd mentioned that Henrietta and Katie both came from Tainwick. We'd been sitting at my kitchen table. She'd been disconcerted and dropped her fork, sputtering around, trying to cover up.

She'd been rattled and for the life of me I couldn't figure out why. At the time.

Now I had a hunch, so I picked up the phone and called the inspector.

"It's Eden," I said.

After a slight pause, he said, "I'm guessin' ye aren't

very happy with me or with recent decisions that I've needed tae make."

"That's beside the point," I said, knowing that he had my best interests in mind. Still, it hurt. "Henrietta McCloud and Katie Taylor are from Tainwick," I continued, "and now I've learned that my grandfather is buried in the cemetery there. I'm wondering if there is a connection of some sort. Is there?"

The inspector let the moment drag out before saying, "Ye're supposed tae be enjoying yer last days in Glenkillen. Why aren't ye plannin' tae do some holiday shoppin' fer yer friends back home? And until the roads clear, make a snowman or bake cookies. Enjoy."

"That's what I keep hearing."

"And so ye should listen tae us."

Bake cookies! Really? "I'd like a rundown of your investigation into Henrietta's past. All I know is where she's from and that she had a lot of bad luck."

The inspector sighed heavily into the phone. "I can't discuss the case with ye."

"And why not?" I wasn't going away easily. "You have in the past."

"Ye were in an official capacity . . ."

I interrupted. "You shared information with me long before that. I distinctly remember certain comments you made to justify it, something about my ability to see things that you couldn't. I'm paraphrasing, of course."

"Look who's the crabit today. And ye thought I was bad!"

"And look who's evading. You refuse to tell me what you've learned about Henrietta's past and whether anything there could have contributed to her death. Maybe you have a theory to explain to me why my grandfather is buried in the same town she hails from?"

"Applefary is a wee place. It's one o' those villages ye miss goin' through it if ye so much as blink an eye. Tainwick is the closest village with a cemetery. Those who live and die in Applefary are almost always buried in Tainwick. There's nothing unusual or mysterious aboot it. Is that a reasonable enough explanation fer ye?"

"It might have been, except how did you know my family is from Applefary?" I demanded.

I'd never told him.

Vicki. They had had words about my connection to Tainwick. What was going on? And why was I being excluded from the conversations?

Another heavy sigh on the other end. "Eden, please, ye're makin' this more difficult than it needs tae be. Let me do my job. It'll all work out in the end. I promise ye that."

I must have made some guttural communication that disturbed him, because his voice grew harder. "And I'm gonna have tae warn ye tae stay away from the case and everybody involved."

"Fine!" I said, disconnecting without a proper good-bye. And "fine" didn't necessarily mean I was agreeing to his outrageous demand. He couldn't stop me from seeing anyone I felt like seeing. And I didn't need the inspector for up-to-date information.

I had Sean. For what that was worth.

I stomped over to Vicki's house unannounced and found Sean dozing on the sofa. Vicki was nowhere to be seen. In her room, no doubt, sleeping. "Where is Katie Taylor right now?" I demanded.

Sean blinked and sat up.

"Katie Taylor? Uh, away with her family," he said.

"Where?"

"I can't say . . ."

"Then I will call the inspector and inform him of the lousy job you've been doing protecting me and will also mention that you've already blabbed when you shouldn't have."

"Ye wouldn't." The thunder on my face must have told him otherwise, even though I wouldn't have made that call. "Okay," he said, "but ye can't go saying how ye found out, if he ever asks."

"I assure you that I won't."

"It's like this," he began.

Katie, according to Sean, had been injured more seriously than initially believed. Even though I'd had several brief conversations with her, and on the surface she appeared perfectly normal, she had several residual effects. After the trauma to her head, she had experienced dizziness, difficulty sleeping without sleep aids, and memory loss, mostly short term.

"She should have remained in hospital in Glenkillen," Sean said, "but her family was worried about her safety. So they moved her tae a rehab facility in Invershnecky."

"Invershnecky? Do you mean Inverness?"

"That's wha' I said."

After a few more threats from me, Sean divulged the name of the rehabilitation center. "Her mum is staying there with her. Her da had tae go back to Tainwick tae work."

"How's Vicki feeling?" I asked.

"She's sick as a dog and will be sleepin' most o' the day. And there's no use all of us getting what she has. I'm runnin' into Glenkillen tae get some medications from the doc." Sean hopped up. "I shoulda been on my way already." He glanced at me. "But I'm tae keep ye in my sights. What are yer plans fer the day?"

"I don't have any," I lied. "The roads are bad. I think I'll just leave my car in the barn for the whole day, putter around at the cottage, do a little writing. Keep me posted on Vicki."

Sean shot me a doubtful look. "Ye aren't going tae Invershnecky, now are ye?"

"Hardly," I snorted.

"Then why did ye press me aboot Katie Taylor?"

I shrugged. "I don't know. I guess I was just thinking about her and hoped everything was okay."

I could see the relief register on his face. Now he could focus all his attention on caring for Vicki.

Vicki's voice came weakly from the direction of the bedroom. "Sean, who's here?"

"Eden, love, checkin' on ye, but she isn't visitin' and gettin' sick, too. I'm going out fer yer medications. Be back soon. Do ye need anything before I go?"

"No," came Vicki's frail answer.

Outside, I waved good-bye as Sean drove off in his Renault. Then I hurried back to the cottage and packed up whatever I might need for the day—laptop, phone, the drawing in case I had time to stop at Bridie's—and while the car warmed up, I made sure my trusty road map was inside it. I also made certain that the pepper spray canister was in my pocket within easy reach.

Braced for a drive that usually takes under an hour but would be much longer due to the road conditions, I set out for Inverness.

I've been to the Highland capital city several times and have even driven it enough to have a smidgen of confidence when it comes to navigating the city center. I could find my way around. The rehab center was easy enough to locate after a brief visit to city hall for directions, and I parked and entered, requesting directions to Katie's room. She wasn't there, but an aide led me to an open, airy sitting room that overlooked a winter garden scene. Only a few branches of the barren ornamental trees were visible under the heavy snow.

Katie was sitting up in an armchair with her mother beside her. The two looked so much alike there could be no mistaking their kinship. Mom, though, looked appropriately haggard as any mother would after the ordeal her daughter had been through.

Katie recognized me immediately, and I wondered about the extent of her ability to remember. It seemed in fine working order as I introduced myself to her mother.

"Elliott?" Katie said, obviously surprised, and I again recalled that I hadn't shared my last name at our prior meetings. "Are ye related to the Elliotts o' Applefary?"

"I am," I said, taking the seat her mother offered. "How are you doing?"

"Pretty well, thanks. Did ye drive all the way from Glenkillen tae see me?"

"I had other business here," I said, becoming more

comfortable in my deceptive practices. "And thought I'd come by and see how you were."

Her mom rose, probably relieved to have someone else to occupy some of Katie's time, and said, "I'll let you two visit." She kissed her daughter on the cheek. "And be back in a few hours."

With that, we were left alone.

"Have you remembered anything from the tasting that might be useful to the investigation?" I said, aware that I was misleading her again by letting her assume I was still part of the team.

She shook her head. "No, and since ye ask, that must mean ye don't know who did it."

"We have a few promising leads."

"I'll feel much better when someone is arrested. Mum is worried about me."

"You think your attack is related to the murder?"

"I'm not sure. At first I didn't think so, but . . ."

". . . but your mom and the inspector are showing enough concern to make you wonder." I could tell that was it. "We just want to be careful. And keep you safe. It won't be much longer and it will all be over."

"Eden Elliott," she said, turning the topic in a new direction. "Ye're Dennis Elliott's daughter, then."

I laughed. "You're good. I remember that you like local history and are even intent on writing a book about some of the more mysterious happenings in the area."

Katie frowned and said, "That's right. Who told you?"

"You did." This was the first indication I had that Katie hadn't fully recovered.

"I don't remember that."

"Well, it isn't important. I hope you aren't planning an exposé on the Elliott clan," I said with a laugh.

Katie gave me a studied look. "Most of my research has been through interviews with family members or neighbors. Stories passed down from one generation tae the next. I'm afraid most of yer relatives were gone before I became interested in clan histories, although . . ." She paused, about to say something, then thought better of it and said, "There are a few Elliotts somewhere in the area, but I haven't pursued them for material."

"Bridie eluded to that. Some distant cousins, I think she said."

So there was nothing to learn from Katie. No names or addresses. Just as well. That hadn't been the purpose of my visit.

She brightened before I could go on. "Once I'm back home, I could take on a new project, find out more o' yer history in a proper fashion, but I can't promise it'll be all roses. Most accounts aren't. And while there's always some truth tae the old stories, they tend tae get twisted with the telling."

"Right now you need to focus on getting well. My family can wait." Hadn't I thought that often enough? "Right now I'm wondering if you did any research into the McCloud family."

"Funny ye should mention that. Before we left hospital fer here, I asked my mum to get some o' my files and I've been reviewing them. Especially the one on Henrietta's family. And I found a few interesting notes." She gave me a sharp look again. "I believe there is a mention o' Elliott in there as well. If ye really want tae take a peek."

"Absolutely," I said, not bothering to hide a high level of interest. Never mind the Elliott, but reading about Henrietta's family might give me some sort of clue to pursue. "Have you discussed this with the inspector?"

"No, I only yesterday was up tae looking at my notes. I've been a wee bit dizzy and not able tae read much."

So I had a head start. I'd take it. Maybe I'd even learn something of significance and use it as leverage for an exchange of information with Jamieson.

"The file is in my room," Katie said, standing up.

"Then what are we waiting for?" I said with a smile that was as bright as the North Star. "Let's do some digging."

And with some luck, I thought, *we'll dig up a little dirt.*

CHAPTER 26

I'm not sure when it occurred to me or the exact moment when I began to suspect that my father's life and Henrietta's were connected. Maybe I'd had an inkling for days, simply because the two subjects—an Elliott disappearance and a McCloud murder—had become intertwined in my mind, and I'd been unable to separate them. But as I drove back to Glenkillen several hours later after poring over Henrietta's past with Katie, that inkling had found a basis in fact and had mushroomed into full-fledged North Star–quality illumination. Just like the smile I'd worn while following the budding historian to her room.

It hadn't taken long for that twinkle of delight to fade away under the harshness of reality.

Katie's notes had confirmed much of what Bridie had shared with me about Henrietta. Neighbors of the McCloud family had been willing to talk to Katie, since the family had moved away and therefore so had any threat of retribution from an alcoholic father who was quick to anger and raise his fists.

"Instead of neglecting his family as many drunks do," Katie had said, "he was a strict authoritarian, with rigid expectations. The girls couldn't possibly be perfect enough tae escape his wrath."

With a mother too frightened of consequences to even attempt to intervene, the abuse had gone on throughout their formative years. Eventually, a relative stepped in on Patricia's behalf. Patricia was five years older than Henrietta. This relative arranged for her to attend university, and she was sent off to Edinburgh, where she met and married Connor Martin. The rest of her story had been public knowledge as Connor climbed the political ladder.

"So what are those points of interest you mentioned?" I'd asked Katie, thinking of Henrietta and wondering how she'd fared once her sister escaped.

"Little gems," she'd replied. "But are they real? Or are they fake?"

"Tell me."

Rumors about the McCloud family weren't hard to come by. Neighbors were quick to supply them. The father had ended up in prison somewhere in Glasgow. The mother had died, battered by her husband. The older sister, Patricia, had given birth to a child out of wedlock, the father of her child unknown.

"Patricia had been away for several years before she had Gordon," Katie said. "She married Connor shortly after, and he claimed the boy as his own."

So Gordon Martin had been a love child. Interesting

but hardly of concern to the case. Or if it was, I hadn't found a connection yet.

"Speaking of love, Henrietta had her own richly described affair of the heart with a local young man," Katie continued. "He was going to be her way out, her escape from a rotten home life, according to the neighbors. They'd watched her sneak out at night, witnessed a few of the trysts between the two. It was how she managed to cope, they said. He gave her hope.

"Then one day he was gone. Henrietta moped around, waiting for him to come and rescue her. For months no one saw her leave the house. She'd become a recluse, pining away, wasting away. Until the day that Bridie Dougal agreed to have her as an employee. That's the last the neighbors saw of her."

"Interesting," I said.

"At one time I'd intended to pursue more documentation, try to substantiate some of those details," Katie said. "But it would have involved speaking directly to Henrietta and it slipped out o' my mind. Not that she probably woulda cooperated. That's the problem with this kind o' research.

"And the lad who jilted her? I suppose ye need tae know." Katie said with a serious expression.

"Yes, who was he?"

And I was thinking maybe he was the key to this whole case. I wasn't sure how, not this early, not yet, but it was one more place to look.

And that was when I found out.

The young man who stole Henrietta McCloud's heart had been my father.

* * *

At first I'd been stunned. Blindsided. Not believing it. Truths, half truths, lies. What was the case this time? Truth gets twisted in the telling, especially over time, Katie had said at the beginning, and she repeated it when she saw my expression.

But the more I thought about it on that slow drive back to Glenkillen along the snowy narrow roadway, the more I accepted their past relationship as truth.

Henrietta had been sneaking peeks at me that morning when we'd met. No wonder she'd been interested in me. She must have seen the resemblance, would have known my grandfather. My presence there must have dredged up more than a few memories. Hopefully some of them had been good ones.

Was that why she'd wanted to meet with me?

Of course. She'd been ready to tell me her story. Maybe she thought I knew where my father was. She would have been hoping for news of him. She would have been horribly disappointed to find out that I didn't know anything about him, hadn't heard from him for thirty-some years. We could have exchanged sad stories, commiserated together, because as it turned out, Dennis Elliott had horribly disappointed both of us.

Thinking of the cad who had been my dad, who had broken a young woman's heart (no matter that he'd left her for my mother), brought a fresh sense of loss, a new pain shooting through my own heart.

I reminded myself that it might not have been what it seemed. Just because a woman falls in love doesn't mean her feelings are reciprocated. It could have been one-sided. Not that it mattered. My father wasn't around to tell his side of the story.

Did Bridie know about them?

I didn't think so. She wouldn't have been able to contain herself this long. Bridie wasn't one to exhibit restraint. No. My guess was that Henrietta hadn't shared that part of her past with her employer.

Halfway to Glenkillen, my mind turned dark, which I'm learning to recognize as a curse of an overactive imagination. What if my father had murdered Henrietta? What if he had been lurking about? He obviously had a gift for disappearing at will. Why not appear at will just as easily?

I forced that thought away mainly because I couldn't come up with a workable motive. He hadn't snuck in and drowned her because she might tell me about their romantic interludes. *And*, carrying that farfetched premise to its end, he'd have had to be the one who attacked me. Even my resentful, bitter mind couldn't imagine that.

So I shelved those gruesome thoughts. I didn't have a high regard for Dennis Elliott, and I didn't want him to fall further than he already had. If that was possible.

Maybe his disappearance and Henrietta's death were related.

Or maybe they weren't.

In the world of the investigator, I would need to prove those two knew each other, then confirm without a shadow of a doubt that they'd been romantically involved.

Did I want to? In the end, would it matter?

I drove into Glenkillen with an hour to spare before taking tea with Bridie, so I drove to the inn and parked. Everything was snow covered and decorated for Christmas, which was only two weeks away. I paused outside the Whistling Inn to imagine the lackluster Christmas awaiting me back in Chicago. Then I opened the door and entered the inn.

"Janet Dougal is back," Jeannie said from the reception desk. "And playin' the part o' royalty in me best suite at this very moment."

"Yes, I know."

"I'd wonder if ye hadn't. It's all aboot town."

What would Jeannie have to say if she knew that she'd supplied at least one of Janet's alibis, the one proving that Janet hadn't attacked me at the hospital, the one leading to the inspector's own moment of doubt and her release?

"Is Patricia Martin here?" I wasn't sure exactly how I would go about confirming the rumors that had been uncovered, but asking her was the logical first step. I'd have to do it gingerly, dredge up more tact than I usually practiced, or she'd react as Florence had the day I'd quizzed her. This would have to be done delicately.

I was almost relieved when Jeannie said Patricia wasn't in. "Stormed out o' here like she'd been launched from a cannon when she found out aboot that other one being let loose. I almost went with her tae voice me own complaint. Tae think I have to put up with the likes o' her again!"

Back in my car with time to spare before tea, I called Vicki.

"How are you feeling?"

"About the same, but I'm going crazy lying around. The Internet is back up and running, so I did some research from the sofa."

I heard Sean in the background. "Against me orders, I might add."

"Ignore him. He's trying to do what's best for me without understanding exactly what is best. Anyhow . . ."

After a split second of fumbling around, Sean's voice came on loud and clear. "Yer car is missing and ye aren't in yer cottage as ye promised. Ye haff no business givin' me the slip. It isn't safe and I took ye at yer word, not that that did me a bit o' good . . ."

Vicki had seized control again. "You're being careful, right?"

"Right."

"I've done some digging. Dennis Elliott was on a passenger list, that much is certain. But he wasn't on that flight."

"That's strange."

"I'm still digging. If he was on a later one, I'll find him. Good thing this happened so many years ago when lives weren't as private. In today's world, I wouldn't have this kind of access. There's a lot online to sort through."

Vicki sounded excited in spite of her illness. She'd discovered she had a knack for historical research.

"Thanks, Vicki, I appreciate it," I said, truthfully, although when she was better, we were going to have to have a serious discussion about some of her recent deceptions. She wouldn't see them as such, but I did. I'd lost some trust in her. Which was one of the reasons I chose not to confide in her regarding the visit to Katie in Inverness.

If I shared with her, she'd tell Sean, and then Jamieson would find out in record time. The inspector would chastise me for interfering in his investigation, and he might well put someone more capable than Sean on my tail.

For now, I was going it alone.

If and when I had anything concrete, I'd turn all that I'd learned over to the inspector.

I drove over to the estate of the Dougal chieftain for a little tête-à-tête.

Except instead of a private audience with Bridie, she was holding court. Again.

Archie met me at the door. I hadn't seen him since the tasting, had only spoken to him on the phone once, but he greeted me with the warmth and charm of an old, dear friend. I was immediately suspicious, remembering well that this man had a good motive for murder.

"You're expected," he said with a smile, leading me down the hall. My heart sank as I heard all the voices ahead. A private chat with Bridie about my family would have to wait.

And, yes, I recognized the irony. I'd been doing my best to avoid the subject, not that my best had been good enough. But I'd put a lot of effort into it. Now I desperately wanted to learn as much as I could.

Go figure.

CHAPTER 27

Leith Cameron rose and came forward to greet me while Archie returned to a chair next to his wife, Florence. "What are you doing here?" I asked Leith quietly as he led me to a vacant seat to the right of his, the last one at the round table, which was mounded with sandwiches, biscuits, and savories. I counted seven place settings, seven of us for tea.

He leaned close and whispered in my ear. "Same as yerself. Doing Bridie's bidding."

The next few minutes were taken up with small talk, although no introductions were necessary. We'd been together Saturday evening when Henrietta's body had been discovered facedown in a vat of whisky.

The only one missing was Katie Taylor, and I knew exactly where she was and why she wasn't here. Someone had gotten very close and almost succeeded in killing the young woman. One of these guests might very well be responsible for that attack as well as the one against me.

Going around the table from my right, Bridie reigned

249

from her position as perfect hostess. Next, a scowling, obviously distressed Patricia Martin. Up in arms about the release of Janet Dougal, no doubt. Gordon Martin sat to his mother's right, his expression neutral. Then Archie and finally his wife with her standard knitted brow.

"Thank you all fer coming on such short notice," Bridie said to the group. "I suppose everyone has heard about Janet Dougal's disturbing release from custody." She turned to me. "I'm afraid our tea fer two has grown by leaps and bounds, but it couldn't be helped under the circumstances." Her eyes darted to Patricia, implying that Henrietta's sister had something to do with this gathering.

"It's a travesty o' justice," Patricia said. Her anger was palpable. "That woman killed my sister!"

Bridie edged back in, and for the first time, I noticed how powerfully she commanded a room in spite of her slight form. "We . . . or rather Patricia . . . thought if we all got together, meaning those of us who were at the tasting that night, maybe we could work on a solution that puts Janet back in jail."

"Where she belongs," Gordon said, loyal to his mother.

"I'd like to know why that menace is running loose," Patricia said, addressing me.

"I'm no longer part of the investigation," I told her, relieved because I wasn't sure what Patricia would have done to me if I'd been responsible for the present situation. I wasn't about to recite the rules of law to her, either. She'd simply dismiss them as another example of foolish bureaucracy, on par with special constables.

"Janet Dougal was also at the tasting," Gordon pointed out unnecessarily. "She should be here tae explain herself and offer an explanation fer what happened tae Aunt Henrietta."

No one mentioned Katie. Good. Let them forget her. She'd been part of the décor for all they noticed her.

Leith gave me a light squeeze at my elbow. When I glanced at him, he winked. The grin on his face was standard Leith, but his eyes were serious. The wink was reassuring, though. He was the only one at the table who I could trust.

"We know what happened, Gordon," Florence said, taking a finger sandwich from a three-tiered server, an indication to the rest of us to follow suit. "She killed Henrietta. Then had the nerve tae show up at the tasting and act like nothing happened. She's a mental case."

"And back on the fair streets o' Glenkillen," Patricia fairly shouted.

"Not on the street, actually." Archie corrected her. "She's been told tae keep a low profile, tae stay in her suite and out o' trouble. The inspector told me when he rang up my mum this morning with the disturbing news that the woman had been released."

Of course, Jamieson would have shown that consideration to the involved parties, advised them of his unpopular decision. I wouldn't want his job for all the homegrown tea in Scotland.

I studied the tiered server closest to me and selected an egg and cress finger sandwich, with a future eye on a smoked salmon, lemon, and dill for my second.

"Delicious," I told Bridie. "Who made all these wonderful treats?"

"Florence gets all the credit."

I gave Florence an appreciative nod. Her scowl only deepened, and I wondered if she ever smiled and if she was still holding a grudge against me for our exchange of words early on.

I'd been alert to the group dynamics from the start in case anyone said anything that might be useful. This was the perfect opportunity to listen and learn. I went over the cast in my head. Archie and Florence were now free from Henrietta's claim to remain on the estate for the long term. They gained by her death. Patricia, Gordon, and Bridie didn't have any obvious rewards based on her death, nothing that I could determine anyway. Patricia and Gordon had lost a family member and Bridie had been deprived of a longtime companion. But images can be deceiving.

I reviewed what I'd learned about Patricia from Katie's research. She'd had a difficult young adulthood, a poor home life, but she'd persevered and had a lot to show for her efforts—a son who seemed to be doing well for himself at the distillery, a husband with a successful career, a good life from what I could tell.

"I'm in the same inn as that murderess!" Patricia went on, and I felt another pang of sympathy for the inspector and the characters in this case he'd had to deal with. "Forced by the local authorities to stay in Glenkillen with a killer free to kill again. I should be allowed to return to Edinburgh. I could be next!"

"I doubt that Janet Dougal is some kind o' serial killer," Leith said, speaking up for the first time. "And our local authorities are the best in all o' Scotland. The inspector wouldn'ta released her without sufficient reason tae do so."

"Good God, man"—this from Archie—"ye aren't suggesting that one o' us knocked her off?"

"That's a cold way of describing it," Patricia said to him.

"I'm not suggesting that at all," Leith said, "I'm tryin' tae say that the inspector knows what he's about."

"Janet Dougal is obviously unhinged," Bridie said. "She's off her head. We've all seen examples of very bad behavior. Before we start off accusing each other, I believe with my whole heart that Janet Dougal killed our dear Henrietta. And Inspector Jamieson had tae let her go because he doesn't have enough evidence tae charge her, is my guess. So . . . how are we goin' tae help the inspector prove it?"

The table went silent as we ate, sipped, and thought.

"Someone called in an anonymous tip," I said. "Somebody saw Janet leave the inn late Saturday afternoon."

Everyone turned and stared at me. That comment hadn't been a slip on my part. I intended to give the conversation a lively boost. I no longer had an obligation to secrecy, although I'd never do anything to jeopardize the case.

"She was seen coming here?" Bridie asked. "While I was having my hair done?"

"Around then, yes," I said. "But the caller didn't mention her destination, only that she'd been out and about."

"Who saw her leave the inn?" Archie said, looking around the table. "It musta been one o' us since no one else in the village knows her. If one o' ye saw her, what direction had she taken?"

No one said anything for a minute. Then Leith said, "I didn't know who she was until the tasting when we were introduced. And I'm guessing the same goes fer most o' the rest o' us."

"That's right," Bridie agreed. "She just appeared at the tasting room door. Who of us had been introduced to her before then? Did any o' you know who she was? Well, the person who tipped off the cops knew her, or else how would they have been able to recognize her?"

Gordon and Patricia exchanged glances and held them long enough that I picked up on the interchange. When Gordon looked away, he saw me watching and gave me a polite smile.

"There's still the issue of how Janet knew about the tasting," I added. "One of us *must* have told her."

Again, no one offered up an explanation. I was disappointed and really wanted to go on to tell them the rest— that Janet claimed Henrietta invited her out before the tasting, then was turned away by the very woman who had extended the invitation. But I couldn't break that confidence. Besides, the only other person who could vouch for or deny that statement was dead.

I asked Bridie, delicately rather than boldly, "You didn't ask Janet out to the house prior to the tasting, did you?"

"I wouldn't think o' it. First off, she was pushy and demanding when she phoned, and secondly, I was preoccupied with the details o' the tasting. So was Henrietta. Neither o' us wanted her underfoot."

"Henrietta didn't invite her to the house or to the tasting?"

"A resounding no! Henrietta held her in less regard than I do!"

That passionate outburst brought a few more minutes

of silence to the table. We focused on our tea and sandwiches. I helped myself to a toffee cupcake.

I had fresh doubts about Janet's guilt. What if Janet Dougal had been telling the truth about her final confrontation with the dead woman? It may have actually happened the way she explained. She might have had a call from someone impersonating Henrietta with the intention of sending her speeding off to the estate. That someone could have been the killer, setting Janet up to take the rap.

If true, that meant a clever murderer, sly and calculating.

My eyes wandered the room. No beam of light from above shone expressly on any one particular person. Except maybe Leith, who radiated his own source of heat. Our eyes met and he gave me that lopsided grin of his.

"I ought tae take matters into my own hands," Patricia said. "And wring the truth out of her."

"Ye need tae calm down, Mum," Gordon told her. "And focus on carrying out Aunt Henrietta's last wishes instead." His eyes swept over us as he explained. "My aunt had very specific ideas regarding her ashes."

"Ye aren't dumping them here, are ye?" Archie said. "Ye aren't scattering them at the distillery? I dislike the idea o' people's ashes thrown willy-nilly."

"Only a little in the gardens," Patricia said. "Bridie doesn't have a problem with that."

"It's only fitting," Bridie said. "Ye wouldn't think it now that winter is upon us, but the gardens are lovely and Henrietta spent hours sittin' out there."

The party broke up soon after that. Everyone departing, subdued compared to earlier. Besides the sadness of the subject matter, I guessed that everyone was stuffed to the gills and needed naps. I knew I did. But I hung around. So did Leith.

"I'd like a private word with Eden, young man," Bridie said. "Ye can wait outside fer her, if ye wish. It won't be long."

"I'm on my way tae get my daughter fer a few days away," he said, his Scot blues trained on me. "Ye take care o' yerself."

When he was gone, I withdrew the sketch from my purse, unfolded it, and handed it to Bridie.

She studied it at length, wiped her eyes several times, and said, "It brings back memories, it does. It's a mighty crest, one o' great honor. Ye should be proud tae carry the Elliott name."

Proud? I hadn't considered anything honorable about my name. Having Bridie feel it was special was something I hadn't considered. At least my grandfather had lived up to her larger-than-life image of what a gentleman should be. "Do you recognize this?"

"I've never seen this particular sketch before. But I have a warm place in my heart fer the Elliott crest and motto, and I'd do anythin' tae make you see it the same way. If only ye'd soften yer heart."

"You loved my grandfather, didn't you?"

"More than life itself," she said with wet eyes. "But it was a long time ago and not meant tae be. We went separate ways and never connected in a way I'd hoped we would. He was a special man."

She slowly folded it along the worn crease, halving it.

Her eyes widened in surprise.

"What's the matter?" I asked.

"'Princess Hen.' I know that term o' endearment. Yer da used it when he was visiting with his new bride. He used it often. He called yer mum Princess Hen."

"Are you saying my father drew this?"

"Aye, who else could have?"

This sketch was a link between the two that I had been looking for, but not the one I'd expected.

"But it would have been intended for my mother. So what was it doing in a notebook belonging to Henrietta McCloud?"

Bridie and I looked at each other.

Neither of us had an answer.

CHAPTER 28

It was late in the afternoon, a little after six o'clock. Evening's twilight had arrived hours ago, along with a steady drop in the temperature that caused me to reach quickly for the car's heater control and turn it up as far as it would go. By the time I drove away from the distillery, I felt weary and ready to relax in front of a warm fire with Snookie. But instead of turning toward the cottage, I resisted the urge to indulge in creature comforts and headed for Glenkillen.

The teatime gathering hadn't produced much new information, but old questions had been raised, and they were foremost in my mind. Until I resolved them, or at least began the process of inquiry, starting the ball in motion, I wouldn't be able to unwind.

I parked and entered the Whistling Inn only to discover that Janet Dougal wasn't in her room.

"She was told tae stay put," Jeanie griped with a sour expression, nervously fingering a hoop ring on one of a multitude of ear piercings. "I suppose I have tae inform the inspector. He won't like it one bit."

All tiredness vanished at this new development and I felt a surge of adrenaline. "She skipped town?" I was ready to run her down myself if need be.

"No, no, nothin' as bonnie as that. Herself is over at the pub."

"I'll apprise the inspector," I said, already turning away to pursue Janet before realizing that he and I were no longer a team. Our friendship had suffered during this investigation, and I wasn't sure that we could find our way back to what we'd once had, especially considering the limited time before I left. The inspector had been cold and detached when we'd spoken earlier, without a hint of the camaraderie we'd once shared.

I went back to the car, hauled my laptop out, and slung the computer bag over my shoulder as a pretense for my presence at the Kilt & Thistle. Not exactly a cover, since I needed the computer to contact Ami, if for no other reason than to make arrangements for my first week back in Chicago. I'd need a place to stay while I regrouped and planned the next phase of my life. Even though I'd originally needed a break from her, the reality was that I needed her now more than ever.

Thankfully, the pub was lively, more so than when I usually hung out here during the day. Entering gave my mood an upbeat swing that matched the atmosphere of the place. There were plenty of customers, and a musical duo— one on the fiddle, one on guitar—entertaining the pub's patrons with some fine traditional folk music. After I ordered a pint at the bar, one song ended and another started up, a song I recognized, "Annie Laurie." I sang along with what seemed like the entire pub. We raised our voices. "Her voice is low and sweet and she's all the world to me / And for bonnie Annie Laurie I'd lay me doon and dee."

This was one gathering place I'd really miss, my home away from home. Where else would a roomful of customers join together and sing like this?

I sipped the ale, my eyes sliding over the patrons until I spotted Janet sitting alone at a table far from the musicians, with her own pint in front of her. That seemed strange to me. I'd never have pegged the American woman as a beer drinker. To me, beer lovers are easygoing, happy sorts who go with the flow. Janet didn't fit with that image.

"I suppose you are going to haul me back to that wretched inn," she said, a bit loud and aggressive when I walked over. This wasn't her first pint. "You can't expect me to stay in my room day and night, eating the same food over and over. And that proprietor! I swear she isn't even trying to make those meals tasty. But what can you expect from the Scotch. Anyway, it's a free country last I checked and I have a right to be here. If you try to arrest me, I will demand to place a call to an attorney."

So she didn't realize I was an ordinary citizen, that my rank had been pulled and I didn't have any authority over her. I decided not to enlighten her and to take full advantage of her inebriation.

"Would you like a dram of whisky with that?" I asked, thinking that Janet spouted off about her rights every time I ran into her. It must be rough when the whole world is against you. "Beer and whisky go together well."

Janet shook her head, and it bobbed a bit loosely. "I never want to see another glass of whisky in this lifetime. I never should have gone to that tasting. Look where it's landed me."

I sat down without being invited.

"It will turn out okay," I reassured her in a best-friend voice. "The inspector released you. That means he has his doubts. The important thing for you to do is to help us catch the real killer."

"I told that inspector all that I know." She looked directly at me with slightly vacant eyes. "I told you, too. You were there."

"Yes, I was. You admitted to driving out to Bridie's home after Henrietta invited you."

"She did! I didn't make that up."

"And when you arrived, she turned you away."

"That's right."

"Let's back up a little and work this out."

"It isn't going to help. I already did that."

"Perhaps you'll remember something more," I said, sounding just like some character on a cop show. "Tell me how you originally found out about the tasting."

Janet's eyes rolled up in thought. I sipped my ale and waited.

"Friday," she announced. "There were two Scotches sitting next to me in the inn's dining room. At first I couldn't understand a word they were saying. You know how they mangle the English language."

I let her outrageous comment slide. And I'd already tried to correct her on several other counts with no luck whatsoever. *They aren't Scotch*, I wanted to say, *they're Scots*. But apparently Janet wasn't going to learn what she didn't want to learn.

"Go on," I said, gritting my teeth and attempting to appear pleasant. "Did you recognize them?"

"Not then, but certainly at the tasting. It was that sister and her son."

"Patricia Martin and Gordon?" Neither of them had offered this information when I'd asked the group directly how Janet Dougal had found out about the tasting. But perhaps they hadn't been aware that she was eavesdropping. And on Friday, they wouldn't have met her yet. She would have been just one more diner.

"They were talking about this whisky tasting out at the distillery," Janet continued. "Hosted by Bridie Dougal. That's when my ears perked up, when I heard her name. And the man said something about Saturday night, and that it was a small intimate group, and that he'd meet her in the reception area a little before seven o'clock and drive her out to the distillery."

That was an easy explanation. Simple. Direct.

"So you decided to join them."

"Not at first. I was put out that Bridie hadn't included me, but that wasn't my initial plan. It was only after the fiasco with that woman, that housekeeper. She'd been cruel, asking me out and then slamming the door in my face. I drove back to the inn, changed my clothes, and demanded a ride when Gordon arrived. Biggest mistake of my life. Oh well, you know what they say about hindsight." She took a chug of her beer. "Twenty-twenty."

"So you didn't speak to Gordon and Patricia when they were discussing the tasting?"

"Not him, no, he got up and left. Then I leaned over toward the table and said something about needing a ride and did she think I could ride out with her. And all I got was a sort of glare and right then another woman joined her. It was that housekeeper sister of hers. Course, I didn't know it at the time, having only spoken with her on the phone, but the next day, when she pulled that stunt on me, then I connected that face to the same one from the night before."

"Henrietta was in the dining room?" I racked my brain and dredged up a little of the conversation I'd had with Patricia when we were establishing timelines. She'd stated that the last time she'd seen her sister alive had been Friday. That fit with what Janet was telling me. But Patricia had still withheld information that I'd asked for a few hours earlier. I wondered why and if the glances exchanged by Patricia and Gordon had anything to do with it.

"The same. Those two put their heads together like I didn't even exist, so I went back to minding my own business, as much as I could."

"You told all this to the inspector?"

"Ad nauseam. A zillion times." I heard neediness in her tone as she continued. "And a few more wouldn't hurt. Do you ever see him with a woman? Does he date?"

"We need to focus." Janet was the victim of unrequited love, something that doesn't enter into my romantic stories. Nothing is one-sided about those relationships even though it might seem that way at the beginning. Real life is much more painful, and Janet was suffering. "Back to answering questions regarding the investigation."

"Don't you and the inspector share information? We already addressed all this."

"You and I are going over things once again with fresh eyes," I told her, the assumption being that the inspector and I in fact collaborated on all aspects of the case. At least my eyes were fresh. Hers were glazed. "Did you overhear any of the conversation between the two sisters?"

Instead of answering, she held up her empty glass. "Bartender," she shouted out during a brief pause in the music. Her glass was quickly replaced with a full one. I was nursing mine. Not that Janet noticed or cared or offered to buy me one.

"Did you hear any more of the conversation?" I repeated.

"Those two sisters lowered their voices. The one who died the next day was facing my table. I didn't hear much, but that housekeeper was upset, I could tell, blubbering and wiping her eyes and shaking her head as though she disagreed with what the other one was saying. She might have been refusing whatever the other one wanted, or something like that. Pretty soon, the one staying at the inn stood up and said they'd discuss this further and the other wasn't to do anything until she said so."

"Is there more?" I asked when Janet didn't continue. "Anything else?"

She thought a minute and said, "No, but those two are like two peas in a pod. Both nasty, if you want my opinion."

And that was pretty much all Janet had to offer. She quickly finished the next pint and teetered out the door. I powered up my laptop, settling in to enjoy the music, and found an e-mail from Ami.

"Don't be angry with me," she wrote. "I'll explain my reasoning, but I want to do it in person. What time should I pick you up at O'Hare? And I insist that you spend the holiday with me. Wait until you see the decorations in downtown Chicago! And we'll shop and wine and dine. Have you gone to Applefary yet? Hope all worked out well. Love and kisses, Ami."

Suddenly, I felt warm and cozy and loved. All the annoyance with her that I'd experienced earlier drained away with the last swallow of the pint of ale. I shot back an e-mail with my arrival time and went on to return her loving sentiments before telling her I was going to Tainwick to the grave site first thing tomorrow.

After that I headed for my cottage, parked the Peugeot in the barn, and popped in to check on Vicki before calling it a night.

She was on the sofa, propped up with a pillow, with her laptop on another pillow.

"You look better," I told her.

"And I feel a little better."

"Have you eaten?"

"Yes, Sean made chicken soup."

"Where is he?"

"Off doing cop stuff," she said vaguely. "I'm loving these ancestry sites I'm finding online."

I laughed. "You're obsessed."

"It's addictive," she agreed. "Still no leads on Dennis Elliott, though. Unless he's changed his name, which I sort of doubt."

"I hadn't thought of that."

Would he have gone to that extent to disappear? He wasn't wanted for any crimes, at least none we knew about. Why else would a man with a richly historic Scottish name change it? I agreed with Vicki. It was unlikely.

"We need more information," Vicki added, "and I'm not going to find it online. I've exhausted those resources."

"What do you suggest?"

"Your grandfather's gravesite might hold some clues. Lots of the older gravestones are like memorials. Sometimes they mention relatives and friends who aren't even dead and buried at the time."

"His grave isn't *that* old. He died in the nineteen eighties."

"If that doesn't pan out, we can visit the Tainwick library. It has a local history section. If nothing else, we might find out where some of your current relatives live and contact them."

"Bridie seems to know a little. She offered to help."

"The more, the merrier. When should we make the trip?"

"When you're up to it. In a day or two?"

"Okay."

I left it at that, intentionally dangling the loose ends. And then I went home to the cottage to the soft welcoming meows of Snookie, with her cute little folded ears and her reassuring purr.

CHAPTER 29

Today was Thursday, December 13.

My flight was scheduled to depart from Inverness on the 22nd with a layover in London, then on to Chicago. Only nine full days left in the Scottish Highlands. In the village of Glenkillen. At the MacBride farm. In my cottage.

Six months ago I couldn't imagine coming here. I remembered vividly, as though it were only yesterday. Ami had to accompany me to the airport to make sure I boarded. This morning, I couldn't imagine ever leaving. Vicki might have to shove me on the return flight.

I'd seriously considered an option—going back and forth, living in Chicago and visiting as often as I could. But I know one thing about myself, at least. I needed to establish a home and get involved in a community. I have every intention of visiting Glenkillen again someday, but what I really wanted was to make my permanent home in these beautiful highlands. It was an impossible dream.

With the bed comforter pulled up around my ears and

Snookie practically wrapped around my head like a fur headpiece, I thought about the possibility of a future alone. Men brought complexity and risk to one's life, even in the alternate world of Rosehearty, Scotland, where my Highlands Desire Series takes place.

There, the men are always strong, rugged, competent, hardworking, pretty much perfect, except they are also damaged by past relationships. Either they've sworn off love because they don't believe in it, or they've lost true love and have given up on ever finding it again.

In my stories, the hero and heroine initially work at cross-purposes, butting heads before falling in love.

In the real world, Leith Cameron has been my inspiration for both Jack Ross and Daniel Ross, each brother appearing in his own story—Jack in *Falling for You* and Daniel in my current work in progress, *Hooked on You*.

But Leith doesn't appear to be damaged by anything. He did have a daughter out of wedlock without marrying Fia's mom, and being a single parent must be hard. But in general, he's easygoing. Lately, I've been suspecting that "easy come, easy go" is his real attitude toward life and women. He's committed to raising his daughter and I respect him for that, but if he has a serious side other than when he's parenting, he hides it well.

And as for the two of us butting heads, I couldn't think of a single example. And even though I think he is one of the sexiest men in all of Scotland, my heart doesn't pound when he is near.

What about the inspector? Immediately the rational part of my brain snorted. He was twenty years older, practically old enough to be my father. A widower, who cared for his wife until the end. Jamieson still wears his wedding ring, an indication that he keeps commitments until death and beyond.

While Leith is outgoing, the inspector is introverted, like me. There's nothing shy about him, though. He just values his privacy. That got me thinking about the home he has somewhere out in the middle of nowhere, a cabin of sorts, according to Vicki. I'd never been invited out and probably never would be.

Talk about butting heads! We've done some of that lately.

Before I could pursue that line of thought any further, someone rapped on the cottage door. I grabbed a robe and opened the door to find Sean standing outside.

"I'm not comin' in," he reported when I extended the invitation. "This is me seein' ye in the flesh so I can report that ye're in me sight."

I grabbed his arm and pulled him inside. "It's freezing out there," I said, closing the door. "And I have a few questions for you."

Sean moaned. "Ye're gettin' me in deeper and deeper. Can't ye just leave me alone?"

"This one is easy. I haven't heard anything more about that threatening note. I know that Bridie's grandson sent it and that he's come clean, but has there been any subsequent follow-up?"

"I don't know wha' ye mean."

"Has he been cleared as a suspect in Henrietta's murder?"

"Aye, the lad caused a wee bit o' mischief and the inspector investigated him further. He had nothin' tae do with the murder."

"What about Florence?" Which was the real question I'd been leading up to but in a roundabout way so Sean's suspicions wouldn't be aroused. "And Archie Dougal?"

"And I suppose ye want all the details on Gordon and Patricia Martin and Bridie herself and the rubbish collector and . . ."

"Any and all," I agreed, seeing the first signs of resistance in Sean's set expression.

"I'm done with bein' blackmailed by the likes o' yerself," he said.

I studied him, searching for a break in his confidence, a way to slip in and gain a firm hold. Then with growing horror I realized I'd been as manipulative with Sean as I'd been accusing others of being with me.

"Okay," I said, taking the first step to correcting my unacceptable behavior.

"O . . . kay?" There was the crack, widening, large enough to squeeze through. I left it alone.

"I apologize for pressuring you," I told him.

Sean's look went blank while he absorbed this strange turn, and then he grinned. "It's all right. You and me, we go back a bit. A little clash now and again is normal."

"Okay, great, how's Vicki?"

"Still not back tae her old self. Another day will see her better. I hear ye're havin' a hen party when she recovers, goin' on a visit tae yer ancestors. What are yer plans fer today, if I might be so bold as tae ask?"

"Oh, I don't know," I said, knowing exactly, thinking the quiet side of my personality needed space today to reenergize, and the only way to get it was through misdirection.

"I'll probably go into Glenkillen and write at the pub for most of the day."

"I can't see ye getting into any sort o' trouble there. Ye'll be on alert, though, won't ye?"

"Of course."

"If ye get it intae yer head tae go further afield, ye'll let me know? I'll go with ye or tag along in me own rattletrap." Sean glanced out the window, up at the gray sky. "On second thought, there's a storm brewin' and it would be best fer ye tae stay within easy drivin'."

"I'll stay put," I said, opening the door and shooing him out, thinking, *So what if a storm is on the way? More snow? What else is new?*

A short time later I pulled out from the lane onto the main road. I'd packed what I anticipated needing for the day—a freshly charged phone and laptop, water bottle, extra outerwear in case of a breakdown, and the map of the Highlands. The route to Tainwick wasn't complicated, a direct shot to Loch Ness and then due north. Applefary was even farther north than Tainwick, and I'd go there if time allowed. Otherwise, I'd save that village for another trip in a few days with Vicki when I retraced these steps for her benefit.

And with her history-gathering expertise.

Remembering that, I decided that the library historical section could wait as well. Vicki would enjoy combing through the files, searching for genealogical tidbits. While I reveled in researching topics myself, I couldn't take the fun away from my friend. She'd be upset enough if she learned I'd left her behind today.

Morning's first light was a spectacular visual display.

Clouds hung low and red over snow-covered hills and frost-coated trees, and as I approached Loch Ness, the colors reflected brilliantly on the icy lake. When I turned due north, a wild deer stood out on the side of a glen watching me.

I took it all in until twenty-some kilometers outside Tain-wick, when my mind turned back to Henrietta McCloud's murder. I attempted to find new angles, fresh perspectives, starting not from the very beginning but after her death. When she'd wanted to speak with me after the tasting. At first I'd assumed she intended to pinpoint the note writer, to send me off to handle this person who had threatened Bridie. Then after I'd learned of Henrietta's link to my father, I'd figured that she wanted to share information about him with me, or that she was seeking word of him.

Henrietta was a dying woman, even before her unexpected murder, after her diagnosis and prognosis. She'd talked to Gordon about regrets, about setting things right. What if she'd wanted to tell me something before it was too late? What if she'd been killed because of what she intended to reveal to me Saturday night?

Setting things right. Weren't those the words Gordon had used, implying that she was going to make amends? There was a distinct difference between making amends and offering apologies. Amends were much more complex than apologies; their intent was to restore justice, to set right a wrong. Amends were more active than apologies.

Henrietta gave those who knew her the impression that she was in denial over her deadly disease, but she'd expressed regrets to her nephew and she'd made some provisions for her imminent death by leaving written instructions regarding her ashes. Was I one of her pieces of unfinished business?

But Henrietta never did anything to me personally. Had she hurt my father in some horrible way that she'd lived to regret? From Katie's account, *he* had been the one doing the hurting. What could she possibly have done to him that she needed to set right?

I felt a growing sense of inexplicable unease and tried to shake it off as I approached the outskirts of Tainwick. But it stuck with me. I turned my thoughts elsewhere.

An online search had informed me that the Tainwick parish churchyard had originally been in the center of the village but had filled up with no room for expansion in the latter part of the nineteenth century. A public cemetery had been created south of Tainwick at the turn of the twentieth century. Since my grandfather had passed away in the early 1980s, that was where I would find his grave.

When I realized that I didn't have an exact location for his site, I considered driving on past the cemetery to the village library. But it was still early morning; not much would be open, certainly not the library. And I wasn't sure that the genealogy section could even supply specific gravesite information. Besides, how large could the cemetery be?

The Tainwick Cemetery signage was large enough that I didn't miss it. I followed the arrow, turning off and driving down a narrow road that had been recently cleared of snow. I pulled into a car lot. Mine was the only vehicle there at this time of the morning.

I placed a call to Bridie, mildly surprised that it went through from this remote location.

"You mentioned that my father and mother visited you right after they were married."

"Aye, Dennis was showin' off his new bride."

"Was Henrietta living with you at the time?"

"She was, but . . . let me think . . . something came up with her family and she went tae Edinburgh."

"That's an excellent memory you have. So Henrietta didn't meet them?"

"Ye can't take away an old woman's memories. The past is clearer than the present when ye get tae my age. I believe Gordon was ill and she went off, and I remember because I wanted everything tae be shiny fer the visit and had tae rely on a local girl. As I recall, she didn't meet yer parents."

"You also said that you and my mother exchanged letters."

"A few here and there."

"Did you receive any from her after my grandfather's funeral, once my father left us?"

"No. And it's a shame. Yer mother was a lovely woman."

After disconnecting I sat for a moment thinking about the letters my mother had written to Scotland in search of information regarding my father. She'd told me about them and that they'd gone unanswered. Who else might she have written to? I didn't know.

My thoughts shifted to plotlines and my frustrating inability to create a full-blown outline before beginning to write a new story. Some writers can do that. They can see the big picture before ever putting pen to paper. Mine have to grow organically, each scene playing off the last. Sometimes I feel like I'm just along for the ride and am as surprised as my characters at the turn of events.

So it wasn't surprising that I'd go at this murder plot in the same fashion. By the seat of my pants.

A bit of information here, something that appears entirely unrelated there.

In a flash, I decided that Archie and Florence probably hadn't had anything to do with Henrietta's murder. They had the best motive, and they'd been "skating on thin ice" ever since that threatening note, even when it turned out to be a prank. But having a motive and actually committing murder were two very different things.

I didn't know enough about Gordon Martin to make that same declaration, but he'd been honest about his aunt's wistful expressions and there wasn't anything false about his pain when he and I discovered his aunt's body.

Janet Dougal might very well end up with a guilty charge and verdict. But it was hard for me to believe that she'd kill another human being over a slight. The inspector would call me naïve. I'm sure he's seen it all.

As much as I tried, I still couldn't shake the feeling that she was being set up.

What about Patricia Martin? The grieving sister? She didn't have an alibi. No one could confirm that she'd been in her room all afternoon, and she was a tall, strong woman who could easily have managed to set up the murder scene.

I shivered, but not from the cold weather, rather from the cold calculation of Henrietta's killer. To shove a washback over to a cask and drain whisky into it . . .

Patricia didn't have an obvious motive for killing her sister. But why was she at the tasting in the first place? If she'd wanted to visit with Henrietta there would have been better opportunities, ones when Henrietta wasn't busy planning gatherings. Afterward would have been preferable.

Had she felt that she had to hurry to Glenkillen? To put a stop to Henrietta's plan, whatever that plan was?

The plot was thickening with suppositions. I could speculate all I wanted, but without evidence, I couldn't write a proper ending.

As I turned off the Peugeot's engine, I heard the crunch of tires on hard-packed snow. Another car pulled in and parked on the other side of the lot. I got out, thinking that it was windier than I'd expected and that I needed to make this a quick exploratory trip. That was when I glanced up and saw Patricia Martin emerge from the other car. I ducked down, reopened my car door, and slid inside.

It wasn't clear why, but instinct guided me.

She came around the back of the car and opened its trunk, shuffling around inside. Then she removed something that looked about the size of a shoebox, closed the trunk, and walked down a shoveled pathway flanked by pine trees that led to the gravesites.

I recognized the object from its cylinder shape. It was a scattering urn, much like the one in which my mother's ashes had been presented to me for my own task of scattering her ashes. Was the cemetery one of those special places Henrietta had designated? Well, why not. She probably had a family plot here.

I followed discreetly, keeping a distance, the wind stinging my eyes, my hands clutching the collar of my coat tighter against it. Patricia walked wide around a hole that had been freshly dug and came to a stop before one of the tombstones on the far side.

Even though the weather had been cold, I could see that the ground at my feet hadn't been frozen more than a few inches deep. Beside the hole, a pile of chunks of ground and rocks remained. The mounded dirt was covered with snow, as was the ground and gravestones as far as I could see.

I paused, reminded of my mother's graveside service. And the hole, much like this one. Except that mound of dirt had been removed, as this one was sure to be before the funeral mourners arrived. I noted snow-covered strips of frozen turf lying like jigsaw puzzle pieces on plywood sheets to be used as covering after the coffin was inserted and the dirt returned to fill in the spaces. Planks had been laid along the edges of the hole to ensure firm footing for the pallbearers.

I wondered who had died. Who would be buried soon in this prepared space?

Moving up behind Patricia, I watched her as she bent and brushed away snow with a gloved hand, revealing the inscription.

My eyes swept over the engraving, and I almost gasped aloud in surprise.

Because the grave belonged to my grandfather.

CHAPTER 30

"Ashes to ashes, dust to dust," Patricia spoke aloud, after I watched her remove a glove and open the urn. She withdrew a handful of ashes and bent down, patting them into the snow so they wouldn't whirl away with the wind.

Rising, she must have sensed my presence because she turned and faced me.

Her face registered surprise, then anger. "What are *you* doing here?"

"I might ask you the same thing. Are those Henrietta's ashes?"

A dumb question. Who else's would they be? But what meaningful reason would an unrelated dead woman have for requesting that her ashes be spread on an Elliott grave? Why would Henrietta want her ashes here? Why?

Patricia's expression didn't give anything away. She turned back as though my interruption were a tiny bleep in the moment. She stared at the grave. I followed her gaze.

The now all-familiar family crest, with the fist clutching the cutlass, was etched into the stonework. And our motto:

Fortiter et Recte

Then:

IN LOVING MEMORY OF
RODERICK JAMES ELLIOT

One *T* rather than the two that I'd always used when spelling my last name. A tiny detail, not unusual really.

Born 29 September 1907, died 10 July 1983
Beloved husband, father, and grandfather

Grandfather to me. My father was his only child, meaning I'd been his only grandchild, at least at the time of his death. I still could be. Who had chosen the words for this stone? My grandmother had already been dead. My father probably decided what should go on the gravestone.

A little below and centered was a short verse.

His Life A Beautiful Memory,
His Absence A Silent Grief.

Until this moment, the Elliott clan had been an abstraction for me.

The wind howled, calling me back, striking sharper and colder.

"Why are you scattering Henrietta's ashes on my grand-father's grave?" I asked.

Patricia remained motionless, still staring at the stone. "She thought of him as family," she said.

I thought about that and still found it strange. If I'd been eternally in love with one man, my wishes would be entirely different. I'd have my ashes spread on the grave of my beloved. If he was dead. Or in a secret place where we once met. But on the grave of one of his family members? I loved my mother, but I'd never consider scattering my ashes with hers.

"Your sister had been in love with my father," I said, chilled to the bone. It wasn't all because of the temperature of the air, which had been steadily dropping. Or was it the harsh wind that made it seem so?

"She was, but she was a foolish young girl."

"She never got over him."

"It was more complicated than a simple infatuation."

"You know where my father is," I said, stating rather than questioning. "And you've been hiding that fact, keep-ing it a secret."

Patricia gave a little laugh, whether of contempt or dis-appointment I wasn't sure. "Do ye know how difficult it is living in the public eye all the time, on guard constantly? Of course ye don't. But I love my life; it's all I ever wanted. And if I could have thrown away the rest of my past, I would have. Instead I buried it. But it never goes away, does it?"

"We all have scars," I said.

Now Patricia turned and faced me, full on. "I loved my sister, would have protected her with my life. I risked everything for her."

I formed my next thought, verbalizing what I dreaded

learning of, forcing it out, thinking if I could only go back to what I believed yesterday . . . but it was too late for that. "My father is dead, isn't he?"

"Let's get out o' this wind and we will talk."

Every red alert in my body was sending signals. I fumbled in my pocket for the pepper spray. But I'd carelessly stored my phone in the same pocket on top of the canister. I slipped the phone out, keeping a careful eye on Patricia. As we began walking back the way we'd come, as we passed the recently dug grave, I must have inadvertently pushed one of the keys because it beeped, alerting her.

She stopped and stared at me. I was afraid to make a move to remove the pepper spray. She looked down at the phone.

"My sister killed your father," Patricia said. Before I had a chance to react, she tossed the urn aside, grabbed the phone from my hands, and forced me backward. She was taller than I. She drove me back like a football defensive player. And before I knew what was happening, I was airborne, flapping my arms, grasping at air.

The earth beneath my feet was gone.

I landed inside the open grave, flat on my back, the wind momentarily knocked out of me. I remained motionless while I did an internal assessment of my body parts, carefully flexing arms and legs until I determined that nothing was broken. I slowly rose.

Patricia stood above, still without expression, my phone in her hand. And well out of range of a shot from my pepper spray. I left it where it was. She didn't know I had it, and I needed that advantage.

"What I told you is true," she called, her words carrying

on the wind. "Henrietta was impulsive and foolish when she was a girl. She took up with Dennis Elliott. I told her he'd break her heart. He had aspirations and wanderlust. He wanted to leave Scotland, but Henrietta set out tae tie him tae her. It didn't work."

The grave wasn't more than six feet deep, but the side-walls were smooth and icy. Standing on my toes, I thought I could reach the top. Whether I had the strength to pull myself up and out was another matter.

"You'll stay where ye are, if ye know what's good for ye," she warned, anticipating my intention. I could hear the cold-ness in her voice.

It probably wasn't the smartest move I've ever made, but I must have been in shock. I'd just heard that Henrietta had killed my father, and her sister had thrown me into a grave. I sprang up and made an attempt to gain purchase, to pull myself out. As I'd suspected, getting a good hold was going to be difficult because of the icy surface.

That didn't matter because Patricia stepped hard on my fingers. When she removed her foot, I sank down, cradling my fingers in my hand, wondering if she'd crushed any bones.

"Your father came for his father's funeral. Henrietta saw that as her opportunity to convince him to stay."

"He was married to my mother. He had me."

"She didn't care. She had her own leverage. She had a son he didn't know about."

I stared at her.

"Aye, Gordon was Henrietta's baby, not mine. She was so young, in no position to raise a child, but Connor and I were. She gave him up. Gordon was about seven at the time that Dennis came fer the funeral. I was his mum fer all intents and purposes, but then she wanted to take a perfect situation and ruin it."

Patricia went on, as though her secret had been bottled up too long and she had to let it out. I was afraid to move a muscle, wanting to hear all of it, and the best way to make that happen was to stay quiet and listen.

"Henrietta waited for him after the funeral, led him to a secluded spot, told him about his son, told him he had to stay. He refused, said he'd contact her later and that he would take responsibility.

"Henrietta had so much rage inside her. When he turned to go, she picked up a large rock and struck him in the back of the head."

I fought tears, feeling a pain deeper than any I'd ever experienced when I thought my father had abandoned me. "She killed him?"

Patricia nodded. "And I had tae help her cover it up. All these years went by with our secret safe and sound. Then she was diagnosed with cancer, given a life sentence, and then she decided she was going to confess her crime to Dennis's daughter.

"I couldn't let that happen. She promised to protect me and never divulge my role, but a new investigation would have been launched, and it would have come out, would have not only ruined my life but also destroyed my husband's career. And Gordon? What would it have done to Gordon?"

"You tried to talk her out of it," I said, thinking back to Janet's account of Patricia and her sister at the inn. Arguing and upset, according to the American woman.

"She refused to listen tae reason. She didn't care what her confession would do tae the rest o' the family."

"So you drowned her in a vat of whisky!" In that moment, I understood how dangerous this woman could be. She'd already cut off my ability to use my cell phone to call for help and had thrown me into a deep hole without any regard for my personal safety. What if I'd broken bones? I was certain if I had, she'd have left me out here to die from hypothermia and shock without a moment of remorse.

"Henrietta was dying anyway. I only sped up the process."

So that was how she was justifying what she'd done? The woman was mad.

"What about the attack on Katie? On me?"

"I didn't intend to kill the girl, but I didn't want to risk the two o' ye putting your heads together and connecting Henrietta tae Dennis. I had tae stop ye at all cost. And if the girl suffered some memory loss and forgot about some o' that history she kept accumulating like a nosy nelly, all the better."

"But I figured out the link between them anyway." She didn't need to know that Katie and I had indeed put our heads together. "It was only a matter of time before I would."

"The attack on yerself, I would have gladly bashed yer brains in. None of this would have happened if not fer yer family."

Patricia had undergone a transformation during the telling of the story. She'd been calm and unreadable throughout most of it, until a few minutes ago. Now she was highly agitated, her face an angry mask, her eyes flashing dangerously.

The only positive thing about this whole situation was

that Patricia most likely didn't have a weapon, or she would have used it by now. She didn't have a gun, since they were hard to come by in Scotland, or a convenient barrel of whisky to drown me in. And if she had a knife, she'd have to come within striking range and then I'd hit her with a blast of pepper spray.

I still had a chance to get out of this mess and figure out how to climb out of this hole, but I'd have to keep my cool. Not try anything foolish. Patricia was taller but she also was older. But if it came to a fistfight or wrestling match, I'm not sure which of us would come out on top. I needed to think of a way to give myself an advantage.

Patricia could have been reading my mind because she said, "I'm sure ye can figure out how tae get out o' there, so I'm going tae disable your car fer good measure. Nobody else is going to come out to the cemetery with the weather forecast calling for severe gale conditions. I wouldn't have risked it myself, only I needed tae get this over and done with, then back tae Glenkillen before the real weather hits. This one is going tae be a red weather alert."

She smiled as she gazed down at me. "Ye didn't listen tae the reports, did ye? The schools and nurseries have been canceled fer the rest o' the day. Everybody is goin' tae be inside fer the remainder o' the storm. Except you.

"It's not the best plan I've ever made," she admitted, "but it'll have tae do temporarily. We're a good distance from the main road. With luck you'll freeze attempting tae make it. Or maybe you'll get run over somewhere along this isolated stretch."

The implication was perfectly clear. Patricia would be watching for me down that road.

"I have one more question," I said, with a dozen on my mind. "What did you do with my father's body?"

Patricia relaxed her features and became less emotional, more matter-of-fact. "Why, he's buried in with yer grandfather. It wasn't hard tae do a little digging so soon after the funeral. The ground had been disturbed already, making it easy."

Then she turned away and disappeared from my sight. But I heard her parting words.

"Ashes to ashes, dust to dust," she said.

There is something powerful about appropriately placed rage. For a good portion of my life I'd resented my father, believing that he'd gone off and abandoned us. His disappearance had affected my mother deeply at a time when she desperately needed his love and support. It had affected my relationships with men, had most likely been the reason I'd chosen a husband so poorly and why I've never been able to manage a lasting relationship. Growing up thinking your father didn't love you wreaks havoc on your soul.

Now I had a new target for all that anger.

I lunged for the wall of the grave and attempted to scale it. But again I slid down. I made several more attempts until I finally jumped high enough that my hands reached the roughness of the wood planks edging the grave and found purchase. I'd never considered myself particularly athletic, but through sheer will I managed to pull my body weight up and rolled out onto the snowy ground.

The wind was fierce outside the hole and snow had begun to fall, not soft and gentle, but forceful, heavy, and wet. Before I could get to my feet, I felt a blow to my side. And another.

Patricia had found a shovel and used it. I didn't have time to react; the pepper spray canister was still inside my pocket. I'd needed both hands to claw my way out. I attempted to get to my feet, but she was strong and fast, and I saw her raise the shovel, directed at my head. My only option was to roll and pitch over the side, back into the hole.

"I came up with a better plan," she said, peering down at me. "It's still a bit makeshift but the goal is tae make yer death seem as accidental as possible. Ye had a breakdown and walked out tae the road. A car, not able tae see ye in the storm, ran over ye. No one will ever know that ye were bludgeoned tae death with this shovel."

I saw movement behind her. Or thought I did. *I must be delusional*, I thought, shivering from the cold. I felt a throbbing pain in my side where she'd struck me with the shovel.

There. I saw it again. Patricia turned and stepped out of my line of sight. I heard voices mixed in with the howling wind. A minute or two passed in which I thought about venturing up. Except the woman had a shovel. If she struck me in the head, I'd be dead.

Then a form appeared above. One I recognized even though he looked more like a polar bear than a human covered in so much snow.

"I had the situation under control," I called up, sure I looked the same.

"I can see that," the inspector replied.

Chapter 31

Patricia refused to speak one word once she was in police custody. The inspector confiscated her keys, brushed a thick layer of snow from the door of her rental car, and handcuffed her to the inside. Producing a blanket from his own vehicle, he threw it over her and said to the silent woman, "We'll be speakin' more in a bit."

Then he and I sat inside his police car, heater on high, while he made a call on his mobile to check the weather conditions and forecast. I've seen plenty of driving rain in my lifetime, but this was the first time I'd encountered driving snow. Pounding, driving, gale-force snow.

"Snow gates are up out on the main road," he informed me after disconnecting.

"The road is closed?"

"Aye, due tae snowdrifts the size o' munros. The patrol gritters are out tae help stranded fools like ourselves, but they won't get tae us fer a spell. So we have plenty o' time tae have a chat."

"How did you know where I was?"

"The lot o' us have been trying tae keep ye in one place and out o' the mix. That was Vicki's suggestion and a good one, tae spare ye in case things went bad fer yer father."

"You all knew something was wrong, that he was involved, and nobody told me?"

"Only that it was a *possibility*. And then only after Vicki found out about yer grandfather bein' interred in Tainwick and the dead woman from the same place. She came tae me with her concerns."

"I wish she'd come to me with those concerns instead."

"We wanted tae protect you," he continued. "Both physically, after that incident at the hospital, and also from any potential o' emotional fallout. But it's been mostly a wasted effort keepin' tabs on ye. I might not have been out here tae help ye, except fer a stroke o' luck."

I saw clearly what had occurred. I'd told only one person where I was going.

"Ami knew that I was going out to the cemetery. She contacted Vicki. Vicki called you," I said.

"I followed ye this morning tae see where ye would end up, thinkin' ye must be ontae something tae be out with the weather about tae turn bad. I stayed a good deal back, not wantin' tae interfere with yer time at yer grandfather's grave. I didn't realize ye had company out there until the snow started falling in buckets and ye didn't come back tae yer car. Imagine my surprise tae find ye fisticuffin' with Patricia Martin."

"And was about to win, I might add," I said. It was easy to insert a little humor into the situation now that it was under control, now that Patricia Martin wasn't a threat any longer. And as to winning, I could only imagine how I looked down in that hole.

The inspector smiled. "Ye're resilient, that's fer sure, and I'll put my wages on ye fer future events."

After that I told my story. I didn't leave anything out. By the time I got to the end, my voice was quivering and I completely broke down when I told him where my father's body was buried. Earlier I'd been in survival mode. Now the full impact of my loss and what might have happened to me sank in.

The inspector produced a box of tissues and made more phone calls, then got out and went over to Patricia's car.

While he was gone, through tears I could no longer control, I reflected on Henrietta's solitary life and her voluntary seclusion. In a way she *had* been a criminal hiding away, imprisoned for life after that one destructive act of violence. Ultimately, neither of the sisters had escaped their abusive home life. They'd perpetuated it with more acts of violence.

I thought of Gordon Martin and how he'd cope when he discovered that he'd been raised by his aunt and that his real mother had killed his biological father in cold blood.

It seemed like forever before the inspector returned. I must have looked an absolute wreck with my damp face and red swollen eyes.

"This is going to devastate Gordon Martin," I said. I wasn't going to be the only one impacted by Henrietta and Patricia's actions.

"Henrietta must not've been capable of raising him," the inspector guessed. "She had deep-seated emotional issues. But that sister over there"—he gestured toward Patricia's car—"isn't even a wee bit better when it comes right down tae it. What a pair!"

"I just realized that I have a brother," I said, and somehow that dawning knowledge made me feel slightly better. "If what Patricia said is true."

"It has the ring o' truth."

"Did you get her to confess while you were in her car?"

The inspector held up a small recorder. "She decided tae talk after I threatened tae leave her out where she'd tried tae leave you."

"You? Coercing a suspect?"

"When it's necessary." He gave me a piercing glance. "And I'll deny that if ye go blathering it aboot."

"I wouldn't think of it."

He let me listen to the tape. Her story was the same as the one she'd given me, but with a few more details. Patricia had been aware that Janet Dougal was attempting to infiltrate the group gathering for the tasting. She'd impersonated Henrietta to get Janet out to the house. Patricia had also been the one who called in the anonymous tip placing Janet outside the inn, that tip leading to the American woman's detention. Patricia was a shrewd, evil woman.

"I wonder about the letters my mother wrote. I imagine she sent them to Bridie, and Henrietta intercepted them."

"'Tis a fair assumption."

"You shouldn't have fired me in the first place," I said. "I understand your thought process, why you did what you did, but we could have worked through this together."

"Aye, it wasn't one o' my better decisions."

To my surprise he leaned over and wrapped his arms around me. I could feel the warmth of him through our coats. He smelled slightly of aftershave. If I didn't know better, I might think he had been really worried about me.

Or maybe I didn't know better. The inspector's innermost feelings were on full display for the first time.

Once he released me, to lighten up what was becoming an awkward situation, I said, "Now that Janet Dougal is a free woman, she'll be coming for you."

Jamieson grimaced.

"Don't you feel any guilt about locking up an innocent woman?"

"I was startin' tae suspect that she'd set herself up fer the fall so she could chase me around the jail cell. Thanks tae yer fine detectin' today, I'll be able tae give Janet Dougal a royal send-off. Or better yet, I'll have Sean see her ontae the first plane out o' here, while I begin a process tae ban her permanently from Scotland."

Shortly after, a snowplow arrived, its enormous blade clearing a swath down the road. Sean descended from the passenger side of the cab and made his way to us through knee-high snow.

"I don't know how Eden got away from me," he said to the inspector through a crack in the window.

"She's a wily one," Jamieson agreed, stepping out.

"I'm sorry," I called out, feeling guilty for having deceived Sean.

Eventually, with the snowplow leading the way, we caravanned back to Glenkillen.

It would have been easy to dwell on the negative, but in fact, I was one lucky woman.

In so many ways.

And I owed a great deal of gratitude to the inspector.

He always seemed to have my back.

CHAPTER 32

The next several days were snowed-in ones. It was a good time for me to reflect on the past and plan for the future. And to grieve for the father I'd lost so long ago.

When the weather conditions improved, a backhoe would dig up my grandfather's grave, searching for my father's remains. I felt confident that the inspector would find what he was looking for and that I'd find closure, although certainly not in the way I'd expected.

I spent those long days and evenings before the fire with Snookie on my lap and the crest sketch my father had drawn on the side table next to me. Between my knitting needles, the most amazing thing was happening. A skein of yarn was slowly growing into recognizable Merry Mittens.

During that time, I turned off my cell and landline, didn't open my laptop at all, and Vicki, somehow sensing that I needed to be alone, kept humanity at bay. She was always hovering nearby, though, in case I needed her.

Once the snow finally stopped falling, I'd had enough

sadness and put away my pain and anguish to focus on the short amount of time I had left.

Vicki squealed in delight when I slipped out of my boots at her entryway and stepped inside her home two days before I was scheduled to depart. I had my laptop along per her mysterious request. Sean arrived moments later and we admired his new police vehicle from the window.

"Sweet," I told him when he proudly showed it off.

"Aboot time," he replied.

Leith's Land Rover pulled into the driveway next. Kelly bounded out first as soon as the passenger door opened, followed by Leith's daughter, Fia. Coco and Pepper bolted to the door, and Sean let them out to play chase with Leith's border collie. I could see Jasper venturing out through a crack in the barn door. Even the tomcat was feeling snowbound. He needed some torment-the-dogs playtime.

Leith gave me a bear hug, then stepped back to search my eyes with his Scottish blues. "So what's the occasion?"

I shrugged. "This is Vicki's party and she's being very secretive."

In fact, my friend was fairly bursting with excitement as we waited for the inspector, who was the last to arrive.

"Okay," Vicki said, the minute we were all seated. "Eden, get your laptop ready. We are going to video-call Ami."

Soon we had my Chicago friend on the screen. She was beaming, and I couldn't figure out why everyone was so happy when I felt like I was about to go to my execution.

Ami began, "Last spring I did some research and figured out where your Scottish family lived. You were so bitter and I'd hoped you would discover some of your relatives and reconcile with your past."

"So the whole idea to set a romance in Scotland really was a ruse?" I couldn't believe she'd go to that extent.

"Not exactly. The two ideas sort of merged. Once you were there, I quickly found out that you weren't doing anything about connecting with the Elliotts."

I glanced at Vicki. Those two had been in this together from the beginning.

"But I could tell how much you loved the Highlands," Vicki went on. "And so I did my own digging and found out a few things, and that's how Ami and I started working together."

My face must have conveyed my puzzlement.

Ami picked up the story. "We used a nationality-checking service, started gathering documents."

"Like birth and death certificates," Vicki added. "And marriage certificates."

"It took over four months," Ami said, "back and forth, digging through boxes of your mother's stored items, getting the application filed, and then we waited for the mail to arrive."

So that explained Vicki's weird behavior, especially the day I'd beat her to the mail. And Ami had been extremely resourceful as always. "But what have you accomplished?" I asked.

Something. I sensed it in their elation.

Vicki answered, "You have Scottish-born grandparents."

"I know that."

"So you are eligible for an ancestry visa."

I frowned. "I'm not following. Is that different from my tourist visa?"

"You can stay here in the Highlands for five years with

these." Vicki picked up several pieces of paper and waved them in the air. "You've been approved!"

Stunned, I took the documents and stared at them, not comprehending until the inspector, who sat next to me, took my free hand. "I believe this means we're stuck with ye."

And that was all it took for another round of tears. This time I wasn't crying alone.

"We'll take a trip to Applefary next week," Vicki said, sniffling. "I know just where to find some of your relatives. Gordon Martin wants to join us. He's having a hard time, but he's a strong man, and he'll see his way through. And Bridie Dougal. We can't forget her."

Later, after we terminated the call with Ami, after thanking everyone and watching Leith pull away with his daughter and his dog, the inspector walked me to the cottage. I still hadn't processed all my good news. So much had occurred. Some awful. Some wonderful.

"I'm rehired?" I asked him.

"Aye," he said with a sigh. "It was inevitable."

"You need to know up front that I work best alone," I told him.

He smiled. I could hear what he was thinking, that this hadn't been Eden Elliott's finest solo job.

And after that was settled, we butted heads for a few more minutes. And as twilight fell, with the inspector at my side, I thanked my lucky stars. Later, in my cottage with Snookie, I indulged in a little wool gathering.

I was learning that anything was possible in the Scottish Highlands.

ABOUT THE AUTHOR

Hannah Reed is the national bestselling author of the Scottish Highlands Mysteries, including *Off Kilter* and *Hooked on Ewe*, and the Queen Bee Mysteries, including *Beewitched* and *Beeline to Trouble*. Her own Scottish ancestors were seventeenth-century rabble-rousers who were eventually shipped to the new world, where they settled in Michigan's Upper Peninsula. Hannah has happily traveled back to her homeland several times and, in keeping with family tradition, enjoyed causing mayhem in the Highlands. Visit her website at hannahreedbooks.com.

From national bestselling author

HANNAH REED

Hooked on Ewe

A Scottish Highlands Mystery

It's early September in Glenkillen, Scotland, when American expat (and budding romance novelist) Eden Elliott is recruited by the local inspector to act as a special constable. Fortunately it's in name only, since not much happens in Glenkillen.

For now Eden has her hands full with other things: preparing for the sheepdog trial on the MacBride farm—a fundraiser for the local hospice—and helping her friend Vicki with her first yarn club skein-of-the-month deliveries. Everything seems to be coming to-gether—until the head of the welcoming committee is found strangled to death with a club member's yarn.

Now Eden feels compelled to honor her commitment as constable and herd together the clues, figure out which ones are dogs, and which ones will lead to a ruthless killer . . .

Also in the Series
Off Kilter
Dressed to Kilt

queenbeemystery.com
penguin.com

Searching for the perfect mystery?

Looking for a place to get the latest clues and connect with fellow fans?

"Like" The Crime Scene on Facebook!

- Participate in author chats
- Enter book giveaways
- Learn about the latest releases
- Get book recommendations and more!

facebook.com/TheCrimeSceneBooks

Obsidian